Cooper

The Splintered Hearts Series

Nicola Jane

Nicola Jane

Copyright © 2019 by Nicola Jane.

Copyright © 2022 by Nicola Jane. (Updated version)

All rights reserved.

No portion of this book may be reproduced in any form without written permission from the publisher or author, except as permitted by U.K. copyright law.

Meet The Team

Cover design: Francessca Wingfield - Wingfield Designs
Editor: Rebecca Vazquez - Dark Syde Books
Formatting: Nicola Miller

Disclaimer:
This book is a work of fiction. The names, characters, places, and incidents are all products of the authors imagination and are not to be construed as real. Any similarities are entirely coincidental.

Spelling:
Please note, this author resides in the United Kingdom and is using British English. Therefore,

some words may be viewed as incorrect or spelled incorrectly. However, they are not.

Acknowledgments

This was the first MC book I wrote. It's probably one of the most controversial.

I have come a long way since this story, and although I'd probably change a few parts, I realise a lot of my readers loved this story, and so I've left it pretty much as it was.

Thank you for reading, and if you were one of the readers who started here, because of you, I'm rocking the author life. Thanks for sticking with me.

A note from the author

Where do I even start? This book contains so many triggers, the warning won't be enough. Please do not read this book if you hate cheating—there's a lot of it.

This isn't a sweet romance. It's MC and we all know that's a trigger warning all by itself!

Have you ever met a guy (or girl) who messes with you in so many ways, you're in a constant state of anxiety? Have you ever been treated so badly by someone who's meant to love you, yet you just can't walk away?

Mila is that woman! She is screwed over so many times by Cooper, but she just can't walk away. She loves him. Despite it all, she loves him.

And so, she becomes a bit more like him, plays the game but never quite wins in the same way he does.

When I wrote this story, it was with past relationships in mind. Not one in particular, but many. Men who lied, cheated, broke me piece by piece. And I put some of those bad times into one character and created Cooper.

I felt the need to explain this because I've been contacted so many times over this book. Readers who hate Cooper, trust me, I'm with you on that. But some say Mila is too weak, that her character is unbelievable, and no woman would put up with it. And I just wanted to say, if you've never met a guy like this, thank your lucky stars, because of course he exists. For some women, he does exist. And some women do stick around. They do fall for the charm, the smiles, the few times they make you laugh, and they hold on to the hope that these men will change and become the Prince Charming they dream of.

In my case, that didn't work out until many Coopers later. Thankfully, I got my happy ever after, but even my prince wasn't always so charming. And in this story, Mila gets her happy ever after, even if you don't agree she should.

I guess what I want to say is, this is my story. It's from my imagination, and I get to form these crazy characters. You don't have to like them, you could write your own, but don't judge and be kind. Kindness costs nothing.

Contents

PLAYLIST	XI
CHAPTER ONE	1
CHAPTER TWO	13
CHAPTER THREE	30
CHAPTER FOUR	42
CHAPTER FIVE	57
CHAPTER SIX	77
CHAPTER SEVEN	89
CHAPTER EIGHT	99
CHAPTER NINE	117
CHAPTER TEN	132
CHAPTER ELEVEN	143
CHAPTER TWELVE	160
CHAPTER THIRTEEN	174
CHAPTER FOURTEEN	187
CHAPTER FIFTEEN	211

CHAPTER SIXTEEN	222
CHAPTER SEVENTEEN	246
CHAPTER EIGHTEEN	257
CHAPTER NINETEEN	272
CHAPTER TWENTY	295
1. KAIN - The Hammers MC	302
2. KAIN - The Hammers MC	308
3. A note from me to you	317
4. Popular Books by Nicola Jane	319

PLAYLIST

Bad for Me – Meghan Trainor ft. Teddy Swims
All That Really Matters – Illenium ft. Teddy Swims
If You Met Me First – Eric Ethridge
Narcissist – Lauren Spencer-Smith
Dancing with the Devil – Demi Lovato
Could've Just Left Me Alone – Alexa Cappelli
Good Enough – Maisie Peters
Wicked Game – Daisy Gray
Broken Strings – James Morrison ft. Nelly Furtado
All For You – Ella Henderson ft. Cian Ducrot
Hold My Hand – Lady Gaga

CHAPTER ONE

I straighten my pencil skirt. I chose the blue one because it wasn't as depressing as black, but now, I feel underdressed and not very formal.

"Well, Miss Coin, it was lovely to meet you. We'll be in touch."

The stuck-up woman in front of me stands, her black suit ironed to perfection. She must spend hours tending to that, I think to myself. She holds out her hand for me to shake, letting me know this meeting is over.

I know she won't be in touch. This is the eighth job I've interviewed for, and I haven't heard back from any of them. At this rate, I'm going to have to take Harper up on her offer of bar work.

I leave the office and pull out my mobile phone to call Harper, my best friend since forever. Our mums were on the same maternity ward, giving birth just one day apart. They began swapping birth stories, discovered they lived just two blocks away from each other, and soon became firm friends. The friendship continued even after Harper's parents moved away for a better life.

"Hey, sweetie, how did it go?" asks Harper. I can hear voices in the background, so she must be at work.

"Not good. The woman who interviewed me looked me up and down as soon as she saw me. I could tell she didn't like me."

"Mila, you're paranoid. I'm sure you did fine. Come to the bar and I'll make you some lunch."

I jump in my car and head to the bar where she works. My car is in serious need of some loving, so it's a miracle I make it. The beat-up red hatchback is my pride and joy, the one thing I saved up to buy during my time at college. It took a lot of waitressing to buy it and I feel a sense of pride that I did it on my own, which makes it harder for me to sell her now.

The car park is full of motorcycles when I arrive. A few bikers are leaning against the outside wall with cigarettes hanging from their mouths while they laugh and joke amongst each other. I used to feel intimidated by them, but since getting to know some of them, I realise they're not as bad as their reputation makes them out to be.

As I approach the doorway, Jase, a member of the Hammers Motorcycle Club, opens the door for me, standing back for me to pass. "Hey, Mila, nice to see you." He winks, looking me up and down with interest. "You're looking smart. You been anywhere nice?"

"A job interview, nowhere exciting."

He grins. "I can take you somewhere exciting."

I roll my eyes. He means no harm, but I'm pretty sure his wife, Kayla, will eat me alive if I touch her man. "Kayla is all the excitement you need, big guy," I say as I head on inside to find Harper.

There're bikers everywhere. Harper is leaning over the bar to talk to Kain, the club's Vice President. She's had a thing for him for months, but he doesn't seem interested, much to her disappointment. It's not like she's unattractive—that girl could cause a car accident with the amount of attention she gets. With her long blonde hair down to her rounded backside and bright blue eyes, she's like every man's wet dream.

I sit beside Kain, and Harper gives me a sympathetic smile. "Don't look so glum, sweetie. You'll find something soon, I'm sure," she says as she places a Diet Coke down in front of me.

"What you looking for Mila?" asks Kain, chugging back his beer.

"A job."

"Doing what exactly?"

"I just had an interview for a nanny position, but I don't think I got it."

"You good with kids?" he asks, a smile pulling at the corners of his mouth.

I shrug. "Yeah, I guess. I have lots of experience, but there just doesn't seem to be any jobs out there at the moment."

"You know, the Pres might need someone. Let me talk to him."

He's referring to Cooper, the President of the Hammers MC. Cooper is the scariest man I've ever met, though I've only actually met him twice. According to Harper, he keeps to himself most of the time, preferring to stay around the clubhouse rather than venture into the bar.

I watch Kain retreat as he heads into the clubhouse. His huge six-foot frame is nothing compared to his President, but he still fits snug in those Levi's, and I admire his backside as he walks away.

"Man, he is so fine. It doesn't matter what I do, the guy just doesn't show me any interest," huffs Harper, making no secret of the fact she's also watching his arse as he leaves.

"You need a cloth to wipe up the drool," I say with a smirk.

"You're not funny," she grumbles. "You see how hot he is, right?"

I nod. "He is gorgeous." He's tall and well-built, his muscles are as big as my thighs, and tattoos cover both arms. His hair is always tied back in a man-bun style, so I imagine it's at least shoulder-length. "Maybe you should pay him no attention. He must get sick of women swooning at his feet. Play it cool."

Harper ponders my suggestion while pouring a pint for Sam, one of the older members of the club. The door to the clubhouse opens and Kain pops his head through.

"Mila, come back here and see the Pres," he shouts.

I've never been in the clubhouse. Harper's been working here for six months now, and she said no one goes back there, not even her. It's strictly club members only unless you get invited.

We walk through a huge open-plan room with couches dotted about and two pool tables. It's not very inviting, but I'm sure it's ideal for the guys who hang around here. A blonde with straggly hair is sitting on one of the pool tables. Her bra is on show and she has short-shorts on, exposing her pale, skinny legs. She tracks my movements with narrowed eyes, a look of irritation on her face.

"Where the hell are you taking her, Kain? It better not be to Cooper's room." Her voice is raspy, like it will run out at any second.

"Shut the hell up, Carrie, and keep your nose outta my business."

A little boy comes running into the room making a siren noise at the top of his lungs. He skids to a halt in front of Kain, tipping his head back to look up at the large biker.

"Asher, stop making that goddamn noise. Your uncle will string me up," yells Carrie, jumping off the pool table and marching towards him. He looks at me with sad eyes, and I wonder if she's his mum. *Poor kid.*

We get to a red wooden door with the word 'President' painted in black. Kain knocks loudly and a gruff voice orders us to come in. Cooper sits behind a large oak desk with his boot-clad feet resting on top of it. His shoulders are straining under his tight, black T-shirt, and I wonder how something so big can fit into normal, human-sized clothes. He's engrossed in something on his mobile phone, so he doesn't immediately look up.

"Pres, this is Mila."

After a few more seconds, he raises his head. His piercing green eyes meet mine and he just stares. I fidget, I hate being stared at.

"No," he finally says, and then looks back at his phone.

"Come on, Coop. She's got loads of experience, and we need the help. The kid's running riot," says Kain, sighing.

"I said no. Now, get her the fuck out of here."

Cooper continues staring at his phone, and I feel a rage burn through my veins. How rude to not even ask me a question before dismissing me. I'm so sick of being turned away, I need a reason. *What am I doing that is so wrong?*

"Why?" I ask. My voice comes out quiet, almost a whisper, and I inwardly cringe. It sounded much louder when I said it in my head. They both look at me, and I suddenly feel that perhaps I shouldn't have spoken to him directly. Maybe in a motorcycle club there are rules about how to address the President, like rules for people meeting the Queen.

His face tells me he isn't used to being questioned when he's made his decision, and that felt like a very final decision.

"Because you aren't what I'm looking for," he grates out.

"But you didn't ask me anything. How would you know?"

He gives me an irritated look. "Get her out of here, Kain."

Kain goes to open the door but stops when he realises I haven't moved to follow him.

"I want a goddamn reason. I'm sick of being told no. I'm a good nanny, I have loads of experience, and kids love me. Is it the way I look? Am I dressed wrong?" He looks me up and down again, which grates on my last nerve. "Oh, just forget it. I'd rather sell my body than work here with someone as rude as you." I stomp towards the door. Kain raises his eyebrows with an amused look on his face and then leads me out of the office.

Carrie is still in the room. She has a hold of the boy's arm and he's crying. She's in his face, whispering angrily at him, when my protective side jumps to attention. "Let go of him right now." I march over to where they are, and the realisation hits me that I possibly just yelled at this kid's mother.

She looks at me in surprise but releases his arm. "Who the hell are you?" she demands, glaring from me to Kain.

I ignore her and pick the little boy up. Even if she is his mum, the boy is clearly distressed, and it breaks my heart. He must only be around three years old. He sniffles a few times, keeping his eyes fixed on me, then he wraps his arms around me and buries his dirty, tear-stained face into my neck. I smile, holding him tighter.

Carrie looks surprised. "He let you hold him," she mutters.

"Fuck," Kain gasps.

"Get back in here. Bring the kid with you," shouts a booming voice from behind me. I turn to see Cooper standing in his office doorway.

I go back in to his dark, depressing office, the manly vibe letting me know that Cooper is, without doubt, a man's man. He sits on the edge of his desk, his brow furrowed.

"That kid's been with me for a month now and not once as he let anyone touch him, let alone hold him," he says, his voice gruff.

I instinctively rub gentle circles on the boy's back. "Maybe if everyone stopped referring to him as 'the kid' . . ."

"Asher. His name is Asher," says Cooper in an almost apologetic tone.

The light snores tell me that Asher has fallen asleep, all that crying must have worn him out. I make my way over to the couch leaning against the office wall and gently lay him down. He stirs briefly before snuggling against the pillow. I pull a blanket from the back of the couch to cover him, taking a moment to stare at his dirty little face, wondering when he last got a bath.

"I need someone to live-in," says Cooper, bringing me back from my thoughts.

I turn to him. "I thought I wasn't right?"

"I reckon you'll last the week before you tell me to shove the job up my arse. The kid's a handful. He hardly sleeps, won't eat properly, and just races around, playing on his own."

I love a challenge, so I smile. "Where will I sleep?"

"You can have a room next to the kid. Anything you need, you go to Max. He's a prospect and his job is to run around. I'll pay you cash, weekly. You can have Sundays off. I'll get Max to show you around."

"Just Sundays?"

"Like I said, you won't last the week."

Cooper sticks his head out the door and shouts for Max, who appears in a flash, looking eager to please.

"This is . . ." Cooper pauses and looks at me.

"Mila," I say with a smile.

"She's Asher's new nanny. Show her to the room next to the kid's. Get her settled."

Max wiggles his eyebrows at me. "Not a problem, Pres." He grins, and I laugh, but Cooper doesn't look impressed.

"Off limits, especially to a prospect," he snaps.

We leave the office, turning left and heading through another door that takes us straight to a set of stairs. I follow Max up to the second floor. There're three doors along the landing, and he opens the first one.

"This is Asher's room."

I step inside. It's decorated in different shades of blue and there're posters on the wall of a cartoon character. A small bed, full of teddy bears, sits against one wall. There's an overflowing toybox in the corner of the room and a small bookshelf full of children's books. It isn't what I expected.

"Surprised?"

"A little."

"He cares about the kid. Just doesn't know how to look after him."

"Well, hiring somebody else to do it won't solve the problem."

Max leads me to the next door and flings it open. It's bright, with cream walls and a huge four poster bed. "Wow, this is really nice. Is this my room?" He nods as I step inside. The furniture is cottage style, also in cream, and there're intricate flowers hand painted onto the walls in random places. There's a double glass door that opens out to a small balcony. It overlooks a field which must be what the club backs onto.

"The Pres' room is the one at the end. He doesn't like to be disturbed, so you're best calling for me and I'll get whatever you need." He hands me a mobile phone. "This is your work phone. It has everyone's number that you'll need. If the Pres rings you, then answer. He hates to be ignored."

"I'll need to go home and get some things. Let Cooper know I'll be back tomorrow at nine and we can go through Asher's schedule."

"Schedule? He doesn't really have one. I can take you to get your things and bring you straight back."

"No, I need to speak to my parents and my boyfriend."

We head back downstairs. I get as far as Cooper's office door, and he appears. "Where are you going?"

"Home."

"Knew you wouldn't last the week," he mutters.

"I need to get my things. I'll be back tomorrow." He raises an eyebrow. "Well, Max will take you to get your things and then you can come straight back."

Max grins. "I already offered, Pres, but she wants to see her boyfriend."

A brief look of annoyance passes over Cooper's face. "I need you here tonight. I've made plans and need someone to watch the kid."

"I literally just took the job. I can't start straight away."

"Then forget it, I'll find someone else," he snaps, heading back into his office and slamming the door.

I'm pretty sure I'm his only option right now, but I need this job. I'm so over attending pointless interviews. "Fine," I huff. "Max, I have my car outside. I'll go and get my stuff and be back in a few hours. Let the grumpy bastard know."

CHAPTER TWO

"Well, I guess it's good you have a job, but I'm not sure working for the Hammers is a good idea." Mum sighs as she sits on my bed, watching me pack a few things.

"A live-in position will earn me good money. If Aaron and I want to move in together, we'll need all the cash we can get."

"I know, sweetie. I just wish it was for someone more reputable."

"All the things we've heard could just be gossip, Mum. We don't know if any of it's true. They've never done anything to upset us."

The Hammers MC, like most motorcycle clubs, has a bad reputation. Money laundering, drugs, fighting... you name it and they've apparently done it or had something to do with it. But Harper loves working the bar and says it's all rumours because she's never seen anything remotely underhanded.

I hear the front door open and close. "Mila?" shouts Aaron.

"Up here." I'd texted him when I left the clubhouse to tell him I'd found a live-in position.

Aaron enters the room and wraps me in his arms. We've been in a relationship for two years and plan on moving in together as soon as we have a deposit and maybe a month or two of rent saved.

We met in a bar, and he'd hit on me a few times before I finally gave in and let him buy me a drink. Our first date was to a burger joint. I should have realised then that he wasn't romantic, but I agreed to go on the next date, and then the next, until we just became a thing. He's tall and preppy-looking, tanned, with straight white teeth and nice brown hair that he sweeps to the side. He's medium build, a runner more than a gym addict, but he's in good shape.

I fill him in on the details, and he and Mum share a concerned look. "Just be careful. I've heard some stories about those guys. Keep your head down and take care of his child, but don't get involved in any of their club dealings," warns Aaron, kissing me on the forehead.

"It means I have to pass on date night. He wants me to start right away."

"That's okay. I'll meet up with Charlie and have a beer or two."

I roll my eyes. Charlie is Aaron's best friend, and as far as I'm concerned, not a good one. Aaron never makes good choices when he's with Charlie. Sometimes I think they slip into their old ways and get beyond drunk and reckless.

"Call me when you get home," I tell him. "You know I worry."

By the time I finally get back to the clubhouse, the car park is almost empty with just three bikes standing lonely. I head in through the bar, finding Harper chatting with Max. They turn to me and smile in unison. "Thank God you're back. He was going mad thinking you had left," says Max with a grin.

The back door leading to the club swings open, and Cooper's large built frame fills the doorway. With his arms crossed over his chest, he looks menacing. His muscles bulge, and I find myself comparing his bulky size to the Hulk, making me smile.

"I don't know why you're smiling. I've got a screaming kid in here that won't shut the fuck up," he growls, knocking the smile right off my face.

"How did he know I was back?" I whisper to Max.

"Cameras everywhere."

Once inside the compound, I find Asher sitting in the middle of the room, wailing. "Did something happen?" I ask Cooper.

He shrugs his huge shoulders. "He woke up and then cried."

"Well, have you tried to hold him?" I ask, heading over to the small child and crouching down in front of him. "Hey, little man, what's all the noise about?" I smile.

"I told you, he doesn't let no one touch him," huffs Cooper.

Asher sniffles but stops his wailing to stare at me. A grin spreads across his face and he reaches for me. I let him wrap his tiny arms around my neck before I stand, lifting him into my arms. He presses his face into my neck and sniffles before settling there like a small baby.

"What the fu—" Cooper begins, but I cut him off with a light slap to his arm.

"No more cursing in front of Asher. It isn't good for him." Cooper stares at the spot where my hand touched him before lifting his eyes to my own, his brow once again furrowed. I guess he isn't used to being told what to do. I ignore him and continue, "I'll also need more details on his background. How old is he?"

"He's three. Just. Birthday was last month."

"I'm going to get him settled with some toys and then I want to see you to discuss him further. Get Max to come to Asher's room. He can watch over him."

I sit on the bedroom floor with Asher pressed into my side. Pulling out a drawer full of small cars from his toy cabinet, I place it on the floor.

"Asher, I'm Mila. I've come to stay with you, to help look after you." He watches me but doesn't answer. I haven't heard him say a word since I first laid eyes on him. I smile to reassure him. "Is that okay with you?" He gives a nod. "Can you use your words, Asher?"

He pauses for a minute, and I'm about to give up hope when, in a small voice, he whispers, "Yes."

Relief washes over me. At least I know he understands me.

I'm holding up cars and asking him to tell me the colours when Max comes in. Asher speaks in single words rather than sentences, but I'm putting that down to me being a stranger and him being shy. He glances at Max and squashes into me tighter. "Asher, this is Max. You know him, right?" He gives a small nod. "He's my friend and he also loves to play with cars. Can he play with your cars for a while? I need to see Cooper."

"Stay," he whispers to me.

"Asher, I'm coming back. I promise." He goes silent for another minute before nodding. "Okay, good boy. You're in charge of Max, so don't let him boss you around, okay?" He hides a small smile.

The clubhouse is empty when I knock on Cooper's office door. I wait for a moment before pushing the door open to find Cooper standing in front of his desk with his back to me. There's a pair of pale legs wrapped around his waist and the sound of kissing fills my ears. I scrunch my face up when I realise it's Carrie, the woman I had the displeasure of meeting earlier.

Cooper spins around, fury on his face, and I stumble back, fear filling my body. "Don't ever come in here unless I tell you that you can," he roars.

I take a few more steps back, my legs working faster than my mind. I almost trip but manage to catch myself by grabbing the door frame. Tears spring to my eyes as I turn away, heading back towards the stairs before he can see my weakness. I don't do well with people shouting at me. I believe in respect and manners.

I'm halfway up the stairs when a strong hand grabs my wrist, halting me mid-step. "Stop," he growls, his voice rumbling through my panic. Cooper gently tugs on my arm until I face him, and he cringes when he sees my tears. "I like my privacy. I should have told you," he mutters.

"I just wanted to talk about Asher. It can wait," I whisper, trying to hide the quiver in my voice. I feel so pathetic.

"No, we'll do it now."

He keeps hold of my wrist, and as we near the bottom of the stairs, he loosens his grip until he finds my hand, and then he holds that until we reach his office. Carrie is still sitting on the edge of his desk, looking flustered. "Out," he snaps, and she glares at me.

Her eyes fall to our joined hands. "Seriously, Cooper?"

"I don't have time for your drama, Carrie. Get out!" She huffs and storms out, shoulder barging me as she passes. Cooper drops my hand and then sits behind his desk, and I lower myself into the chair opposite.

"So, Asher," he begins, releasing a tired sigh and rubbing his forehead. "He came to live with me a month ago. Very withdrawn, and he won't talk to me. He screams when anyone touches him and hardly eats a thing. The club doc reckons he's suffering some sort of trauma after what he's been through, so I've arranged for him to see a therapist once a week. It starts next week."

"I assume you and his mum split up, then? Unless she's his . . ." I glance over my shoulder as if Carrie might appear, but I guessed she wasn't his mum the second Cooper told her to leave.

He looks at me confused. "No, he isn't mine, or hers."

"Oh, I just assumed—"

"Lady, I don't do kids, not mine and not anyone else's, as you can probably tell. He's my sister's kid. To cut a long story short, she died."

I sit like a goldfish. It wasn't what I was expecting to hear. "Poor Asher."

"Not really. She was a waste of space. Asher's dad is a member of a rival club. He got her into all kinds of shit, drugs, alcohol, prostitution. He probably ain't even the dad."

"So, social care gave him to you?" I ask doubtfully.

"Let's just say I was the better option, and the kid ain't got many." Cooper hands me a piece of paper with an address on it. "Every Monday from next week, he needs to go there. Max will take you and bring you back. That goes for anything you do. Max is now your personal driver. The kid doesn't go anywhere without a club member, so unfortunately, that means you too."

"Don't you think Asher may feel a little intimidated by you all?"

"It's not up for discussion princess. Who's your boyfriend?"

I'm taken aback by his question. "I don't see what that's got to do with you."

"It's got everything to do with me. I've requested a full background check on you, so if he's anyone I should know about, now is the time to tell me."

Most jobs like this require a background check, but none have ever gone into enough detail to check my associates. "There's nothing you need to know," I confirm.

"Max will show you around the kitchen."

"Do you require meals too?" I ask, because usually when I live-in, I cook for the whole family, but I don't like the thought of cooking for a whole club.

"No, Carrie does all that for the guys. You just look after the kid."

I give him my best 'are you kidding me' look, wondering what the hell she cooks, and he laughs. His face looks much more handsome when he isn't frowning.

Max shows me around the clubhouse properly. There's a large bathroom just for Asher and me on the same floor as our bedrooms. Cooper is on the same floor but has his own en-suite. The kitchen is big, with a modern-looking island in the centre. I can't wait to get Asher in there and bake.

I decide the first thing to do after my tour is bathe Asher. He's filthy, and I guess if no one was allowed to touch him, he hasn't been bathed properly in a while.

To my surprise, he enjoys bath time, splashing and laughing, although he still doesn't speak much. He looks like a new child once he's clean and dressed again. His blonde hair is soft and a lot lighter than I first thought.

"What do you like to eat, sweetie?" I ask, rubbing lotion into his pale cheeks. He shrugs, and I decide to take him to the kitchen, so he can see what's in there. Thankfully, it's empty. I was dreading bumping into Carrie.

Opening the double fridge, it's full of food but nothing that really stands out as healthy or wholesome. I find some peppers, onions, and eggs. "Omelette?" I suggest and Asher nods.

I sit him on the worktop and pass him a plastic knife. I cut the peppers into strips and then show him how to chop them smaller. He looks at me with delight as he sets about chopping.

Cooper saunters in and freezes. "Wow, did he get a bath?"

"Yes. It's basic childcare one-oh-one."

"Well, Carrie sorted all that," he mutters, shrugging.

"He hadn't been bathed in days, maybe longer."

He sits at the counter watching us chop vegetables. "What are you making?" he asks, screwing his face up.

"Well, we looked in the fridge and it's full of junk food. We managed to find this stuff to make an omelette, but we'll need to go to the supermarket tomorrow and buy some healthier stuff."

Cooper looks at me like I'm crazy. "There's stuff for burgers in there. Carrie always makes us burgers."

I notice Asher screw his face up in distaste. "You don't like burgers, sweetie?" I ask, smiling.

He shakes his head. "Yuck," he whispers.

"Why didn't you say?" asks Cooper. "Is that why you haven't eaten?"

"She said I had to eat them," he mutters, and we both gasp at his short sentence.

"Well, I think we need to try lots of different foods before we can find all the things you like. I don't mind if you don't like something, and I won't make you eat as long as you try it." I smile, and he nods.

"Good to hear him speak. I was giving up hope," mutters Cooper.

I sit Asher on a stool next to Cooper while I set about cooking the omelettes. I glance up every so often, noting how cute they look together. Words aren't spoken, but Asher is playing with a toy car on the worktop and every so often he runs it near Cooper's fingers and peeks up at him. Cooper realises and takes the car from him, gently driving it back in his direction, and then they take it in turns, pushing it to each other. My heart warms with pride. I've been here only a few hours and already we're making progress.

I plate up the omelettes, pass one to each of them, and they both tuck in. Cooper looks at me in amazement. "Wow, this tastes good."

"It's just an omelette. You must have eaten an omelette before?" I laugh.

"I haven't eaten anything but fast food and burgers for a long time."

I feel a small buzz in my stomach, I love to cook, and the thought of cooking for someone who will really appreciate it makes me excited. If he thinks an omelette is amazing, then the standards are low, and my mind is already planning what I need to buy.

"I love to cook. Maybe I can do extra for you and the guys when I do," I offer casually.

"Not for the guys, but for me, yeah."

"Why not the guys?"

"Carrie can look after them, it's her job," he mutters. "She's gotta pay her way."

"Won't she mind me cooking for you, if you're her man and the boss around here?"

"Stop digging for information, Mila." I roll my eyes seriously, like it isn't obvious that she's something to him.

After they've both cleaned their plates, I pull a stool to the sink and Asher helps me wash the dishes. He's smiling, and I love that he's already responding to me.

Cooper is staring at his mobile phone when the door swings open and Carrie comes in. She glares at me but then snuggles into Cooper's side. He looks mildly irritated by her display of affection, but I pretend to show no interest. She's clearly doing it for my benefit and marking her territory.

"I'm going to cook up some burgers, baby. How many do you want?" She smiles sweetly.

"I've just eaten, but thanks anyway," he says, not looking up from his phone.

"Eaten what? You can't cook."

"The new girl made me an omelette."

"An omelette? You hate shit like that," she almost screeches, clearly outraged.

He stands, still staring at his phone. "You wouldn't know what I like."

"I know exactly what you like, especially in the bedroom," she snaps, and he laughs, finally looking up at her.

"I wouldn't say that. You think you do, but you don't actually know," he smarts and leaves the room.

Carrie turns to me, scowling. "Listen up, bitch, you keep your hands and eyes to yourself. Cooper is mine. I'm his ol' lady. He ain't got room in his life for you and your stupid fancy food."

I lift Asher from the stool, but he won't let me place him on the floor. Instead, he clings to me until I sit him on my hip.

"Asher, come to me," demands Carrie, approaching us.

He shakes his head, his floppy blonde hair shaking with the movement. "Don't tell me no, you little shit. I've looked after you for the last month." Asher snuggles his face into my neck, and I walk around her towards the door. "Hand him over, new girl," she growls.

"Not a chance," I say, leaving the room.

We go back to his bedroom and collect some toys before making our way back down to the main room. He sets up a space by the sofa and plays quietly while I sip on a coffee.

It's a little busier in here now. I assume many of the guys have finished their day jobs and are hanging out here. A few guys play pool, and there's a couple snuggled together watching the large screen television that hangs from the wall. The woman looks about my age and keeps glancing over, so I decide to break the ice. After all, if I'm going to be around here more, then I need to make friends. It's clear Carrie won't be a fan of mine.

"Hey, I'm Mila," I introduce, "Asher's new nanny." She returns my smile and pushes to sit upright. Her blonde hair falls loose around her small shoulders. She's a tiny build and sitting next to the huge biker makes her look even smaller.

"Hi, I'm Brook. This is Tanner, my husband." He glances my way and gives me a nod before turning his attention back to the screen. Brook tries to move closer to me, but he pulls her back and wraps his arm around her waist. She laughs, playfully slapping at his strong, tattooed arm. "Baby, let me up so I can talk to Mila." He grunts but releases her begrudgingly, and she moves to the armchair nearest me. "How did you end up here? You with one of the guys?"

I shake my head. "No, my friend, Harper, works the bar. She kind of got me the job."

"I love Harper," she says. "She was born to run that bar. She keeps these guys in line." I laugh because she's probably right. I can imagine Harper not taking any bullshit, even from these big, burly men. "So, who have you met? Apart from the grizzly bastard." I stare at her blankly cos that description could mean any one of these bikers. She giggles and clarifies, "Cooper."

"Oh," I laugh, "erm, just Max and Carrie." At the mention of Carrie's name, Brook's smile disappears. "Not a fan then?" I ask, and she visibly shudders.

"Watch her, she's sly. Almost came between me and Tanner a few months back. I don't know why Cooper keeps her around. None of the ol' ladies like her, but the guys don't seem to see her like we do."

"Well, she certainly doesn't like me," I say. "She warned me off Cooper just now. And poor Asher seems scared of her."

"She's horrible to him. She's nice in front of Coop, though. She couldn't wait to play mum, hoping Coop would make her his ol' lady."

"Hope you ain't gossiping, B," growls Cooper, appearing in front of us.

She grins up at his huge frame. "Me, gossip?" she says innocently, and a small smile tugs at his lips. "I was just telling Mila to take no notice of Carrie. She's stamping her territory around you."

He looks annoyed. "What's she said?" He directs the question at me, and I shift uncomfortably. I don't want to stir shit up, especially not with her.

"Don't worry. I can handle Carrie. I'm here to do a job and that's it."

"What. Did. She. Say?" he asks, punctuating every word.

"That she's your ol' lady, of course," jumps in Brook, looking pleased with herself.

Cooper huffs and pulls out his phone, shooting off a text message before sitting down near Tanner.

Carrie is chatting to some guys at the pool table when a leggy brunette enters. All eyes go to her because she's stunning. Her hair hangs in loose curls past her waist, her skin is tanned, and her smile is wide, making her whole face look radiant. She makes a beeline for Cooper. He watches her, and I find myself shivering. His eyes go dark, his face unreadable, but I know without a doubt that he's fucked her.

She stops in front of him, and he stands, taking her hand and tugging her the last step so that she's pressed against him. He bends slightly, moving his face so it's inches from hers. I find myself holding my breath, like I'm watching a romance movie. Then their mouths collide, and I suck in a gasp. It's the hottest kiss I've ever seen, hungry yet gentle.

Brook nudges me and it takes me a second or two to look away. She's nodding towards Carrie, and when I look over, her face is red with anger.

"He's showing her that he doesn't belong to anyone," whispers Brook.

"Why doesn't he just tell her?" I ask, confused.

"These guys don't do well with words or emotions. And he probably has told her but she wouldn't listen."

I watch as the girl wraps her legs around Cooper's waist, and he carries her from the room, their lips still connected and his large hands cupping her arse.

"Careful, Mila. You look like you want to be that girl." Brook laughs, and I feel myself going red with embarrassment. The whole exchange was hot. I haven't ever seen it like that before, not unless it was in a film. Aaron and I don't even hold hands in public let alone kiss like we want to eat each other.

CHAPTER THREE

Asher finally falls asleep around nine in the evening. I had tried to tuck him in at seven after reading him a story, but he cried when I tried to leave him, so I sat with him for another half an hour. Then, when I finally got away, I found myself watching him on the baby monitor from my bedroom. He's so adorable, and my heart breaks for his lost little soul.

Max gave me the baby monitors, saying that sometimes things in the club can get loud, so if I'm downstairs, I can keep a constant eye on Asher.

Eventually, I decide to go down to the bar. Harper texted me to say she's working a double shift, and it beats sitting up here alone watching a sleeping child.

I find a stool at the end of the bar. It's a good spot because I can see everyone. I love to people watch.

Max joins me, ordering us each a drink. He looks too clean-cut to be a biker. Most of the guys look mean, in a grizzly kind of way, all beards and hard stares, but Max is clean-shaven, his hair cropped short and brushed to one side. He has the tatts and the size like the rest, with thick, muscled arms, and he clearly works out. Most of these guys would make Aaron look tiny.

"Stop looking at me like that, new girl," says Max, sliding a gin and lemonade towards me.

"Like what?"

"Like you want to eat me."

I flush with embarrassment. "I do not. I have a boyfriend."

He grins wider. "That just makes it even more exciting." I roll my eyes at his teasing.

Thinking about Aaron makes me pull out my phone and send him a text asking how he is and what he's up to. It was supposed to be date night tonight. I leave my phone on the bar cos Aaron never texts me straight back.

Harper comes over to where we're sitting and leans against the bar. "Hey, gorgeous, you over Kain yet?" asks Max.

She scowls at him. "There is no me and Kain."

"Then why won't you let me take you out?"

"Come back when you're a real biker, little boy."

Max takes a gulp of his beer. "You wound me, gorgeous, but I know you don't mean it. I won't hold it against you when you're begging me to fuck you." He gets up and walks away.

I laugh at his boldness, but Harper looks annoyed. "He means no harm," I defend.

"Please, the boy is annoying as hell."

My phone flashes, indicating Aaron has texted me back. I unlock the screen and try to decipher the text. It's clear that he's drunk. I feel a tingling sensation across my back, like someone is behind me, and then Cooper leans over my shoulder, his face almost pressing against my cheek.

"You begging the boyfriend to rescue you from this biker hell?" His voice is deep, sending shivers down my back.

I press my mobile to my chest. "It's rude to read my private messages."

Cooper sits beside me, and my body sags with relief. He makes me so nervous prowling around me like that. He waves a finger to Harper, and she sets about making him a drink.

"How long have you been together?" he asks, staring directly ahead.

I shrug. "A couple of years."

"You live together?"

"Not yet. We're saving to rent somewhere."

He looks amused. "The man can't even buy you a house? He ain't for you."

"Money doesn't buy love," I say indignantly, resenting how he's mocking Aaron.

"He can't take care of his woman."

"I don't need a man to take care of me. I can take care of myself." His old-fashioned beliefs piss me off. "Is that how you like things, Cooper?"

He shrugs, knocking his whiskey back and waving the empty glass in Harper's direction. "I admire a woman who can take care of herself, but I don't want my woman to have to do that. I want to give her the option to let me care for her. Isn't that what women want? A man who can provide, who can treat his woman like a queen?"

"Some women, maybe," I agree.

"But not you? You want a man who lets you pay the bill after a meal? Who lets you take control and sort out your half of the rent?"

I've never really had a man who's offered to pay for anything. Aaron is my first serious relationship, and we've always split the cost of meals and shopping, even the cinema.

"I haven't really had a man who's wanted to pay for things," I admit, and he shakes his head in disgust.

"My mum raised me to respect a woman and treat her like a queen so that she'll always look after me when I need it."

"Is that why you don't have an ol' lady yet?" I ask, taking a sip of my gin.

"I had an ol' lady, but she died. No one even comes close to her, and no one ever will. I'm not looking for a replacement."

My heart twists in my chest. Cooper's clearly had a lot of heartache. He looks too young to have lost the love of his life. I can't imagine ever losing Aaron like that. "Focus all that love you have inside on Asher."

He gives me a side glance. "Love inside?" he repeats, raising an eyebrow.

"Pass on what your mum taught you. She obviously did a good job."

My mobile rings and I answer it.

"Hey, Aaron." I smile. Cooper stiffens beside me, and I look around, trying to work out why. My attention is pulled back to my call when I hear Aaron's voice. I realise quickly that he's butt-dialled me.

"Aaron," I say loudly, trying to get his attention. There's a giggle and my blood turns to ice when I realise he's with a girl. I go silent, trying to listen, but it's difficult with the bar being so loud. Someone has started up the juke box, so I head outside to the carpark.

There's more giggling and I hear Aaron laugh. "Shh, you'll wake my mum," he whispers. I go cold. Surely, he wouldn't be with another woman. There's more giggling, and then a few moans, followed by a definite noisy kiss.

I disconnect the call, staring blankly at the screen. It wouldn't be the first time he's cheated. At the start of our relationship, he slept with a woman at work.

It was an office party and he had just started at the company in property sales. I think he wanted to get noticed, but he felt guilty and confessed what he'd done the second he saw me. I gave him another chance because I was falling hard for him.

My thoughts are disrupted when the door opens and Cooper comes out. He sticks a cigarette in his mouth and lights it. I watch it glow before he turns to me, looking annoyed. "You shouldn't stand out here alone, new girl. Where's Max?"

"Actually, Cooper, I need to get out of here for an hour. Can I leave Asher with Max? He's already sleeping."

"Where do you need to go so urgently on the first night of the new job?" When I don't answer, he looks even more pissed. "Oh, I get it. One call from lover boy and you need to go. Does he want you to pay a bill for him?"

I look down at my phone and then back to Cooper. Tears fill my eyes and I swipe at them angrily. "I need to check on something. I won't be long." I make my way towards my car and pull the door open. It slams shut before I can get in, and I turn to Cooper, who has his hand pressed firmly against it.

"You can't just walk off the job for your boyfriend," he snaps.

"He butt-dialled me. He's at his mum's with another woman, and I need to see it for myself."

He raises his eyebrows and then takes the car keys from my hand. "I'll drive." I'm too upset to argue, so I hop into the passenger side. I almost smile as Cooper squeezes himself into my small car. After spending a few minutes adjusting my seat to accommodate his long legs, he seems satisfied and starts the engine.

I direct him to Aarons mum's house. We park just up the road, and Cooper turns off the engine. He opens the car door to step out, but I shake my head. "I can't go in there."

He settles back in the seat. "Well, what's your plan? Sit here and wait? She might be in there all night."

I smirk. "Trust me when I say she won't be in there all night,"

He laughs, and I immediately like how his face lights up when he smiles. It makes me smile too, and I momentarily forget about my heartache. "He ever cheated before?" Cooper asks.

I nod, not taking my eyes from Aaron's front door. "In the beginning. It was before we'd had sex. Does that still count?"

"Hell, yes, it counts." He surprises me with the venom in his voice. Cooper looks like the type who would cheat and not give two thoughts about it.

"Have you ever cheated?" I ask, and then realise it sounds sexist, like I assume all men cheat. "Or been cheated on?" I add.

"No. I don't think any man would be stupid enough to take what's mine."

"You know, women aren't possessions, Cooper. You talk like they are."

"When I love a woman, she wants me to possess her," he says, and I roll my eyes. "But since Anna, I don't feel that urge anymore. The thought of having another woman on the back of my bike . . ." He lets the sentence hang in the air but shakes his head like the thought alone kills him inside.

"I've never lost anyone that close to me. It must be hard."

"It becomes a way of life for people like me. If it's not through drugs or drink, it's some rival bastard. Can't take your eye off the ball for a second cos if you do, it hits you even harder." He has a faraway gaze in his eyes, and I feel like the conversation has taken on a whole new turn.

"And which one took Anna?" I ask quietly.

He glances at me briefly before staring straight ahead again. "I reckon that's enough bonding tonight, newbie."

We sit in silence for another thirty minutes. "How long do you plan on waiting?" he asks. I'm about to answer when Aaron's door opens and a brunette steps out. She stops and turns back to the door. That's when it hits me hard in the gut. Up until now, I was trying to convince myself that it was a misunderstanding, but there is no more denying it as Aaron steps out in his boxer shorts to lean in for a kiss.

"That your man?" grumbles Cooper. I nod, tears rolling down my cheeks as I watch the only man I've ever really loved kiss another woman.

"Aww, fuck, newbie, don't do that crying shit. I can't cope with all that. Get the fuck over there and sort the bastard out." He must be crazy if he thinks I'm getting out this car. I can't confront Aaron. "So, what? You're going to pretend you haven't seen it? See him tomorrow and act like nothing's happened?"

I haven't really thought about it. Maybe? I didn't plan what would happen once I'd confirmed my suspicions, but before I can answer, Cooper is out the car and marching around to the passenger side. He yanks the door open and grips my arm, but I hold onto the seat so he can't drag me out. "Get the fuck over there," he growls. I shake my head, clinging on for dear life.

"Cooper, I can't," I whisper hiss. Luckily, we're far enough away for them not to hear.

"Then I will," he snaps, closing my door and heading in Aaron's direction. I stare after him, horrified, and then my brain kicks into gear and I scrabble for the door, practically falling out of the car.

"Cooper, wait," I hiss, but he carries on striding towards the kissing fuckers. By the time I've caught up, he's at the edge of the pathway that leads up to Aaron's garden. They both turn to him, confused as to why this mountain of a man is glaring at them.

"You forgetting something, Romeo? Like the fact you have a girlfriend?" Cooper growls. Aaron's eyes fall to me, and he freezes. "Yeah, shithead, she's really here."

"It's not what it looks like, baby," Aaron says to me with a pleading look in his eyes.

The girl glares at Aaron in disbelief. "Are you shitting me?" she screeches.

"Not now, Kit," he hisses. "Baby, come inside so we can talk about this," he adds, looking directly at me.

I remain behind Cooper. "She doesn't want to hear your crap."

"How long?" I ask quietly. "Just tonight, or do you do this all the time?"

Aaron shakes his head. "No, baby, it was this one time. I'm so sorry. I was missing you, since you ditched me on date night, and I got drunk."

The girl turns to him and slaps him hard across the face and then turns to leave. "Sweetheart, he's lying to you. He's cheated on you plenty with me. I've been meeting him for at least a year," she throws my way before marching off.

"That's a fucking lie and you know it," yells Aaron. He rushes towards me, grabbing my hands in his. "I love you. I want to marry you and give you babies. So, I've had a few slip-ups, but it doesn't mean anything. It's just sex." I yank my hands away from him. Pain must be evident on my face because I hear Cooper let out a string of curses.

"A few?" I repeat. Aaron grabs me by the shoulders, pulling me into his arms, but I remain stiff and unresponsive.

"Baby, please, just come inside so we can talk," he begs.

I shake my head. "No, Aaron. We don't need to talk. It's over."

"Don't be fucking stupid, Mila. It's over when I say it is," he snaps, holding me at arm's length now and glaring at me.

Cooper steps closer. "I think that's enough excitement. Let the lady go."

"Who the fuck is this guy?" Aaron growls impatiently.

"The man who's gonna show Mila how a queen should be treated," snaps Cooper, shoving Aaron out of the way and taking my hand. "Let's get you home, newbie," he says to me gently.

I let him guide me back to the car and sit me inside. He straps me in and checks it's secure before softly wiping a thumb over each cheek, rubbing the tears away. "Fuck that prick, Mila. He doesn't deserve you."

I know he's right, but I can't hear that right now. My heart hurts, and I feel like I need to vomit. How many times has he jumped from someone else's bed into mine? These thoughts plague me as we drive back to the clubhouse.

When we arrive back, the car park is full of motorbikes, way fuller than when we left. "Shit, looks like a party," mutters Cooper, and I glance at my watch. It's eleven in the evening. I hope the noise hasn't woken Asher.

Inside, the place is heaving. I follow Cooper through the crowd until we reach the bar. Max gives me a thumbs-up to indicate Asher is fine, and I respond with a grateful smile.

"You want a drink?" asks Cooper. Before I can answer, the brunette he kissed earlier sidles up to him. He smiles and kisses her on the head, so I decide to slip off and go to bed. It's been a long day.

CHAPTER FOUR

My first week as Asher's nanny flies by. Each day, he's showing me a little more of himself, and I think he's trusting me more and more. We've ventured out to the park, much to Max's disgust, as well as to the store to stock up on various ingredients. Asher has helped me most days in the kitchen, trying lots of different foods, and so far, he hasn't disliked any. Our cooking time is a welcome distraction from Aaron and I find myself teaching Asher how to bake too.

I've had non-stop calls and texts from Aaron. He ran straight to my parents and gave them a sob story, and somehow, they seem to be on his side. I know my parents were happy that we were looking to settle down together, but I thought they would listen to my side over his. My mother's response was that all relationships hit problems and that couples must work at it. I've ignored everyone's calls because I'm too hurt to speak to any of them right now.

I take Asher down to the bar to see Harper for a while. It wastes some time, and I need the adult interaction to keep myself sain. Kain stands at the bar, waiting to be served, but Harper ignores him and comes straight to me. Taking a seat, I place Asher beside me so he can run his cars along the bar.

"Kain was first," I tell her.

She glances back to Kain before shouting, "Joe!" The other bartender comes out from the back, drying his hands.

"Yeah, Angel?"

"You have a customer."

"Oh, right," he mutters before grabbing a bottle of beer and snapping off the cap.

"I'm doing what you suggested, toning down the crazy and paying no attention," she whispers when she notices my confused expression.

"Well, I hate to be the one to break it to you, honey, but he just looks pissed off."

She grins. "Does he? What's he doing?" Her tone is far too eager for my liking, and I'd say she's enjoying this. I glance over.

"Erm, well, he's glaring over here, for a start. Can you feel his eyes burning into your back?" She giggles. "Wow, seriously, Harps, he looks really mad."

"He tried to chat with me last night, and I just stared at my phone the whole time, pretending to text. It drove him crazy and he threatened to smash my phone."

"Well, maybe it's actually working then," I say doubtfully.

"You gonna keep this up much longer, Harper?" Kain suddenly shouts. She glances back over her shoulder again.

"Sorry?" she asks in a bored tone.

"Yeah, you should be," he grumbles.

"Sorry, as in what do you mean, not as in an apology," she clarifies.

He scowls at her. "Cut the bullshit. What the hell did I do?"

"Nothing. What's got you so paranoid?" I have to hand it to her—she's playing a good game. He looks fit to explode.

"You've been ignoring me for days now."

She gives a laugh. "Seriously, you bikers," she tuts. "You think the whole world revolves around you. I've got myself a new man, and he doesn't like me flirting with other men."

Kain curls his huge hands into fists. "What did you just say?" he grates out. I can see a pulse ticking in his forehead and his jaw clenches.

"Too far, Harps, too far," I whisper.

"Would you like your missus flirting with other guys?" she asks innocently.

"You got a man? Since when? Who the fuck is he? Do I know him? Is he one of the guys?"

She laughs. "What's with all the questions?"

"Answer me," he yells, slamming his fist down on the bar. We both jump, and Asher begins to cry. I sweep him up and hug him to me, whispering words of reassurance in his ear.

"Jesus, Kain, what's gotten into you?" Harper hisses, reaching over and stroking Asher's back.

Kain slams his empty beer bottle down and stomps out.

"Wow. I think you made your point," I say, wide-eyed. "You need to give me some pointers so I can bag myself a hot arse man like that."

"Try it with Cooper. See if you can get under his skin."

"No way. He scares the shit out of me on a normal day. Didn't your mum ever teach you not to poke a bear?"

"Where's the fun in just looking at the bear when you can rile him up and make him take you back to his cave?" Harper laughs, walking away to serve some customers.

―――⁂―――

By the time I get Asher into bed that evening, I'm so tired, I could literally fall asleep while standing. I'm watching the big screen in the main room, one eye on the baby monitor just in case Asher wakes, when Brook joins me, her face crumpled in annoyance. "What's up?" I yawn.

"Tanner's pissing me off," she mutters, glancing at the door.

"Not another love drama. I can't deal today." I quickly fill her in on the Harper-Kain drama from earlier, and she laughs.

"Kain is mad about Harper. He warned all the guys off her within the first week of her being here."

The door crashes open and Tanner stalks in, his eyes scanning the room until they fall on Brook. She stands quickly, taking on a stance that looks like she's ready to fight.

"Get the fuck upstairs, now," he orders.

"Don't you tell me what to do, Carl Tanner. I don't even want to look at you right now," she yells. For such a tiny person, she sure can shout.

"You're mad at me?" he yells. "How the hell does that work?"

"I was giving him directions, not riding him."

He marches towards her, anger making his expression crazed. She backs away and around the side of the couch so he can't get to her. I briefly wonder if I should intervene, or at least get Cooper.

"You were practically eye fucking him."

"He was a good-looking guy, and eye fucking is not cheating."

"I make up the goddamn rules, Brook," Tanner growls. "You can only eye fuck me," he adds, moving towards her again. They begin circling the couch, like they're stalking each other as prey.

"So, what, you gonna poke my eyes out for looking?"

"If I have to, darlin'," he drawls.

"You're ridiculous. You eye fuck girls all the time."

He makes a sudden dive over the couch, almost knocking into me. He grabs her by the waist and pulls her to him, despite her failed attempts to hit him away. When she finally stills, giving in to her fate, he tilts her head back to look at him. "You make me crazy," he mutters, gently pressing a kiss to her nose. I see the anger melt away from both of them, and they grasp onto each other as their mouths crash together in a hungry kiss similar to the one I watched just last week between Cooper and the pretty girl. I sigh. I need to find me a man who's this passionate about his woman. Maybe Cooper was right, a man who can take care of me for once is probably just what I need, and these bikers seem to have possessiveness by the barrel load.

Max joins me soon after the love birds have disappeared to eat each other's faces some more. "What's up, buttercup?" he asks.

I shrug. "Just missing Aaron, I guess."

"He was a dick. You can do so much better, Mila. I don't know if you realise this, but you're actually pretty fine." He grins, making me smile.

"Yeah?"

He nods. "Hell yeah."

"You gonna take me on a date?" I ask.

"I would love to, but I like my balls attached to my body," he states.

"Max, I'm not after your balls."

"It ain't you I'm worried about. If Pres gets wind of us doing anything other than babysitting that kid, well, I don't even wanna think about it." He shudders.

"Since when does he get a say in my love life?"

"Since you got that kid to laugh for him. He don't want any of us near you like that. Trust me when I say, none of the guys will touch you, even if they all have blue balls because of it."

Well, great, there goes my plan to bag a hot biker for face eating and possessive loving.

It's late and I can't sleep, so I decide to get my Kindle and read a few chapters of the latest romance novel I've downloaded. My bedroom door is slightly ajar in case Asher wants to get to me, and I hear the floorboards creak outside my room. Glancing up, I see Cooper standing there watching me.

"Sorry, didn't mean to disturb you," he whispers, pushing my door open farther.

"That's okay. I can't sleep."

He enters my room, and I pretend not to notice the blood staining his grey T-shirt. "I just got in. It's been a long night." He sighs, glancing down at the blood and then his hands. He looks troubled, so I shift up, making room for him to sit down.

"Wanna talk about it?" I ask as he lowers himself onto my bed.

He gives a short, unamused laugh. "I wouldn't want to darken your pretty little head with my shit."

"Well, the offer's there. If you leave that shirt, I can get the blood out." It's all I can come up with because I'm not sure how to react to a man standing before me covered in someone else's blood.

Cooper sits quietly for a moment and then kicks off his boots and stands. He pulls off his cut and chucks it onto the little white chair in the corner of my room. He lifts the T-shirt over his head, exposing the hard, muscled chest that I've been wanting to see since the moment I met him. I watch with wide eyes and an open mouth. He catches my expression and gives a small smile.

"Can I just lay here for five minutes? When I'm with you, the noise ain't so loud in here." He sighs, tapping is temple. I nod because, quite honestly, he looks so vulnerable right now, it breaks my heart.

He lays next to me, on top of the duvet, and I pick my Kindle back up and continue to read, even though I'm taking nothing in because my heart is pounding at a hundred beats per second.

"Max tells me you warned the guys off me," I say quietly.

He gives a laugh. "I bet he did. Why would he have to tell you that, I wonder?"

"I may have asked him on a date." I smirk.

He quirks an eyebrow up. "You like Max?"

I shrug. "Just feeling lonely, I guess. I wanted a night out."

"You know they call him Mad Max, right? That guy is crazy."

"Says the man who just came into my room covered in someone else's blood," I scoff.

"I warned the guys off because I know what they're like, Mila. I didn't want them to fuck you over and mess everything up for Asher. He likes you, and he's finally looking settled."

I nod, I guess that makes perfect sense, but my heart does a little squeeze. Part of me was wondering if he was warning them off for another reason, and I can't help but feel disappointed. Sometime later, I wake and realise I can't move. The room is dark and I'm too hot. I try to shift, but something beside me groans before pulling me closer. I snuggle into the warmth and drift back off to sleep.

I open my eyes and blink a few times. The light makes me squint as I look next to me at the empty space Cooper left. There's no evidence he was ever here apart from the faint smell of his aftershave on my pillow. I wonder what time he woke and left my room. After Asher and I are up, washed, and dressed, we head down to the kitchen. There're a few guys chatting at the kitchen table in the centre of the room while Carrie is frying up some bacon. She does this most mornings, and Asher and I usually wait until she's out the way so we can make our usual pancakes–something Cooper usually hangs around for. Today, I notice he's tucking into bacon while reading a newspaper and sipping coffee. He glances up but doesn't really acknowledge us. I sit Asher next to him on a stool before getting the ingredients out for pancakes.

"Morning, Mila. Good night's sleep?" asks Max. I feel myself blush. It's not an unusual question, in fact, Max asks me this every morning, but today, I feel like everyone is gossiping because Cooper spent most of the night in my bed. Not that anything happened. One minute, he was chatting to me, and the next, he was fast asleep. I didn't have the heart to wake him and kick him out, so I placed a pillow between us and went back off to sleep. When I woke in the night, Cooper was definitely wrapped around me. The pillow wasn't the best barrier, and while I'm sure he must have thought he was with one of his women, you can't hold people responsible for their actions when they're asleep. Anyway, no one would know—no one comes on to our floor, and Cooper doesn't look like the type to gossip.

I realise I haven't answered and the room has gone silent. Everyone is looking at me, including Cooper.

"Sorry, daydreaming. Erm . . . yes, thanks. Did you?" I stutter, making myself blush further. Max looks between me and Cooper and smirks.

"Got something to say, prospect?" growls Cooper, putting his newspaper down.

"No, Pres, of course not. Did you sleep well?" he asks.

"I was out late, clearing up other people's mess. Wasn't I . . . Mad Max?" he grates out, giving him a pointed look. Max looks sheepish and then goes back to eating his bacon.

Asher helps mix a pancake batter. "Would you like any pancakes?" I ask Cooper quietly, so Carrie doesn't hear. The last thing I need is her smart remarks.

"No, I'm good, thanks. Carrie sorted me out this morning." He winks in her direction, and I pause, pressing my lips together. This is a message, his way of him telling me not to look too much into last night.

"Okay. Did you leave your shirt out?" I ask, going back to mixing the batter and trying to sound friendly.

"What are you, my mother?" he asks with a laugh. I'm a little taken aback, but I know this is him acting the boss, so I brush it off. "Carrie can clean my shirts. I reward her well for all that shit." I give a nod, avoiding his eye.

I feel slightly humiliated by his dismissive attitude. I didn't wake up thinking we were married or anything, but he must really think he's something. Message received loud and clear.

I go about cooking pancakes, ignoring the conversation in the room, ignoring the fact that Carrie and Cooper are practically acting like lovesick puppies, and ignoring the fact that my heart feels a little bruised, even though it has no right to.

Later, I decide to take Asher to the fields that back up to the clubhouse. We pack a picnic and take a football. Max insisted on tagging along for safety, though I'm not sure what he thinks will happen to us in a field this close to the clubhouse.

It's peaceful here. I came on my first Sunday off last week to read my Kindle and knew Asher would love it too.

I'm lying on the picnic blanket in my shorts and a cropped vest, letting the sun heat up my skin, while Max and Asher kick a football back and forth to each other. Asher has finally warmed to Max. The fact that he must come everywhere with us has helped. He lets Max pick him up now, something he rarely lets anyone else do, apart from me.

A shadow blocks my sun and I open one eye. "Did you forget to put your clothes on?" growls Cooper, standing over me with his thick, tattooed arms folded.

I lean up on my elbows. "Did you want something?"

"Yeah, I'm going away tomorrow, for a few days. You'll need to take care of Asher."

"It's Sunday tomorrow," I point out. "That's my day off."

"Well, aren't you clever," he mutters, rolling his eyes. "That's my point. You'll have to have Asher tomorrow on your day off."

"No, you can't do that. I'm entitled to a day off. Get someone to have him or take him with you. I have plans."

He raises an eyebrow. "You have plans to, what, sit in this field, reading some fake love story where there's a happy ever after?"

"No, actually, I'm meeting Harper so we can get totally wasted on gin."

He snorts. "Not happening, especially when I'm not around."

"I think you're blurring the lines a little here, Cooper. You're my boss Monday to Saturday, and I have one day to myself. I intend to take it. What I do with that day is nothing to do with you, and as you so kindly pointed out earlier, I am not your mother, therefore, mind your business." I flop back down and close my eyes again.

"Jesus, Mila, I didn't come out here for a lecture. Take the rest of today off and Max can watch the kid tonight."

Asher comes barrelling towards me with Max hot on his heels, chasing him. I sit up just in time as he throws himself at me, and I make a dramatic show of falling back, wrapping him in my arms. Max drops down next to me on the blanket, out of breath and laughing. Cooper stares down at us.

"Fine. I'll take tonight and maybe you could give me one night in the week to make up for it. We have plans today, don't we, kiddo?" I smile at Asher.

"Ice cream," he squeals excitedly.

"Yes, you owe me ice cream." Max grins, shoulder-pushing me so I almost fall back again.

Cooper looks annoyed. "Actually, I need Max for a run this afternoon."

"Oh, well, looks like it's just me and you, kiddo," I tell Asher. Cooper doesn't miss the disappointed look on mine and Asher's faces.

"I'll take you," he snaps. "You can't go out alone." We watch in silence as he stomps back towards the clubhouse.

Max raises his eyebrows. "Message received," he mutters.

"What do you mean?"

"Pres isn't happy with me spending time with you both." He sighs, standing and holding a hand out to pull me up.

"You were just doing what he told you to," I say defensively. "Aren't we allowed to have fun too?"

"Apparently not. I could do without him crushing my balls, though, so don't take it personally if I'm more distant when he's around, okay?" I nod, but inside, I'm annoyed. Max is one of the very few who

I really get along with here, and he makes being here a lot easier each day.

CHAPTER FIVE

"Thought I gave you the night off?" snaps Cooper, observing me and Asher from the kitchen doorway.

"Well, you asked Carrie to take over and Asher doesn't like being with Carrie." I pour the homemade sauce over the pasta. "I can get him to bed and then have a night off. Max should be back by then to take over."

"The wonderful Max," he mutters sarcastically, taking a seat next to Asher and peering into the pot of food.

"Yeah, he is pretty wonderful." I smile, knowing full well this will annoy Cooper even more. "He wouldn't have let us down this afternoon." I'm referring to the fact that Cooper backed out of ice cream with me and Asher, sending another prospect instead.

"Something came up."

I roll my eyes. "How are you going to build a relationship with Asher if you never spend any time with him?"

"Look, Mila, I don't pay you to lecture me, and it seems you're doing a lot of that lately. Look after Asher. That's all I need you to do."

"Fine, apologies for overstepping," I snap sarcastically, slamming the bowl of pasta onto the worktop.

By the time Max returns, Asher is fast asleep in bed and I'm almost ready to meet Harper in the bar. We don't plan on going far, so I've stuck to skinny jeans and a low-cut bodysuit. With my hair hanging in loose curls and enough makeup to hide all my imperfections, I feel nice. I'm adding one more layer of mascara to make my lashes extra thick, when Max pokes his head in.

"Wow, Mila, you look amazing."

I stand and straighten my black jeans. "Thanks, Max. Let's hope Mr. Right is out tonight." I grin, wiggling my eyebrows.

He twists a lock of my hair around his finger. "And what a lucky guy he's gonna be."

Cooper sticks his head in and immediately looks annoyed when he sees me and Max. "What are you doing in here?" he growls.

Max drops the lock of hair and takes a step back. "Just letting Mila know that I'm here to take over with the kid, Pres."

With a smile across my face, I hand Max the baby monitor. I can see Cooper's eyes on my arse, and it feels good to know someone so hot is checking me out. Max leaves, and Cooper sits on my bed.

"Where are you heading tonight?" he asks.

"Not sure. Harper knows the bars around this way, so she's taking charge."

"Call me if you need anything," he mutters, clearly uncomfortable.

"Just say what you want to say, Cooper. You're making me feel uneasy."

"Will you be coming home tonight?" he asks casually, not meeting my eyes.

"Erm, I'm not sure. I might go back to Harper's. Depends where we end up. Why?"

"Just checking."

―――*ell*―――

Harper takes us to a quiet bar to start us off. We order a bottle of wine and take a seat by the window. It's a cosy bar with low lighting and fairy lights. Candles flicker on all the tables, and there's classical music playing in the background.

"How's things going with the job?" she asks.

"I like it. Asher is amazing, and I love that he's coming out of his shell. He's started therapy and seems so much happier."

"And what about Cooper?" She wiggles her eyebrows, and I laugh.

"What about him? He's moody and snappy and, wherever possible, I avoid him."

"And he hasn't mentioned last night's bed hopping?" I filled Harper in this morning when she arrived for the early shift at the bar.

"No. If anything, he's been weirder, asking me if I'm coming home tonight."

"Interesting."

"Not really. He made it perfectly clear this morning that he prefers the company of club whores over me. Carrie, in particular. He just pissed me off acting the way he did when it was him who came to me last night." I shrug, deciding I won't spend my night overanalysing Cooper. "How's your plan going to get Kain?"

"I haven't seen him since he stormed off in a mood yesterday. I think he's gone ahead on whatever job Cooper is on from tomorrow. I don't think we'll see them for a few days."

My phone flashes, indicating I have a text. I open it and groan. "It's Aaron."

"Wow, is he still bothering you?"

"Yep, every day, multiple times." I turn my phone off and tuck it into my bag.

By the third bar, I'm suitably drunk. "I'll regret this tomorrow morning when I'm looking after Asher," I giggle, knocking down a shot of sambuca down.

"I think we should head back to the club bar."

"What, so I can watch Carrie drool all over Cooper? No, thanks."

"Why do you care?" Harper asks, and then her smile gets wide. "Oh my god."

"What?" I ask innocently.

"You fancy Coop?"

"No . . . well, doesn't everyone? The man's a god. I'd have to be blind not to. But that isn't the reason I don't want to watch him with Carrie. I just hate her, and she hates me."

"Then we definitely need to head back to the club," she screeches, grabbing me by the hand.

The club bar is heaving when we get there. A few of the members from the Hammers MC are dotted about, but it's mostly full of people I've never seen before. Although the bar is owned and run by the MC, it opens to the general public most evenings, especially on the weekends. The club members usually take their party out back at the clubhouse.

Once we have a drink, we find a spot at the back of the bar. Harper decides to text Brook to see if she wants to join us.

"I need to dance, Harper." We put some money in the juke box and play Kings of Leon's 'Sex on Fire'. We jump about like the crazy drunk people we are, and then Brook joins us.

After a few more songs, my feet decide they need a rest, and I find a stool by the dance floor. A large man who I've seen around the club places a drink down in front of me. He isn't a Hammers member, but he's on friendly terms with Cooper because I've seen them together a lot.

"You're the nanny, right?" he asks.

"Mila." I smile, shaking his hand. He could easily pass for a biker—he's big-built with a well-shaped beard and tattoos. He would fit right in.

"You belong to anyone in there yet?" he asks, nodding to the door that leads to the clubhouse.

I laugh. "No, I'm not looking to be claimed."

He gently runs a finger across my wrist. "Just checking I'm not gonna get my balls ripped off when I do this," he says, and before his words have penetrated my drunken brain, his lips are on mine. He presses them firmly, testing my reaction, and when I don't push him away, he takes the kiss deeper. He places one hand to the back of my neck, gently tugging on my hair while his tongue caresses mine in a slow, sweet dance. My heart rate picks up and I feel heat in all the right places. When he pulls away, I'm breathless. I've never been kissed like that!

"You sure no one's claimed you?" he asks, looking over my shoulder. "Because the President of the Hammers MC is looking like he wants to rip my head clean off my shoulders right now." I try to glance behind me, but the guy grips the back of my neck a little tighter. "Don't let him see we've spotted him, or I'll have to acknowledge that he looks pissed, and that will lead to difficult conversations involving me leaving you alone, and that's something I don't feel like doing right now." He winks, pressing a gentle, quick kiss on my lips. "Brick, by the way," he introduces himself.

The girls join us. Brick kisses them both on the cheek, and I'm surprised to see they already know him. He buys us each a drink and then asks for my mobile number, which Harper gives him without hesitation. "I have to go and see Coop now. I can feel his eyes burning holes in my head." He grins and gives me another heart-stopping kiss.

"Bad news," warns Brook as soon as he's out of ear shot. "Like, really bad news. He's a walking STD, and that's not the worst of it. Steer clear of him, Mila."

"What? No way. The way he just came over here and took control . . ." I fan my face with my hand. "He's the best kisser," I whine.

"Because he's had a lot of practice," she says, laughing. She pulls out an antibacterial hand spray and squirts it in my general direction.

"Ew, Brook." I laugh, waving my hand about to blow the spray away.

"That's how serious I am. There must be someone else who's caught your attention. We're surrounded by gorgeous men in here."

I swivel slightly on my stool to get a better look at my surroundings. My gaze lands on the angry beast standing in a hulk-like stance and glaring at me, even though Brick is in front of him, clearly talking to him. I give a small wave and smile, but he doesn't respond. Maybe he isn't staring at me after all. Perhaps he's lost in thought but happens to be looking this way.

"That looks serious," remarks Harper, nodding towards Brick and Cooper.

"Cooper never comes into the bar on a Saturday night. He's spent most of the night in the clubhouse staring into his whiskey glass," says Brook.

"Maybe Mila can cheer him up," Harper suggests, dragging me from the comfort of my stool and pulling me towards the men.

"This is not a good idea, Harper. He looks like he's in a vile mood," I panic, trying to loosen her grip.

"His bark is worse than his bite. Well . . . sometimes."

"I don't want to find out. He's my boss." She stops in front of them, and they both stop talking to look at her.

"Can we get you gentlemen a drink?" she offers, smiling sweetly.

"Good night?" grits out Cooper, looking at me, and I suddenly feel more drunk. Maybe the sambuca was a bad idea.

"Yeah, it's been a very good night." I smile at Brick, who smirks but hides it well.

"How's your wife, Brick?" Cooper throws in, and Brick laughs.

"Shit move, Coop," he replies with a grin.

"Oh my god, you have a wife?" I screech, wiping my mouth like that will somehow undo the kiss we just shared.

"I've never known such a scary-ass woman. I'd hate to get on the wrong side of her," warns Cooper.

Brick rolls his eyes. "That's a lie. Sandra wouldn't care what I was doing or with who, seeing as we separated over two months ago."

"But you still go around there for your dinner, and isn't she pregnant with your kid?" Cooper asks innocently.

Brick smacks him on the back, laughing. "You made your point, Cooper. I'm stepping away." He kisses me on the cheek. "If it wasn't for this piece of shit, I'd be balls deep in your sweet little pussy right about now. If he hasn't claimed you by the time I'm next in town, I'm putting you on the back of my bike."

I watch him leave, my fingers lingering on the spot where he just kissed me. Despite what Brook or Cooper have said about him, I'm lightheaded at the thought of him coming back for me.

Cooper slams his glass on the nearest table, bringing my attention back to him. We stand in an awkward silence while Harper gets us a drink from the bar. "Not met your Mr. Right tonight then?" he asks.

Harper returns and pushes a drink in my hand followed by another sambuca. I knock it back and wince. Cooper continues to stare at me. I lick the sticky sambuca from my finger, and he groans.

"I need fresh air," I mumble, pushing my other drink into Cooper's hand and rushing outside. The cool air hits my skin and my head spins. I grip the wall to steady myself.

"Too much to drink?" asks Cooper, standing in the doorway, watching me take deep breaths.

"Maybe a little. I've had a crazy few weeks and needed to let loose."

"You like Brick?" he asks, coming to stand in front of me.

"He kissed me." I smile, touching my lips again. "I've never been kissed like that."

"Get your fingers off your lips and take that dreamy look off your face," Cooper grumbles in disgust. I lean back against the wall, looking up slightly. It's a clear night and there's millions of stars twinkling above us.

"He said he's coming back and putting me on his bike if no one claims me." I smile dreamily.

"Jesus, no one is claiming you, and he definitely is not putting you on the back of his bike," he snaps.

"Why do you care? I won't leave Asher," I huff. He stands in front of me in silence. "Why are you so grumpy all the time?" I add.

He places his hand against my cheek. I close my eyes and lean into his touch. For such a large, scary-looking man, his touch is warm and gentle. "I wanted it to be you," I sigh, "who kissed me."

"Yeah?" he asks. I nod, keeping my eyes closed, enjoying his touch.

I feel his shadow fall over my face and then his breath blowing lightly over my lips. I open my eyes and find myself staring into the greenest eyes I've ever seen. Before I can talk myself out of it, I lean closer, pressing my mouth against his. I part my lips slightly, and that's all the invitation he needs to thrust his tongue into my mouth. I groan because *this* is the best kiss I've ever had, even better than Brick's. It's forceful and demanding, and I find myself gripping his T-shirt, scrunching it up in my hands.

He pulls away, and I rest my forehead against his chest. His racing heartbeat tells me he was just as affected by the kiss. He rubs gentle circles on my back, and I can feel my eyes growing heavy.

"Let's get you back inside. It's getting cold out here." I follow him and head over to the girls, and he disappears back into the clubhouse.

"Oh my god, I've just kissed Cooper," I whisper. Their eyes widen in shock.

"Oh, you lucky bitch," groans Harper. "Was it as amazing as I've dreamt it to be?"

"Toe-curling."

"What perfume are you wearing tonight? You have them falling at your feet," says Brook, grinning. "Let's go through to the clubhouse. Tanner is blowing up my phone with texts. In case you haven't noticed, he doesn't like to be away from me for too long."

"Doesn't that drive you insane?" I ask.

She smiles. "You get used to it. He just loves me. These Hammer men love fiercely."

The clubhouse is pretty busy tonight. There're half-naked club whores hanging around and bikers all over them, not in the slightest bit bothered that there are people around. A couple of the guys are leaning on the pool table, getting full-on blowjobs.

"You get used to this too," sighs Brook, nodding towards them. "The guys need to let off steam, especially before they go on a job."

Tanner stalks over to where we're standing and wraps his arm around Brook's tiny waist. "You were gone too long," he grumbles, kissing her hard.

"I was just through that door, and I think I was gone for no more than an hour," she says, smiling gently and running her hand over his cheek.

"Bed, now," he orders, swatting her on the backside. She squeals and runs for the stairs, Tanner hot on her heels.

"Oh shit, Kain's here," whispers Harper, gripping my arm. "I thought he'd gone."

"Well, isn't this a good thing?" I ask.

"No. I haven't planned to see him. I haven't got my game face on."

I roll my eyes. "Just go and snog his face off," I suggest. As if he senses her near, he looks up, his face pales slightly, and he looks panicked. It doesn't take long to see why, as a red-haired girl hands him a drink before kissing him.

"Son of a bitch," Harper growls, turning her back on him.

"Who is that?"

"Ginger. They were a thing once upon a time."

"Oh, right." I follow her to a free couch and plonk myself down next to her. "Maybe these guys aren't the loving kind. Perhaps we need to look elsewhere," I suggest.

Harper looks thoroughly miserable. Cooper is by the snooker table, talking with Carrie. He keeps glancing over to where I sit but shows no signs of coming over. I know that kiss got his blood pumping. Carrie leans up on her tiptoes and pulls his face down to meet hers. He keeps his eyes open and fixed on mine as she kisses him full-on.

"Yep, I think we are definitely looking in the wrong place, Harps." I sigh. "Why don't you take one of the spare rooms tonight? Saves you getting a cab. I can't watch any more of this porn show tonight."

I feel his eyes track me as we leave the room. I won't allow myself to think about Cooper or the amazing kiss he just gave me. It was a passing moment that meant nothing. I repeat those words as a mantra as I climb the stairs to my room, after showing Harper to a spare room.

I stumble about, pulling at my clothes. I manage to get my shoes and jeans off before falling onto my bed. All the jigging about has done nothing for my dizziness and I lay spreadeagled on the bed in my bodysuit. I'm not sure how long I'm there before my stomach decides to protest at the amount of alcohol swimming around in it. I bolt upright and make a dash across the landing to the bathroom, just managing to get my head over the toilet before I spill the contents of my stomach.

Pressing my head against the tiled floor, I daren't move from the toilet even though I'm shivering with cold. The door opens and Cooper peers in. "Jesus, Mila, are you okay?" he asks, concern evident on his beautiful, rugged face.

I roll onto my back, giving him a full view of my bodysuit-clad self. Once I realise, I sit up quickly, trying to cover myself. "Oh god, my head," I groan, pulling my knees up to my stomach and resting my head there.

"Let's get you to bed." I feel one strong arm go under my legs and the other around my back, and then he picks me up with little effort and carries me back across the landing and into my room.

Cooper gently lays me down and pulls the blankets over me. "I can't sleep in this," I whine, kicking them back off and trying to sit up.

He hesitates before sighing and sitting on the edge of my bed. "How exactly do I get it off?" he asks, scanning me for an opening. I reach for the poppers between my legs, and he groans, turning his head away. I pull them apart and try to tug the bodysuit up, but I flop back down in frustration.

Then, I feel his warm hands glide up my ribcage. "I'm too drunk to be in here, Mila," he mutters. I lift my arms so he can help me out of my top and watch his conflicted expression as he battles with himself. He finally lifts it higher, exposing my pink lacey bra. It's practically see-through, but at this point, I don't care. He sucks in a breath and pulls the top over my head, dropping it to the floor. I reach around, fumbling to find the back of my bra. "No!" he says firmly. "Don't remove that, Mila. I can't promise to walk out of here tonight if you do."

I smile smugly when I find the clasp, unclipping it and pulling it away from my body. He groans and places his head in his hands.

Laying back down, I pat the space beside me. He thinks about it for a few seconds before losing the battle. Kicking off his boots, he climbs into the space at my side. I pull the covers over us and back up until my arse hits his thigh and I feel his body stiffen.

"You're making this impossible, Mila," he growls. I smile to myself, reaching for his arm and wrapping it around my waist. "Stop fidgeting." I feel safe in his arms, and that's my last thought before I drift off to sleep.

I feel the bed shift. It's light outside, so I open one eye to check the time. It's five in the morning. I groan, flinging my arm across my eyes. My head is spinning, and my mouth is dry. I turn onto my side to find that Cooper is still in my bed. He's fully clothed and staring up at the ceiling. "Cover yourself up, Mila," he mutters, and I pull the sheet tight around my body. *Why the hell am I naked?*

Cooper sits up, swinging his legs over the side of the bed. "Where are you going?" I ask.

He stands, stretching his arms out above his head. "I've got to go and do something about this," he tells me, gripping his evident erection through his jeans. "I'm on the road from today and the image of you laying there naked is gonna play on my mind on a fucking loop." He doesn't look pleased about it.

"Coop," comes a voice from the hall. It takes me a second to place it.

"You have got to be shitting me," I whisper-hiss when I realise it's Carrie.

"I know it's a real shit thing to do. I'm not proud right now, but I can't go on the road in this state."

"I don't mean to sound like a princess, but you'd rather fuck a club whore than me?"

"Don't do that, Mila. I'm your boss. You're Asher's nanny, and I just don't want to overstep that mark with you and fuck it all up for Asher."

"You know what, it's fine. You're right," I say. He gives a nod, then heads for the door. "But before you go . . ." I say, standing. He sucks in a breath, staring at my naked body. "Can you just write down Brick's number for me?"

His face turns to fury. "Don't fucking play games with me, Mila. It won't end well," he warns.

I give him my best innocent look. "Who's playing games? You think you're the only one with needs, Cooper? I'm a single woman right now," I remind him, pulling a T-shirt over my head.

"Cooper?" Carrie shouts again.

"Can you shut her up before she wakes your nephew," I snap.

"You aren't fucking Brick," he says firmly.

He watches me pull my underwear up my tanned legs, so I make a slight show of it by taking my time. "Have a great trip," I say with a smirk.

"Mila, are you listening to me?"

"I heard you, but I'm not listening. I'm not playing games with you, Cooper. You creep into my bed for two nights running. You give me a mind-blowing kiss that I know got your blood pumping. You wake up with an erection in *my* bed and decide that you'd rather have sex with the club whore over me. I'm very insulted and extremely pissed off."

He sighs. "I can't deal with this shit right now, Mila." He leaves, slamming the door behind him.

I flop back on my bed. I need to just concentrate on the job I'm here for. I didn't come here to meet a man. I was happy with Aaron, and we've only just split up, so there's no way I'm ready for anything new. Getting involved with Cooper is not what I need in my life right now. I can just imagine my parents' faces if I ever took him home to meet them. He isn't exactly the type of guy who screams marriage, kids, and security. But there's something about the man that has me so intrigued, I find myself not being myself at all around him. I turn into some sex-crazed monster. I groan aloud again, so frustrated, I can't think straight.

I decide to go for a shower to sort out my fuzzy head and then get breakfast sorted because my stomach is crying out for bacon. I take the baby monitor with me even though it's still early and Asher doesn't usually wake up until after seven.

I'm just tucking into my bacon at the kitchen table when the door flies open and Carrie and Cooper come stumbling in, laughing. It's quite clear from their dishevelled appearance and flushed faces what they've spent the last hour doing. Carrie has her arms and legs wrapped around him like a baby monkey, kissing his face as he tries to carry her. He sits her on the counter with the promise of feeding her to give her more energy. I roll my eyes and pick up my phone to give the impression I don't care about their sex marathon, or the fact that I'm horny as hell and I came close to being wrapped around him like a baby monkey. Scowling, I scroll through my emails, not noticing any of them.

"It was nice to see Kain and Ginger back together last night," says Carrie, smiling as she takes the coffee that Cooper hands her.

"Coffee, Mila?" he asks, turning to me. I shake my head, not looking up from my phone screen. "And I take it you were responsible for her showing up last night?" he asks Carrie.

"Oh baby, they belong together, like me and you." I feel her watching me before she says, "I noticed Brick hanging around you last night, newbie."

"Brick sniffs around anything with a heartbeat these days," mutters Cooper.

"Thanks," I say sarcastically.

"He's decided to stay around for a few more days. I could put in a word for you," Carrie suggests, smiling. She's trying to keep me occupied so I don't take her man.

"Mila can sort out her own shit," Cooper snaps before I can respond.

"That would be great, Carrie, thanks," I say, grinning.

He scowls at me, and she jumps off the counter. "I'll sort it asap. I need a shower. You coming, Coop?"

"I'll be there in a sec."

He waits for Carrie to leave before stalking over to me. "I'm not kidding. You aren't dating any of my guys, Mila. If you do, I'll fire you."

My mouth falls open in shock. "You can't fire me for that. There're laws in place."

"Sweetheart, round here, I am the law. You're here for Asher, not to whore yourself out for my men. If you want to be a club whore, I can change the job description and hire someone else for Asher," he warns, smirking. "And I don't want to hear of anymore performances like last night."

"What?" I ask, my voice low and weak. I feel humiliated because I know exactly what he's about to say.

"No slipping into bed in a drunken state and offering yourself out," he says, a disgusted look on his face. "A future tip—I like my women with a bit more class, and so does Brick. You reminded me of Carrie last night." I feel a stabbing pain directly in my heart, and my face flushes a deep red with embarrassment. He stomps out, slamming the door behind him as I stare after him in shock.

CHAPTER SIX

The week passes relatively quickly. I thought it would drag, seeing as I worked the Sunday, but it's been quiet around the clubhouse with just a handful of bikers remaining. The rest left on their run on Sunday afternoon.

It's been great not bumping into Cooper or having to see him and Carrie together around the club. The man sets me on edge just being in the same room, and after the way he spoke to me on Sunday, I'm relieved to have the break from him.

I've also reflected on the Saturday night incident and concluded that even though Cooper is gorgeous, he isn't good boyfriend material. He's much better suited to Carrie. With that in mind, I've treated Carrie exactly as I would if she was Cooper's ol' lady. It's working, because we've been getting on much better.

Cooper took Max on the run and left me and Asher with a new prospect. He's been with the club for a couple of months and is nothing like the rest of the bikers. He must only be around eighteen years of age, and he's skinny and pale-looking. He hasn't got much about him in the way of conversation and doesn't really interact with Asher, which I find disappointing.

Luckily, we've spent a lot of time with Sam. He's been around the club for over thirty years and is one of the oldest members. He's great with Asher and insists that he call him Grandpa. He told me he practically brought Cooper and his sister up.

Carrie gave Brick my number and we've sent some texts back and forth. I haven't been able to meet with him because of Asher. I thought about asking Sam to watch over him last night while I met him for some dinner, but then I thought about how Cooper would react and I really don't want to lose this job. Carrie said she can handle Cooper, and once he gets back, she'll talk to him.

It's Friday night and Asher is safely tucked up in bed. I decide I can't sit in my room all night, so I go down to the main room. Brook is moping about because Tanner has been away all week with the guys. She's sitting on the couch, staring at the large screen television.

"Any news?" I ask, sitting next to her. She shakes her head. Apparently, this is the hardest part of being a biker's wife. They go off-radar for days, and she just has to wait until he contacts her.

As if she conjured him up, the door opens and the guys pile in. Brook jumps up and runs to Tanner, flinging herself into his arms and wrapping herself around him. I watch them wistfully, a smile on my face. She looks so happy, and I'm pleased for her. She's been miserable without him these past few days.

I feel Cooper's presence as soon as he enters the room, but I avoid meeting his gaze because I know that somewhere in this room is Carrie. And because of our unspoken truce, I don't want to ruin it.

When I eventually see him, Carrie is by his side chatting to him, but his eyes are on me. I decide to make it work-related, to save any awkward looks from Carrie. "Welcome back, Cooper. Asher's been fine while you were away. If you want a rundown about him, just let me know and we can schedule a meeting." Carrie smiles like she's happy with that, but Cooper lets out a roaring laugh.

"I'm sorry, did Mary Poppins take over while I was away?" I feel myself blush. "Only, before I left, you were bending my ear like a nagging wife, and now, you're all professional and talking schedules?"

"Sorry, I didn't mean . . . I, erm . . ." I trail off, not sure what to say.

"Could it be anything to do with the fact that you got Carrie to put in a word for you?" he asks, his sudden change in tone unsettling me. Carrie looks annoyed and says something to him quietly. "Well, you wanted me to discuss it with her, so I am," he snaps at her. "So, you want to see Brick?" he asks, glaring at me. People are starting to look, and I feel embarrassed. "I'm pretty sure I hired you to look after my nephew, and now, you want to switch roles? That's fine, I mean, the job prospects aren't as good, and there's not really any benefits, but at least you get to keep a roof over your head."

I look at him, confusion on my face. I'm not sure if we're on the same page. "The guys will be pleased. There's a queue wanting to get in your pants." He grins and then turns to the gathering crowd. "Guys, good news, we have a new club whore. Brick's called dibs first, but after that, Mila is fair game." There's a few cheers and Carrie stares at me in shock.

"Mila, I didn't tell him to do that," she says in a panic.

I give her a small smile and stand. "It's fine. He's a prick," I mutter.

Suddenly, I feel hands wrap around my throat. I'm pushed back onto the couch, the breath knocked from my lungs, and I gasp, trying to prise the hand from my throat. I stare into Cooper's cold eyes. This is the Cooper that everyone is scared of. I can see why.

He rests a knee between my legs and leans over me, still gripping my throat. "Who the fuck do you think you're talking to, whore? I'm the fucking President of the Hammers MC and I've killed people for disrespecting me," he hisses in my face. "Club whores should show respect at all times."

I hear him before I see him. Asher is screaming from somewhere out of my view. It's a toe-curling scream of panic and fear. I haven't heard anything like that before.

Cooper looks up over my head and his expression is one of regret. His grip loosens, and I gasp for air, clutching my sore neck. He slowly gets off me and is replaced by a sobbing Asher, who jumps up and wraps himself around me.

"Leave Mimi alone," he screams. That's the nickname he's honoured me with. Mila was not suitable, apparently. I hug him to me, trying not to cry as the awareness of what just happened settles in.

"Hey, kiddo, I'm fine. It's okay," I reassure him.

Cooper watches us both. He looks like he wants to say something, maybe even apologise, but instead, he just stares.

His apology isn't wanted. He'll never be able to undo what he just did, and the fact Asher saw makes it ten times worse. I won't stick around to be humiliated by him.

I stand with Asher still in my arms. "I'll leave first thing tomorrow morning," I say coldly. I head for the door, the silence in the packed room eerie.

I'm sat on my bed, my bag half packed, when there's a small knock at the door. I stiffen at the thought of seeing Cooper. I had planned to sneak off early to avoid him. I would have liked to have said goodbye to Asher, but I'm not sure either of us could take that. Maybe when the dust settles, I can come back and visit him.

I open my door to find Brook holding a bottle of vodka. "Hey, doll. Fancy some company?"

"Tanner just got back. Go and see your man."

"This is more important at the minute. He isn't going anywhere."

I open the door wider, inviting her inside. She plonks herself down on my bed and unscrews the bottle cap, taking a swig. "So, that was pretty intense. I've never seen Cooper go off like that at a woman."

I sit next to her, shoving some clothes aside to make room. She hands me the bottle, and I take a swig. "He's an arsehole."

"Yeah, he is. But to see him so affected like that, makes me wonder if he's battling something deeper."

"Like psychopathic tendencies?" I ask, smirking. "He's unhinged."

"Well, according to Tanner, he hasn't acted this crazy over a woman since his wife."

"That means nothing. He told me himself that no one could ever come close to her. You're reading too much into all of this."

She takes the bottle back and drinks. "Maybe, but for Tanner to notice something like that..." she trails off.

"I'm outta here tomorrow. I won't be attacked or humiliated. I'd rather stack shelves in the local shop than put up with him for another second."

"What about Asher?"

"Don't put that on me, Brook," I mutter, sighing.

"I'm not, I'm just asking. I thought you were made of stronger stuff."

I glare at her, snatching the bottle and drinking the vile liquid. "He just humiliated me in front of everyone. He told them I was a whore."

"Do you even want Brick? Because he's probably only trying to piss Coop off."

"I don't know. I haven't had a chance to get to know him, but the more Cooper tells me no, the more I want to rebel. Why would he want to piss Cooper off?"

"Well, he's never really forgiven Cooper for marrying his sister." She slams her hand over her mouth. "I shouldn't have said that. He hates people knowing his business."

"I'm not around from tomorrow, so it's not like I'm going to say anything," I remind her.

"I guess," she mutters. "Cooper whisked her away and they came back married. Never even said he was with her like that. Brick was mad. Mad enough to hit the road alone. He was a big part of the Hammers before all of that, but he sees it as betrayal. Cooper should have spoken to Brick about it."

"Oh." I take another drink. My head is feeling a little lighter, the anxiety of the evening slipping away.

"Look, being in this life isn't a choice for most of us. We were born into it or dragged into it for whatever reason. But you, you have something, and I feel like you were meant to come into Cooper's life for a reason. I've actually seen him smile since you came. He drinks in the bar and hangs out with the guys more. Before you, he hid away, and the only time he came out of that office was to rip into someone."

"He'll find a new nanny."

"Just stay, Mila. You love Asher, and you've been amazing with him. At least stay until he finds a new nanny."

I shrug, not sure I can ever look him in the face again without having a panic attack. "He grabbed me by the throat," I remind her.

"He did, and I told him exactly what I thought of him. But stay for Asher." When I don't respond, she flings her arms around me.

"Just until he finds a new nanny," I snap, and she nods.

By the time we are halfway through the bottle, we're both suitably drunk. "Let's go back downstairs. Fuck Cooper and his moody ways," suggests Brook.

I'm doubtful of this new plan, but my drunken brain buzzes to life, along with my heart, the alcohol numbing the fear I felt earlier.

When we get downstairs, Tanner comes over and kisses Brook before leaning down and kissing me on the top of the head. "Ignore him baby girl, none of the guys will ever treat you like a club whore, I'll make sure of it." I'm grateful for the reassurance.

Cooper is sat on the pool table, looking into a bottle of Jack. He glances up, but I look away.

Brook sticks some music on the old juke box sitting in the corner of the room. Aerosmith's 'Crying' blasts out and we both jump around, singing to each other at the top of our lungs. I'm aware that Cooper is watching us, a small smile tugging on his lips, but I take no notice because I'm still really mad at him, even if my heart is trying to sway me otherwise.

Brook grins. "He can't take his eyes off you."

"It's guilt."

"Get ready for his apology then." She winks, moving away from me in time for Cooper to step in front of me.

"Oh, for heaven's sake," I groan. "It's taken half a bottle of vodka to chill me out and now you've come back for another go."

"Can I talk to you, in my office?"

"No!" I snap, turning away from him. I feel his huge arms wrap around my waist, lifting me off the floor effortlessly and throwing me over his shoulder.

I scream out, more in surprise than anger. Tanner steps in front of him, stopping him in his tracks.

"Are we gonna have a problem here, Pres?" he grits out.

"No, Tanner, we're all good," Cooper says calmly.

"Yes, we have a problem," I screech, but Tanner moves to one side, letting him pass with me over his shoulder like some caveman. Tanner winks at me as Cooper passes. "I thought you were going to protect me?" I say to him, and he shrugs. "Traitor," I hiss.

Cooper places me back on my feet once inside the office. "I'm sorry," he says firmly. "You won't hear me say it often, but I really am sorry." I nod, not wanting to engage in conversation. I'm hurt by his behaviour, and I can't just forget it like that. "Will you stay?"

"I'll stay until you find another nanny," I tell him.

"That's fair," he agrees, "but I'm hoping I'll change your mind before that happens. Asher really loves you, and I know it hasn't been long, but I've never seen him so happy."

"Most nannies will do amazing with him. He's an easy kid to love."

"I promise to keep my nose out of your personal business from this moment on," he vows.

"And no more sneaking into my room. It's not appropriate," I add, and he nods in agreement. I head for the door, and he makes no move to stop me. "And Cooper, don't ever lay your hands on me like that again."

The following day, Asher is more clingy than normal. He shies away from Cooper, scared at what he witnessed. I tell Cooper that he needs to take things slow and show Asher that he can trust him, but Cooper isn't convinced. I feel like he doesn't know how to behave around children.

We invite him to the park, but he makes up an excuse, and he does the same again when we invite him to the cinema. At this rate, Asher will have a better relationship with the club prospects than his own uncle.

Once Asher is in bed, I decide to try and win Cooper around. I knock gently on his office door. "Come in," he shouts. I find him hunched over some paperwork, looking serious and moody.

"Hey, you have a minute?" I ask hopefully.

He chucks his phone on top of the papers and leans back in his office chair. "You any good at numbers, Mila?"

"Not really. I failed maths," I admit, sitting opposite him. "I came to talk to you about Asher."

He sighs but gives a nod for me to go ahead. "I think he needs to see photos of family, maybe his mum and grandparents."

He scowls. "Why?"

"Because he's a lost little boy and asks questions a lot."

"He does?" Cooper looks surprised.

"Yeah. He asks where Mummy is and if Nana is with her."

Cooper pulls open a drawer and brings out a large photo album, passing it over to me. "There should be pictures in there of his mum before she turned into a mess."

"Why don't we all sit together tomorrow and go through this," I suggest casually.

"Maybe, but I've got a lot on," he mutters.

I leave the office feeling dejected and sad for Asher. The poor kid is relying on this guy to bring him up and yet they can't even look at each other right now.

CHAPTER SEVEN

It's been four weeks since I asked Cooper to go through the photo album with us. We're still waiting. I've given up asking him to join us for anything now because he never comes, and if he isn't bothered about his relationship with Asher, then why should I be?

It's a hot day today, so we decide to head out to the field and read a story. I've set up a parasol to shade Asher and laid out a blanket and some cushions. I'm hoping he has a nap out here so I can enjoy the beautiful sunshine and read my Kindle.

When we get to the field, I'm surprised to find Cooper there. He's laying back on the blanket I set out earlier in his comfy blue jeans and no top. I try not to drool over his tattooed abs. His body is amazing.

"To what do we owe this pleasure?" I ask. We haven't seen Cooper much at all these last few weeks. He's gone back to hiding out in his office all day. Sometimes I pass him in the hall when he's heading to his room, but we only converse in passing, and he hardly ever asks me about Asher.

"I brought the photo album and thought I'd spend some time with Asher."

"Wow, you hear that, Asher? Uncle Cooper is going to show us some pictures," I say in my best excited voice. Asher picks up on my tone and immediately smiles. We sit next to Cooper on the blanket, and he pulls out the album.

"I haven't looked at this since my wife passed," he admits.

He opens to the first page and the first picture is big enough to fill it. It's of Cooper when he was young, with a younger girl who I assume is his sister. There's no mistaking it's him, even though he's just a teenager in this picture. His green eyes are piercing.

"This is me and Kyla, my sister, Asher's mum." I smile. She's beautiful, with the same green eyes as Cooper surrounded by long, dark eyelashes. Both of their smiles are wide with perfect white teeth.

I point her out to Asher. "It's Mummy when she was a little girl," I tell him. Cooper turns the page and it's a family picture with his parents. His dad was clearly a biker too, and he looks the part. He has his cut on, 'Hammers MC' proudly displayed on the badge, and he has a long beard and a bandanna.

We go through various photos. Asher is enthralled, even though I'm not sure he really understands what we're looking at. Cooper freezes when he turns the page to a photo of him and a gorgeous blonde girl. She's looking up at him with complete love in her eyes, and he's got her tucked into his side like she's the most important possession in his life.

"Wow, Cooper, she's stunning. She looks so happy and . . ." I trail off when he abruptly turns the page. "I was going to say in love," I finish.

"Look, Asher, this is you and your mummy," he says gruffly, completely ignoring my comment and pointing to a picture of his sister holding a tiny bundle. She looks so proud, it breaks my heart.

Asher runs one of his little fingers over the face of his mother, looking so intently at it, like he's saving every detail. "Mummy." He smiles suddenly, looking up at Cooper. He throws his little arms around Cooper's neck, clinging onto him, and then he runs off towards his football, leaving us both stunned into silence.

After a few minutes, Cooper closes the book. "I think he needed that," I say quietly, and he nods. "I bet you miss them both so much, your sister and your wife."

"We aren't talking about that, Mila. You're not my therapist or my ol' lady."

He never misses an opportunity to remind me that I'm nothing to him, and it actually annoys me more than it should.

"Any luck on finding that new nanny?" I ask casually. "It's been a month." I have asked before, but he always seems to dodge the question or mutter about being too busy. I don't understand why he wants me around when he clearly can't stand being near me.

"Is that what you want still?" He lies back on the blanket, placing his hands behind his head. His sunglasses shield his eyes, so I can't see if he's looking at me, but I give him my best annoyed look.

"Cooper, you were supposed to sort this out weeks ago."

"I've been too busy, Mila. I was hoping you would change your mind if I left you alone. Asher will be heartbroken."

"Like you actually care," I mutter.

"Of course, I care. He's my nephew and he's terrified of everyone but you. Who will he run to if you go?"

"Carrie will willingly help you out."

"Carrie and I aren't a thing. She's a club whore."

I feel him tug on the back of my vest, gently guiding me to lay down beside him. Once I'm down, he rolls onto his side, propping his head up with his hand. "Let me take you out tonight."

I frown in confusion. "Why?"

"Because I want to. Because I haven't been out for dinner in ages. Why do I need a reason?"

"But you hate me," I state, and he laughs.

"When did I say that?"

"Erm, I got that impression when you grabbed me by the throat and threatened to kill me for disrespecting you. Or maybe the fact that you avoid me and Asher like the plague."

He falls silent for a few minutes, gently twisting some of my loose hair around his finger. "I don't hate you, Mila. When I'm next to you, I feel calm. All the raging thoughts flying around my head, they just stop, and I can breathe. So, come for dinner with me. I just need to breathe for a few hours."

My breath stutters. How can he be so cold and then say stuff like that? He makes my heart melt when he looks so vulnerable, and I wonder if he's feeding me a line or if he actually means what he says. Do I calm him?

It's eight in the evening and Brook is flapping around me, twisting the curls she spent an hour on, insisting that she help me get ready for my 'date' with Cooper. I keep telling her it isn't like that, but she won't listen. I told her what he said about me calming him and I saw a tear in her eye. From that moment on, she's brushed, fluffed, and prodded every inch of me.

"Asher shouldn't wake at all, but if he does, stick him in my bed. It always works," I say as she sprays my hair yet again.

I glance at my outfit in the floor-to-ceiling mirror. I opted for ripped skinny jeans and a black vest top. I didn't want to look like I was expecting a date night, especially with Brook trying to squeeze me into skirts and low-cut tops. I add a coat of lip gloss. I've kept the makeup to a minimum, preferring a natural look to enhance my golden tan. Slipping into my black heels, I do one final check.

"Have a great night. Show him what he could have won." Brook smiles, and I roll my eyes. Like he would ever look at me like that.

I get down to the bar and Cooper is already there, chatting to Sam. He looks hot in a pair of jeans and a white T-shirt. No kutte tonight, though, which makes him look out of place. He glances up, catching my eye, and smiles as I approach.

"You kids behave tonight," says Sam, grinning as he stands and indicates for me to sit in his seat. Cooper orders me a gin and lemonade, which I nervously sip. I suddenly feel like I'm going on a date. Damn Brook for sticking ideas in my head.

"We best get out of here. Carrie is giving us death glares from over there," he mutters, and I groan.

"Why? It's just some dinner."

"She gets like this, but who can blame her?" He grins, adding a cocky wink.

He drives my car to the restaurant. It's a little less conspicuous around here, even though most people know Cooper, and so he still gets stopped a few times from the car to the restaurant.

Once seated, the waiter hands us menus, and Cooper orders us each a beer. We settle on steak, and once the waiter leaves us, we sit in silence for a few minutes. Eventually, Cooper laughs. "Usually, I can't shut you up, Mila. You follow me around, nagging about what I need to do with Asher, and now, you sit here like a mute?"

"I do not nag," I defend myself with a laugh. "I merely point out what Asher needs. Not that you listen."

"Sorry about earlier. I was snappy when you asked about my wife, and I was out of order. I just don't handle talking about her well." I nod, understanding. It's not like we're close enough to talk, and if there's one thing I've learned about bikers, it's that they don't do feelings or talk shit through.

"I guess you heard that she was Brick's sister?" he continues, and I give another nod. "So, you can see why I got pissed when he hit on you. I felt it was payback."

"Payback? I'm your nanny, not your girlfriend."

"Yeah, well, Brick's good at noticing the shit I don't say," he mutters, knocking some of his beer back. "He won't ever forgive me for marrying her without talking to him first. I don't blame him—my sister did the same to me and I hated it. But Brick won't settle until he feels we're even. It kills him that I'm the Pres, and it's not easy for him to go up against me, so he'll do sly shit like hit on my nanny to piss me off."

"Thanks, and there I was thinking I was special," I say sarcastically, adding a laugh.

"Brick doesn't do special, Mila."

"Do you?" The words are out and I inwardly groan because it totally sounds like I'm hitting on him.

"I didn't think I'd ever meet anyone as special as Anna, but who knows, maybe one day." I don't know why that thought makes my heart flutter. It isn't like we could ever be anything other than employer and employee.

"So, Carrie, she isn't your happy ever after?"

He rolls his eyes. "Carrie is a laugh and we have fun together, but it's nothing more and she knows it deep down."

"Not very fair, though. You're kinda keeping her hanging on even though you know she isn't your forever."

Cooper shrugs. "She knows the score. If she wants to keep making herself available, knowing there's nothing at the end of it, then that's her problem."

Harsh, I'm certain she thinks he will change his mind one day. She talks like she's in a relationship with him.

The rest of the meal runs smoothly, we manage to eat and chat about childhoods, and I tell him about my parents and how they were disappointed when

I split up with Aaron. They still see him and invite him around to their house on Sundays for dinner.

I feel more relaxed as we both open up about past relationships. Cooper makes me laugh with some of his tales of mishaps about climbing up trees to sneak into girls' rooms. The description of the teenage Cooper is exactly how I imagined him to be, cheeky and sex-crazed. It's nice to see another side to him, one that's removed from the President of the MC.

When we arrive back to the club, the bar is heaving, and Cooper goes off to the bar to get us each a drink. I head over to Brook and Tanner, who are sitting in a booth by the window. "How was the date?" asks Brook with a grin.

"The *non*-date was really nice. It was good to get to know Cooper without him rushing off to answer his phone or making excuses."

Cooper joins us with a drink and his kutte firmly back in place. I smile because it suits him and I actually prefer to have him in it than not.

"How did you think the date went, Coop?" asks Brook, mischief sparkling in her eyes.

"Brook," grumbles Tanner in his gruff voice, clearly trying to give her a warning.

"Ever the matchmaker, hey, B?" Cooper sighs, shaking his head.

"Well, when two single people go out for dinner together, that's usually seen as a date."

My mobile rings and I pull it out my bag, Aaron's name flashing on the screen. I sigh and cancel the call. "So, you are ignoring my calls then." I swing around in fright to find Aaron standing beside our booth, looking handsome and fresh and nothing like the rough, hard-cut men I'm surrounded by lately.

"Aaron, what are you doing here?"

"I needed to see you, seeing as you won't return my calls," he says pointedly.

"I didn't see the point. We're over, so what's to discuss?" I glance around the table, and no one looks pleased to see Aaron, least of all Cooper.

"So, you seeing him now?" asks Aaron, glaring in Cooper's direction. I stand abruptly. The last thing I need is Aaron and Cooper arguing.

"Outside, now!" I growl, storming towards the door.

CHAPTER EIGHT

Spinning around to face Aaron, I realise I haven't missed that preppy-looking face. He's smug, probably because he thinks he can talk me around. "How dare you turn up here? This is my job," I hiss.

"You wouldn't answer my calls," he huffs.

"Why would I? I caught you cheating on me," I say exasperated.

"Your mum is really upset that you won't talk to her."

"Why are you here talking about my mum? You cheated on me and we've split up. Stay away from my family."

He sighs. "It's been my family too, for years, I can't just cut them off."

"Oh really? Were you thinking about any of that when you were having sex with that woman? Was family on your priority list then?"

"I made a mistake. I got too drunk," he explains, trying to reach for my hand. I pull away angrily.

"Aaron, I don't want to see you. Please don't come here again, and stay the fuck away from my parents. It's weird."

I turn to head inside, but he catches my arm, pulling me towards him. "Please, Mila. I realise what a mistake I've made. I love you and I miss you so much." He places a bony finger under my chin, lifting my gaze to meet his. It makes me shudder, feeling nothing like Cooper or even Brick. I think he mistakes my shudder for desire because his lips crash to mine and he pushes his fingers through my hair, holding me there while he assaults me with his sloppy kiss.

I place both hands on his chest and push him back. "Christ, Aaron, what the hell was that? That sort of crap might work on your one-night stands, but I'm after a real man. One who doesn't cheat!" I wipe my lips on the back of my hand, showing how disgusted I am. Then, I leave him standing in the car park and make my way back to the bar.

Jase is leaning against the wall, talking to a few other guys. "New boyfriend, Mila?" he asks, and I shudder again.

"No, a past mistake."

"Well, you'd better go and tell Cooper that. He didn't look too impressed with that kiss he just witnessed."

I groan. How did such a good night turn into this? Not that Cooper will care about me and Aaron. It's not like there's anything between us, and Aaron isn't part of his club, so he can't be upset, but I'm sure he will find something to lecture me on.

When I get back to the booth, Cooper isn't there. "What happened?" asks Brook eagerly.

"I sent him packing, obviously. The creep kissed me. I feel violated. Where's Cooper?" I ask, looking around. I notice the shared look between her and Tanner, and then I see why. Cooper is at the bar with Carrie, his arm around her shoulder, leaning in close to her, whispering and laughing. It bothers me, but I'm not going to let anyone see that.

"Sorry, honey," mutters Brook, touching my arm with a gentle squeeze.

I laugh. "Don't be silly, Brook. I told you already, it wasn't a date." My smile faulters slightly, but I hide it with a well-timed cough.

I take a sip my drink and smile in all the right places while Tanner and Brook throw banter back and forth. Cooper hasn't returned, and it's been half an hour. I felt silly going straight up to my room, not wanting Cooper to think I was upset that he had left our evening to see Carrie.

Harper joins us after her shift, plonking herself down next to me. "I am so tired," she huffs. "Kain is a total prick, by the way," she adds, glancing back to the bar where he has a girl pressed up against him.

"The plan not going well then?" I laugh, and she rolls her eyes.

"Fuck him. I can do so much better."

Tanner clinks her glass with his own. "Tank is still available. Said I'd put in a good word with you."

"Not a chance, Tanner. Not a fucking chance," snaps Harper, knocking her vodka back in one go. "Was that Aaron I saw?"

I nod. "I sent him packing after he decided to suck my face."

She giggles and screws up her face. "Gross."

Cooper interrupts our conversation, sliding into the booth next to Brook, Carrie by his side. He stares at me, his green eyes shooting butterflies straight to my stomach. He plonks a bottle of vodka on the table and some shot glasses.

"Actually, I was about to call it a night," I mutter, going to stand.

"Somewhere better to be?" he snaps. I lower myself back into my seat. The last time Cooper was snappy with me, he ended up grabbing me by the throat. He must sense my uneasiness because he looks away.

"Sorry about Aaron turning up like that," I say quietly. He slams shot glasses down in front of each of us and unscrews the cap of the vodka.

"Not my business," he grunts, pouring everyone a shot. He knocks his back and refills his glass. Once

Carrie drinks hers, she turns to him, brushing her lips against his. My stomach ties in knots, and as much as I want to deny it, this feeling is pure jealousy.

I bite my bottom lip hard as I watch him ease her head back, gently kissing along her jaw line. He reaches her lips before I realise that he's looking directly at me. I feel like he's goading me, like he can read my mind and wants to evoke these jealous feelings inside me.

I reach for the bottle of vodka, drinking directly from it. He pulls away from Carrie, grinning at my lack of manners.

"You okay?" he asks, cocking his eyebrow.

I slam the bottle down. "Yep, I need to dance," I say firmly, standing on the booth chair and climbing over the back so that I don't disturb Harper, who is still staring at Kain.

There're a few ol' ladies dancing, so I join them, and they welcome me with cheers as I wiggle my way in. Fuck Cooper and Carrie. I have no business being jealous, but the heart wants what it wants, and I can't help that.

I turn to Woody, the club's enforcer. We get on well, and he's always doing little jobs for me, like putting up shelves or fixing something that Asher has broken.

"You gonna dance with me, big guy, or have I gotta beg?"

He hesitates for a second, glancing at Cooper, but he must give him the nod because Woody grins and joins me, his big arms wrapping around my small waist.

"You trying to get him to confess his undying love, Mila?" he growls into my ear.

"Who?" I ask innocently.

"Like you don't know." He laughs, pressing me closer to him.

When the next song begins to play, I pull away. "I need to pee," I explain, before heading for the toilets.

I pee and then spend a few minutes checking my face in the mirror. I spent so long sitting still so Brook could perfect these curls, it feels like such a waste now. I had no intention of letting anything happen with Cooper tonight or any expectations that anything would happen, but I still feel so disappointed that it's ended like this.

I step out of the bathroom and straight into a hard, firm chest. Placing my hands on his chest, I steady myself and look up into those brilliant, green eyes that I'm becoming to know so well.

Cooper backs me into the corner of the waiting area just outside the bathrooms. My back presses against the cool wall and I'm holding my breath, scared that if I make a sound, it will startle him and he'll run away.

His large hand cups my chin and he lowers his head until our lips are almost touching. "You are driving me crazy tonight," he whispers. He presses his lips to mine, and within seconds, we go from a gentle, unsure kiss to something desperate and passionate.

His hands run through my hair, pulling and tugging like he needs this to breathe. He lifts me, and I automatically wrap my legs around his waist. Something about feeling him pressed so close to where I need him has me grinding against him, making him groan. "Shit, Mila, you make me feel like a horny teenager," he growls, lowering me back onto my feet.

He straightens my hair. "We need to go back out there. Keep this between us." Hurt must fill my face because he takes my hand. "I don't mean it like that. Make your excuses to Brook and Harper, and I'll follow you up." He places a quick, light kiss on my head and disappears into the men's bathroom.

Once I've said goodnight to the girls, I head to my room, avoiding all eye contact with Cooper. I quickly brush my teeth and as I swing the bathroom door open, I run straight into him. He reaches for my wrists and pushes me back against the wall, pressing his mouth hard against mine again, bruising me with his lips.

He guides me towards his room. I've never been in there, and I'm surprised when he doesn't take me to mine, especially as I left the door open. He punches in the key code to unlock his door, still kissing me hungrily. The door swings back, crashing against the wall. He pushes me into the darkness, and I don't get chance to look around because he leaves the light off and slams the door shut.

Our heavy breaths fill the silence as he pulls at my clothes. I thank the heavens that I chose my best underwear tonight, the only matching set I own from Victoria's Secret, something I treated myself to recently. Maybe subconsciously I was hoping that Cooper would get to see the black lace set one day.

When I'm finally down to my underwear, he lifts me against the wall. I wrap my arms around his huge shoulders, trying to keep myself up as he fiddles with the button on his jeans. When he finally pops it open, his mouth returns to mine and his tongue pushes against mine.

I don't remember a time when I was so turned on. All I can think about is him and the need I have to get him inside me. It's taken over and I'm now shamelessly rubbing against the hardness I feel in his jeans.

Cooper places me back on my feet and rummages around in his pocket. I don't even want to think about why he has a condom at the ready, so I push that thought to one side while he rips open the packet and places the it on. He lifts me again, but this time, he lowers me so that his hard cock is pressed against my wet entrance.

My breath hitches as he slowly pushes inside me, then he pauses, resting his head against my shoulder and breathing deeply. "Fuck," he mutters. I run my nails up and down his back, making him groan and push forward in one quick movement. He stills for a second before picking up the pace and ramming into me. I don't have a chance to adjust properly, but the burning, tight sensation is a welcome pleasure and I find myself screaming and gripping onto his shoulders to stop myself from collapsing to the floor.

My orgasm rips through me, it's the first time I've been able to orgasm from intercourse—usually, after sex with Aaron, I'd have to finish myself off.

Cooper grips my hair and pulls my head to one side, biting at my neck before suddenly stopping his movements and groaning. He stills, and I feel the odd jerking movement as he finishes his release.

Lowering me to the floor, he slips out of me. Still keeping me imprisoned against the wall, he presses his forehead against mine, his breathing matching my panting.

"I've been wanting to do that since the day you walked into my clubhouse," he mutters.

I smile. "Then what took you so long?"

He reaches over and flicks the light on, the space bathed in bright light, making me shield my eyes. It's clear this isn't just a bedroom like mine and Asher's. It's an apartment with three doors leading off from the hall where we stand.

"Best room in the house?" I ask. He takes my hand and leads me to the first door, opening it to reveal a small bathroom with a sink, toilet, and a shower. "Get cleaned up. I'll get us a drink."

Once he's left, I jump in the shower. There's a pile of white fluffy towels on the side, and I can't resist making use of the facilities. After a quick shower, in which I use Cooper's shower gel, I'm wrapping myself in the huge towel when the door opens and Cooper appears. He looks relaxed in just his jeans, holding two glasses with an amber liquid. He hands me one, and I wince as the whiskey burns my throat. He places his glass on the side and pushes his jeans down his muscly legs, revealing more tattoos that run down the backs of his calves.

I watch as he steps into the shower, turning it on and rinsing himself clean, using the same shower gel I just used. Once finished, he gets out and wraps a towel around his waist. I watch the water droplets run down his tattooed chest. "So, now what?" he asks, breaking my daydream.

I take another sip of my drink. "I go back to my room and get some much-needed sleep?" I ask, even though that's the last thing I want.

"Not a chance. I haven't finished with you yet," he says, picking up his drink and taking me by the hand.

He leads me into his bedroom. It's a lot bigger than mine, decorated in dark colours, making it an obvious man's room. Large oak furniture placed carefully makes me wonder if there was a woman's touch at some point. A four poster bed stands sturdy against one wall, black sheets strewn across it as it lies unmade.

"Sorry about the mess. I don't usually bring anyone back in here," he mutters, switching on the nearest lamp.

"Except Carrie," I say, raising an eyebrow.

"Except Carrie," he agrees with an awkward smile.

I hadn't thought about Carrie, and the mention of her makes my heart squeeze. It isn't like we're best friends or anything, but she was growing on me, and I think she had started to like me too. Now, I've done exactly what she thought I would, and guilt and shame hit me all at once.

"We can't mention this to anyone," I say quietly.

Annoyance crosses his features. "I'm not watching my men drool all over you anymore, and the only way to stop that is to tell them we're sleeping together."

A pang of hurt hits my chest. I didn't expect the whole girlfriend speech, but seriously, talk about laying it out there. All I've done is replace Carrie.

"I don't want all the hassle from Carrie or any of the other girls here just because we had a one-night stand," I snap. It comes out harsher than I meant it to, and he raises his eyebrows.

"One-night stand," he repeats, nodding his head. "Fair enough." He drops his towel and heads over to the bed, throwing the covers back and sliding in. "Are you sleeping in here or your own room?" he asks.

I find my feet moving forward towards his bed. It's selfish and my brain is screaming for me to leave, but my heart won't let me, and I shut it off as I climb in beside him. He tugs at my towel, unwrapping it and leaning over me, sucking a nipple into his gorgeous mouth.

I wake sometime during the night because I'm too hot. Cooper has his arm around my waist, and I feel his erection pushing inside me once again. His movements are slow and lazy as he takes his time fucking me into oblivion, and then I drift back off to sleep.

The sunlight shining in my eyes wakes me and I turn to the bedside clock. It's only six a.m. I have at least an hour before Asher wakes up. Cooper is asleep beside me, his arm thrown over his eyes.

Feeling brave, I slide my hand over his abs and down towards his cock. I've only ever been this forward once with Aaron, and he turned me down. It was enough to knock my confidence to never try it again. My hand grips around him and I feel him swell, so I begin to move my hand back and forth until he feels hard. I carefully move over him and rub myself against him. He groans as his hands move to my waist. "Mm . . . what a way to wake up." He grins, keeping his eyes closed.

I reach for the condom on his bedside table and open the pack. I've never put one on before, but now is a good time to learn, so I pull it over his shaft and once I'm satisfied, I lift myself over his erection and slowly lower down. This way feels more intense and I'm fuller. I give myself time to adjust before moving again, taking pleasure in the groans and grunts coming from Cooper. I watch his face as I move, the strain on it making him look fiercer than normal.

I think it's taking all his control not to throw me down and fuck me senseless. He is definitely a man who likes all the control, but I like that he's letting me lead.

As my orgasm builds, I move faster. He pinches my nipple, and it sends me spiralling into my release. I flop onto his heaving chest and let him take over the movements. He holds my waist, thrusting up into me at a fast pace until he shouts out and then stills. His grip on my waist is bruising, but I don't move. This is going to be the final time this happens between us, and I don't want it to end.

"Fuck, how the hell am I gonna stay away from this?" he mumbles, running his fingers up and down my back. The movement sends me drifting back off to sleep, and when I wake again, Cooper isn't next to me. My heart squeezes, and I'm not sure whether I can be around him if we go back to how we were.

When I eventually pluck up the courage to leave his room, it's almost ten a.m. I run to my room, just in case anyone is lingering in the hall, and then I rush to get dressed. By the time I get downstairs, the clubhouse is busy. Asher is sitting on Cooper's knee, watching something on the big screen. It's the first time I've ever seen them sitting this close together and it warms my heart.

Cooper catches my eye and gives me a wink before scowling at me. He's putting on an act for the others, especially Carrie, who is sitting nearby. "Wondered when you would climb out your pit, newbie. Heavy drinking leads to late starts," he snaps.

"Sorry, Cooper, I was sick this morning, I did send you a text message," I mutter. I'm terrible at lying, and I feel like everyone is watching me, even though they aren't.

"Well, luckily for you, the kid's been very good this morning, so I'll let you off, but don't let this be a regular occurrence."

I give a nod and then head to the kitchen to make myself a much-needed coffee.

I'm in a daydream, thinking about Cooper's hands on my body, when his arms wrap around my waist from behind. "You thinking about me?" he growls into my ear, making me jump.

"What are you doing?" I whisper-hiss, trying to escape his arms.

He holds me firmly, his hands running up towards my breasts. "I miss these already." He grins.

"I thought we were going to keep this between ourselves. Someone might come in."

He kisses my neck, and I sigh, leaning into him. "I don't think that's going to be possible," he groans, pushing his erection into my back.

"You're like a beast," I joke.

"Maybe we can come to an arrangement," he suggests, turning me to face him. "It can be our secret, if it makes you feel better, but I can't give it up. I can't give *you* up . . . not now I've had a taste," he says.

My heart skips a beat, and a smile breaks out across my face. "A secret," I confirm, and he kisses me, causing me to sigh again. Maybe this could work. I nod, and he smiles too before stealing my coffee and leaving the kitchen.

The rest of the week flies by. Every night, Cooper has crept into my bed, sometimes before I'm asleep, and other times, it's in the middle of the night, once I've been asleep for hours. To everyone else, we look like we hate each other. He snipes at me, and I roll my eyes and huff. Carrie is frustrated because he isn't giving her any attention, and secretly, I'm over the moon, even if I feel guilty because I'm the reason for his lack of interest in her.

It's Friday and most of the guys, including Cooper, have been away for a night. It's been quiet in the clubhouse, but I know how Brook feels when Tanner is away. I missed Cooper in my bed last night and that worries me. I tried to convince myself it's because it's all new and he's the only man who's ever made me orgasm, let alone three or four times a night. The feeling is addictive, but I am not falling for him. Definitely not.

I'm at the bar keeping Harper company. Asher went to bed at a decent time tonight, so I'm enjoying the peace. The bar is quiet, mainly because most of the guys are still away and it's pouring with rain outside, keeping the usual party revellers away.

Carrie comes in and sits on the bar seat next to me. "Have you heard from Cooper?" she asks.

"No, why would I hear from him?" I ask defensively. She looks at me, confused.

"I don't know, maybe about Asher or something?" I shake my head and sip my drink, not trusting myself to speak. "He slips out of my bed on Thursday morning and then disappears for a few days, not a text or a return day. I'm sick of this life," she grumbles.

My mind is still frozen on her remark about him leaving her bed. That can't be right—he's been with me every night. He hasn't paid her any attention.

"You okay?" she asks, moving her hand in front of my face. I give a quick nod. Brick is sitting across the bar from me, and he gives a small wave, which I return. "He's still got it bad for you, yah know," she adds, nodding towards Brick, then she gets up and leaves. Harper tops up my wine.

"Ignore her. I'm pretty sure that was total bullshit," she says. I've told her about me and Cooper. She's my best friend and the only person I can trust to keep it quiet.

"I doubt it. We didn't say we were exclusive. I shouldn't be upset because it's a casual thing," I say, not sure who I'm trying to convince. She pats my hand and then goes to serve another customer.

Brick seizes the opportunity to fill the vacant bar stool next to me.

"How're you, beautiful girl?"

"I'm good, Brick, how're you?"

He nods. "Not bad, not bad at all." We sit in silence for some time, both drinking and watching Harper serve the odd customer. "So, he didn't claim you?" he finally asks.

"Who?"

He rolls his eyes. "Cooper, the big bad President."

"No, why would he? He's my boss." I laugh, hoping that I'm not blushing.

We continue to talk for some time, drunken talk about relationships and being cheated on. I open up about Aaron and his cheating, and he tells me his wife recently cheated on him.

"Did you kill him, the other guy?" I ask, and he laughs.

"Not exactly. Look, let's cut to the chase. I'm drunk, you're drunk, why don't we make a drunken mistake together?" he asks, wiggling his eyebrows, making me laugh.

"That was a swift change in subject there," I point out, and he holds his hands up.

Harper rings the bell, indicating last orders, and Brick buys a bottle of wine. "Why don't we take this upstairs to your room and open it?" he suggests, and for some stupid reason, I nod.

We walk through the clubhouse and get a few raised eyebrows—not because anyone knows about me and Cooper but because it's not the sort of thing I've ever done, take a man back to my room. Carrie grins at me in a knowing gesture.

CHAPTER NINE

I'm naked. I'm naked, and Brick is on top of me, thrusting back and forth. It's not a bad thing, I like Brick, but it isn't the same as Cooper and my heart knows it. I feel cheap and dirty, because not twenty-four hours before, I was doing the exact same thing with Cooper and it felt so right. This doesn't, and I can't tell if I feel guilty or if revenge just doesn't suit me, because let's face it, this is payback for what Carrie told me. I'm hurt that Cooper went to her.

Brick finally finds his release and rolls off me, not caring if I've found mine. *Typical.*

We lay silently for some time and then Brick gets up and begins dressing. "Can I call you?" he asks, and I hesitate. Do I want him to call me? Not really.

I shrug my shoulders. "I think Cooper will flip his shit if we try and make this a regular thing. Maybe it's best if you don't and we keep this quiet," I suggest hopefully.

He gives a nod. "Whatever you want, Mila."

I feel like I can sense relief in his tone. Maybe he didn't feel it was right either.

It takes me a while to fall asleep. Guilt eats at me. When I finally drift off, it feels like I've been asleep just minutes before my door opens, letting in the hall light which wakes me. I lean up on my elbow and turn on my bedside lamp. Cooper stands there. Blood stains his light grey T-shirt and his jeans. He has that lost look about him again and I feel my heart rate kick up.

"Cooper, you okay?" I ask, rubbing my eyes.

Silently, he shuts the door behind him and begins to undress. He climbs into the bed, shoving me over. "It's a mess in here again," he mutters, tapping his head. I lay on my back, and he rests his head on my chest. Something about my heartbeat must calm him because his light snores fill the room within minutes.

I wake hours later feeling stiff. I must have fallen asleep in this sitting position. Cooper is still glued to me, his head pressed against my stomach. He stirs, running his hand up my thigh. There is no way I can have sex with him, not after Brick.

I clamp my legs together, and he lifts his head, looking at me with amusement on his face. I know I need to tell him, but the thought makes me sick. He probably won't be bothered, but I don't want to risk him flying into a rage, especially after the last time he got mad with me.

"What's up?" he asks.

"I just don't feel like it." I shrug, and he laughs.

"You haven't seen me since Thursday morning," he points out.

"So, I'm not a nymphomaniac," I snap. "Go and see Carrie if you need it that badly."

He sits up. "What's gotten into you? Has she been stirring up shit?"

"That depends," I ask. "Did you have sex with her on Thursday before you left for your run?" He laughs, "I was with you Thursday morning, I'm good but not that good. Is that what she said?" I nod, picking at my quilt. "She's probably worked out what's been going on, Mila. This is purely to cause trouble, and look, it's working because now you're pissy at me and refusing to help me out." He grins, waiting for me to smile. He sighs, seeing the uncertainty in my eyes. "Trust me, I won't go there again." He leans in and places a gentle kiss on the end of my nose. It makes me feel even worse.

"Are you just having sex with me?" I ask. He smiles and gives a nod. "Am I supposed to just have sex with you?" I ask casually. A look crosses his face and I shiver, it isn't a happy look.

"If you don't want to witness a murder."

"You didn't say we were exclusive," I mutter.

"I didn't say we weren't, either," he says firmly. "Do you want to have sex with someone else?"

I shake my head, and he stands, looking irritated. "Good, I'm glad that's sorted. I'm going to go and have a little word with Carrie." He stomps out of the room and panic sets in.

I scramble around, getting dressed. What if Brick's down there? I need to tell Cooper before he or someone else does.

When I get down to the main room, Cooper and Carrie are in full argument mode, and I cringe. "Tell her now!" booms Cooper in her face.

She looks at me, annoyance in her features. "I lied," she snaps.

"Get your shit and get the fuck out of my clubhouse," he yells, shoving her away from him.

"Cooper, don't do that. No damage done," I say quickly.

"Don't worry about me, I'm done being his whore," she yells, pulling her boots on. "But you're making a huge mistake. Brick's fucked her already, and there's a queue of your own men waiting to get in there." He looks in my direction and my face pales. "The minute your back was turned, she dragged him into her bed," she adds and smiles, realizing that he didn't have a clue.

I watch in disbelief as she saunters out, leaving me to face the hulk who is now snarling and huffing like he's going to explode. Brick leans back against the pool table, amusement on his face, and I know instantly that he did it all on purpose. It was revenge, just like Cooper warned me it would be.

"You have two seconds to get the fuck out of my sight," he snarls in my general direction. I feel Brook take me by the arm and pull me from the room. As we head upstairs, I hear shouting and wood breaking. *That can't be good.*

"What the hell were you thinking?" snaps Brook. I shrug, because I honestly don't know. This isn't the sort of thing I do.

"Carrie said Cooper had been sleeping with her. I was hurt and angry and Brick was there doing that thing he does with the eyes and the sexy smile. And did I mention that she said she'd slept with Cooper," I rush out.

Brook glares at me like I'm crazy. "You didn't even tell me *you* were sleeping with him."

I'd forgotten that bit. I give her a guilty shrug, "Sorry," I squeak out.

The bedroom door crashes open, and Cooper stands there, his breath heaving in and out of his raging body. His fists are curled tight by his sides and there's blood splatters down his T-shirt. I don't make a move. Something tells me I need to stay still and quiet. He stares at me without even blinking, a wild look in his eyes, and I wonder if he's possessed because he looks so crazed.

"Get out," he snaps, and I'm unsure if he's talking to me or Brook. I glance at her, and she shrugs then makes for the door. He doesn't say anything, just continues to stare at me.

"Cooper—" I begin, but he slams the bedroom door, silencing me.

He stalks towards me. "Perhaps I didn't make myself clear before I left on Thursday. You belong to me," he growls so low, it feels menacing. His hand goes to my hair, and he tugs my head back so he can see my face. He runs a finger down my throat and then suddenly spins me away from him, planting my back against his front. I hear his belt buckle and his zipper, then he's tugging at my shorts until they're to my knees. He bends me slightly and moves my underwear to one side before plunging straight into me. I shout out because I'm not ready for him, but he doesn't stop to check. He rams into me, shoving me forward with every push. Then, he places a hand around my throat and a thrill shoots through me, helping to build that warm feeling in the pit of my stomach. Over and over, he pounds into me until I finally scream out.

"Shout my fucking name," he growls into my hair. He's claiming me, there's no mistaking it, and so I shout his name as I shake my way through an intense orgasm. He follows me with a roar, tightening his grasp around my neck.

He stills and then pulls out of me and tucks himself back into his jeans.

"Cooper, you didn't use a condom," I hiss, glancing at him over my shoulder.

He doesn't speak, so I pull up my shorts. I'm on the contraceptive pill, I have been since I started seeing Aaron, but Cooper didn't know that, and how am I supposed to know if he's clean? He's been sleeping with Carrie for a long time, and she's been sleeping with anyone who'll have her.

Cooper heads for the door and leaves without looking back. I stand like a goldfish, my mouth opening and closing. Everything's such a fucking mess.

Once I'm cleaned up, I go downstairs. Asher rushes over to me. "Hey, little man, you hungry?" I ask, glancing around in the hope I see Cooper and get some clue of what to do next. Asher nods eagerly.

He follows me into the kitchen, where I find a few of the guys and Cooper drinking coffee and reading the newspapers. Cooper glances up at me, then stands and leaves the room. I realise that Cooper just kicked Carrie out and these guys are probably sitting here waiting for their breakfast. At least that will keep me busy.

After cooking up some bacon and eggs for what feels like an army, I sit next to Asher, smiling as he shovels the scrambled eggs into his mouth.

"So, you and Cooper then, finally?" asks Max, grinning. I shrug, and the movement feels heavy with everything that's happened so far today. "Well, the fact he's just told everyone to stay away from you and that he'll kill anyone who tries anything on with you indicates that he's claiming you," he says, wiggling his eyebrows.

I'm still sitting baffled and going over everything when Cooper stomps back in. "Brook is going to watch Asher. Get your coat. We have somewhere to be."

Cooper picks Asher up and carries him out the room, again leaving me wondering what the hell is going on. He returns and hands me a Hammers jacket and a helmet. When I just stare at them, he sighs and begins to get me into the jacket and secures the helmet. "We're going on my bike," he says in way of explanation.

Outside, Cooper leads me to his bike. It's huge, and I've never really been on anything like this, so I'm a bit apprehensive. "Keep your feet on these bits," he instructs, pointing to the side of his bike. "All you have to remember is hold onto me and lean when I lean." He swings his leg over and gets on the beast of a bike, then he looks at me, waiting.

I lift my leg over and slide onto the seat. Pressing against him, I place my hands on his shoulders. He takes them and places them around his waist, pulling me so I'm practically flat against his back.

I jump in fright when he starts the engine, clinging to him tighter. "Relax," he says with amusement. His voice is in my helmet, which makes me jump again, causing him to laugh.

He pulls away and out of the car park, and I hold on for dear life. It takes me most of the journey to relax and begin to enjoy the ride. I can see why it appeals to him so much.

We stop outside a row of stores. "This is us," he announces, nodding to a tattooist. He must be getting some more ink.

Once inside, a large man stands to greet Cooper. "Pres, nice to see you as always." He grins, slapping Cooper on the shoulder.

"Hey, Jay, long time no see. How's things?"

"Good, good, this must be Mila." He smiles, taking my hand and kissing it. "So, is this what I think?" he asks. Cooper gives a nod and indicates for me to follow Jay into the back room.

There's a leather chair and lots of drawings on the wall. Jay sits on a small stool at the side of the chair and pats it, looking at me. I look back at Cooper, and he nods for me to sit.

"What? Why?" I ask, confused.

"Next best thing to a wedding ring, baby," Cooper says with a smile, pushing me gently to sit in the chair.

"I don't want a tattoo. What's going on?" Jay reaches for my arm and places it onto a leather cushion, then sets about cleaning my inner wrist.

"Cooper, explain," I say, more firmly this time.

"You're mine now, and you need the tatt to prove it, so no one will go near you. I made a mistake letting you talk me into keeping us a secret. That isn't going to happen again."

I can feel my breathing begin to get heavy, realising he must have lost his mind. I remember the tattoo that Brook has, and nothing against her, but I do not want marking.

The sound of the tattoo gun buzzing brings me back to the situation. "This is permanent," I say, panic setting in.

Cooper leans into my ear. "You better believe it, baby. Now, if Brick so much as looks at you, I can kill him."

I watch helplessly as Jay grips my wrist and brings the gun to my skin. I hold my breath. It doesn't hurt, but it irritates, causing me to grit my teeth. After a few minutes, the gun stops buzzing and Jay places it on his trolley. He sprays my wrist and wipes it roughly with a paper towel. "All done. It wasn't so bad, was it?" He grins, wiping cream over the ink.

Cooper lifts my wrist and studies the tattoo. He smiles, seemingly satisfied. "Thanks, Jay. Swing by the clubhouse this weekend. The guys would love to see you."

Jay wraps my wrist in clingfilm and sticks it down using medical tape. I don't even want to look at it right now. I think I may be in shock.

We arrive back at the clubhouse and I leave the jacket on, keeping my wrist covered from prying eyes. Harper is working the bar, and she looks up and smiles when she notices me behind Cooper.

"Hey, stay and have a coffee with me," she says. Cooper kisses me lightly on the head and disappears into the clubhouse. I sit on a bar stool, and Harper pours me a cup.

"What the hell has been going on? There're rumours of Cooper claiming you today," she whisper-hisses as she hands me the coffee. Tears fill my eyes, though I'm not sure why. It's been a crazy morning.

"I slept with Brick," I whisper, and she slaps her hand over her mouth in shock.

"What the fuck, Mila?" she screeches.

"I know, alright, you don't need to say anything. I feel bad enough."

"So, Cooper knows?" she asks. I nod, and she pours herself a coffee while shaking her head.

"He came home during the night, it all got out of hand, and Carrie told him everything. He revenge-fucked me—or maybe he just marked me, I don't know—and then he took me to get this," I say, holding out my wrist. She grips it, and I wince. "Careful, it hurts!"

She lifts the covering and her mouth falls open. "Well, shit," she gasps.

"I can't even bring myself to look at it, Harp. Is it awful?" I ask.

She smiles and shakes her head, not taking her eyes from the tattoo. "It's really pretty, Mila." She turns my wrist to me. It's curly, intricate lettering of Cooper's name, small and in black ink. I don't hate it. It's identical to Brook's but smaller, and hers obviously says 'Tanner'.

I study the tattoo for some time. "So, you know what this means, right?" asks Harper. "Are you actually ready for what this means?"

I look at her blankly. "I don't even know what day it is. One minute, Brick is in my bed, and then the next, Cooper is there telling me I belong to him." My heart rate is picking up again and panic is setting in.

Harper takes my hand. "Mila, Cooper is gorgeous. Most women would be happy to be claimed by the President of the Hammers MC. You are one lucky bitch."

Brook comes running in and throws herself at me. "Oh my god. He made it official?" she screeches, grabbing my wrist and examining the small tattoo. "You lucky cow."

Cooper, Tanner, and Kain enter and sit at the bar. Cooper still doesn't look at me, and I feel my heart crack a little. Yes, he's claimed me, whatever that means, but he's still mad, and I hate that feeling. I just want one smile, something to know that he's forgiven me, but I know deep down, that's not going to be an easy thing to do.

Harper pours three pints from the pump. "Where's Asher?" I ask.

Cooper doesn't look over when he answers, which burns me even more. "With Max. Take the rest of the day off."

"Yes, because we need to organize a party," says Brook, clapping her hands together like this idea has suddenly just occurred to her.

"A party? Why?" I ask.

"It's tradition, Mila, when any of the men claim someone, but especially if that man happens to be the President," she says excitedly.

A party is the last thing I feel like having. I can't shake this guilt. "No, that's the last thing I want, Brook." She looks crestfallen, but I really can't face a party when I'm not even sure what this claim business means.

"Arrange it for tonight," says Cooper, still not looking at me. Brook looks between us uncomfortably. "Tonight," repeats Cooper, "and make sure that shithead, Brick, is here."

The realisation this is a pissing contest hits me hard. I don't blame him, he's angry, but it makes me feel even shittier. I take myself outside, thinking putting space between me and Cooper for a few hours might help.

The fresh air hits me and I take a huge lungful, hoping it will clear my racing thoughts. I look around the car park. It's empty, so it isn't hard to spot my mum's car as she pulls in. I haven't seen her since we argued about Aaron and she sided with him.

She pulls up alongside of me and winds down her window. "Mila," she greets me, smiling sadly.

"What's up, Mum?" I ask.

"Your dad and I would really love to talk with you. Would you consider coming over for dinner tonight?" Cooper appears in the doorway of the bar, his large arms folded across his huge chest. His eyes find me, and he watches.

I sigh. "I have something on tonight."

"Come before," she insists.

"Fine, I'll see you at six, but I can't stay long." She smiles and gives a satisfied nod before driving away.

"Who was that?" asks Cooper, staring after the car.

"My mum. She wants to see me tonight."

"Invite her to the party."

"Yeah, cos my mum would really understand that. Look, Cooper, the party isn't a good idea. It's clear you're really mad at me still."

He smirks. "I'm not mad. I'm fuckin' raging!"

"Then why have a party? I'm not even sure what's happened today. I feel like a pawn in a game between you and Brick," I snap.

"You're the prize, baby, and I won. I want Brick to know that. Invite your parents tonight because I don't want you out of my sight for a second."

"Don't be ridiculous. I'm seeing my parents before the party."

He looks even more mad, if that's possible, and if he thinks that by claiming me, he's going to be bossing me around, then he is mistaken.

"Final time, Mila, you aren't going anywhere tonight." And then he stomps inside.

CHAPTER TEN

I'm sulking in my bedroom, something I haven't done since I was a hormonal teenager. All the ol' ladies are in the kitchen cooking up a storm. Everyone is so excited, but I don't feel it, not while Cooper is so mad at me, and I still feel like this is one big game. What the hell did he mean, I'm the prize? Is that supposed to be a compliment, because it doesn't feel like it. I look at my watch. It's half past five. I could sneak out, and he wouldn't even know. It's not like he's been up here to see me at all today. In fact, I don't even think he's left his office.

I pull on my trainers and decide to go and see my parents. I'm not going to be bossed around by anyone.

It's busy downstairs, but Brook sees me and smiles. "I'm coming to do your hair in a second."

"Actually, Brook, I've booked into a salon. They're doing my nails too. You're busy enough." I smile sweetly, but she scowls at me. She isn't convinced, but I can tell she doesn't want to call me out on it in front of everyone. She throws me her keys—her car is more reliable than my little run-around—and I smile at her gratefully before rushing out. I don't want to risk bumping into Cooper.

I get to my mum's at exactly six o'clock. Her car isn't out front, which I find odd. I try the door, but it's locked, so I get out my key and let myself in. I hope she isn't out because I did tell her I can't stay long.

"Mum, Dad, is anyone home?" I shout as I enter. There's no answer, so I go in farther and peek around into the sitting room, but there's no one there. I make my way to the kitchen, which is usually where everyone is because it's the biggest room in the house. Mum spent a fortune doing it all up to accommodate parties and Christmases.

I groan when I open the door to find Aaron sitting at the table. He looks rough, tired, and possibly drunk. "Where're my parents? What are you doing here?" I snap. He stands, smiling at me.

"You've been set up. Your parents understood my need to talk to you, and I can't ever seem to get you on your own. There's always that pesky little brat or one of them biker bastards with you," he slurs. *Great, he is drunk.*

"We have nothing to talk about, Aaron. Jesus Christ, get it in to your head. We're over." He stumbles over to me, and I can smell the alcohol on his breath.

"We were meant to be. Who cares if I screw around? Men do that."

"Well, not to me, Aaron. It's not the life I want." I realise how patronizing I sound right now and my heart aches some more. He rolls his eyes in a mocking gesture, like I'm talking utter crap.

"Well, we can't have little miss perfect upset, can we?"

"I want you to leave, Aaron."

"Well, unfortunately for you, I live here now. Your mum's been kind enough to put me up until I can get my own place. Of course, that would have been sooner if you hadn't cleared out the savings account."

"That was my money, Aaron. You didn't pay a penny in to it," I snap, annoyed that he would insinuate that I'd taken what didn't belong to me.

"It was our money, and we were going to buy somewhere."

"Until you ruined it all. This is your fault, Aaron, not mine," I point out. He never accepts responsibility for his own actions, it's been the cause of many rows over the years.

"It can't possibly be your fault, you and your frigid ways. Maybe if you were more adventurous, I wouldn't have looked elsewhere."

"Me, frigid?" I screech. "Seriously, Aaron, get the fuck out." I'm shocked he would even go there. I tried so many times to spice things up with sexy outfits and daring suggestions, and he brushed me off.

He lunges towards me, gripping my wrist. It's the one with my new tattoo, and I try not to show that he's hurt me. I don't want him to see it when he's like this.

"Let me remind you how good we were," he slurs, pulling me against him. I push at his chest, but his grip is tight. He tries, unsuccessfully to kiss me. "Come on, Mila, I know you miss me. You're just mad." He pushes me until my legs hit the table, and then he pushes my chest until I'm laying down. I shove against him, but he doesn't budge, placing a hand on my chest to hold me there while he uses the other to grope at me. *Jesus, I can't believe I am in this situation. Where the hell are my parents?*

"Don't do this, Aaron. I don't want this," I plead, panic lacing my words. This just seems to spur him on, and I feel his erection pushing against me. He lets go of my chest to undo my jeans, and I take the opportunity to try to get away. I don't expect the blow he delivers to my side—it cripples me and I fall to the floor, hitting the side of my head as I go. He drops to his knees and grips my ankle hard, pulling me towards him. I lash out because now I'm truly panicking. Aaron's never shown any violence towards me, not even when he's been this drunk. I manage to get my leg up and shove it towards his chest, sending him flying back.

I scramble to get to my feet just as the kitchen door opens and my dad appears. I run into his chest, and he holds me up. "Mila," he says in surprise. He takes in the situation before him and then looks towards Aaron. "What the hell is going on?" he snaps as I burst into tears.

"He was going to rape me," I sob.

Mum rushes in. "Mila," she gasps.

I pull away. "This is your fault! You set me up," I accuse. Dad looks between us.

"Is that true?" he asks her.

"I just wanted them to talk and sort things out. He said he just needed to talk," she explains.

I straighten my clothes and wipe my eyes. There's a trickle of blood down my cheek where I hit my head, and I wipe it on the sleeve of my jumper. "Goodbye," I mutter, storming out. Thank God my dad came home when he did.

I get in the car and sort out my tear-stained face. I can't tell Cooper about this. He told me not to come and I did anyway, but more secrets aren't going to help our messed-up situation. I sit for five minutes, trying to calm myself while wondering when the fuck my life turned into this crazy shitshow.

When I arrive back, Cooper is at the bar. I try to sneak past him, noticing how handsome he looks in his shirt and jeans. His hair is combed back into a bun and his beard is freshly trimmed. "Been somewhere nice, Mila, because you sure as hell don't look like you've had your hair and nails done." I freeze. How does he do that? It's like he can sense me without even moving.

"It was closed when I got there," I say, consciously wiping at my head to make sure there is no more blood. When he doesn't reply, I head for my room.

I find a black jumpsuit and quickly apply some makeup. I have a small bruise forming just under my hair line, so I decide to keep my hair down. I curl the odd bit to make it look like I've made some effort.

When I get downstairs, there's a lot of people in the clubhouse. It's so busy that I can't see Brook or Cooper. I push my way through and head straight for the table where all the alcohol is stacked. Pouring myself a large gin and lemonade, I glance around at the unfamiliar faces. My eyes finally land on Cooper, who's chatting to a young-looking woman. They look cosy and it pisses me off, but I'm not really in a position to make a scene after what I did last night.

Harper approaches, looking amazing in a short, flary skirt and fitted black top. Her hair hangs in loose curls, reaching her backside.

"Wow, check you out." I smile, and she does a turn. "Kain is going to be grovelling on his knees," I add, and she rolls her eyes.

"I doubt that very much," she says, nodding to where Kain is chatting to his ex, Ginger.

"Oh, so you're giving up on him?"

She gives a smirk. "I didn't say that, now did I?"

Asher comes over with Max. He reaches for me, and I pick him up. He looks cute, dressed in jeans, a black T-shirt, and a tiny leather jacket. "Wow, stunner," I say, kissing his cheek.

I end up chatting with Tanner, Brook, and a small group of club members. Cooper hasn't approached me so far and it's driving me insane. Asher hasn't left my side, and I'm beginning to feel like this party is more about Cooper than me.

Max takes Asher and says, "I'm going to put him to bed so you can enjoy the rest of your evening." Like that's ever going to happen. I never wanted this stupid party in the first place.

I notice Brick leaning against the wall, watching me. One of his eyes is swollen shut with a cut under it and he has a busted lip. I feel bad for a second until I remember that he used me in his revenge plot.

An arm snakes around my waist. "Don't even look in his direction," growls Cooper, pulling my attention away from Brick.

"You haven't spoken to me all evening," I say sulkily.

"I'm still mad as hell."

"When will that stop?"

"I'm not sure. Get that jacket off, stop hiding the tattoo." He tugs at the jacket, but I'm trying to cover the bruises and avoid all the questions that will inevitably follow.

"I'm cold," I argue, but he pulls it off anyway.

His eyes freeze on the finger bruises on my wrists. "Explain."

I rub them nervously and shrug. "I'll tell you later, now isn't the time."

We're interrupted by a group of rowdy club members who congratulate Cooper and slap him on the back. I'm not sure they even know who I am, and Cooper makes no effort to introduce us. I stand by silently while he catches up with them. Every time I go to move away, he pulls me back to his side, clearly keeping me away from Brick, who still hasn't taken his eyes from me.

The night continues in the same fashion. Since Brick's arrival, Cooper hasn't let me out of his sight and it's getting ridiculous.

"I'm going up to bed," I say, interrupting his conversation with Tanner. I go to walk away, but he pulls me back, pressing a bruise accidentally and it makes me wince.

"The party isn't over yet," he says.

"Funnily enough, Cooper, I'm not really enjoying it," I snap. He gives a nod and releases me.

Brick pushes off the wall and catches up with me. "Have you got a death wish?" I hiss, not stopping.

"He married her, yah know. Didn't tag her like some fucking dog. He did this to you purely to stop me pursuing you."

I swing around to face him. "A bit like you and me last night? Did it make it better, you getting your revenge?"

"That isn't what I did," he defends. "If he really liked you, he would have married you."

Shaking my head in annoyance, I stomp off. Fuck Brick and fuck Cooper. I must have lost my mind. When I get into my room, I put on some shorts and a vest and scrub off my makeup. I take in my tired appearance and sigh. There are bruises appearing on my arms, wrists, and legs from my earlier struggle with Aaron.

I decide to unwind and read a book on my Kindle. My mobile phone flashes with a message. It's from Brick. There's a photo attached of Cooper chatting to the same girl he was talking to when I first went down to the party. I ignore it. I am not playing these games. So what if he's talking to someone? It doesn't mean anything.

A few minutes later, it beeps again. Cooper is kissing the girl. Full on, tongue sucking kissing. I have no right to be mad, as I slept with someone else, but in fairness, I didn't know Cooper and I were exclusive. He didn't say we were, and he only officially claimed me this morning, so surely, it only counts from when I got the tattoo. I pace the room, trying not to let it bother me. Another text flashes up.

Brick: I told you, he tramp stamped you just to piss me off!

I throw my phone onto the bed. Why did he make me get the tattoo? Am I the only one with it? I can't hold it in anymore. I'm upset that he's ignored me all day, and I'm mad that he tattooed me and revenge-fucked me. I am so sick of being used by men, first by Aaron, then by Brick, and now by Cooper.

I storm back downstairs, anger coursing through my veins. It's still busy in the clubhouse. A few people look my way as I approach, probably because I'm in shorts and a vest, hardly party attire, even for bikers.

Cooper is sitting in his usual armchair with the girl on his knee. She's kissing his neck, and he has his eyes closed. *Piece of shit.* I grab a glass of beer from the nearby table and chuck it over them both. The girl jumps up screaming, and Cooper sits up spluttering and wiping the beer from his face.

"What the fuck are you playing at, you crazy bitch," he yells, jumping up out of his seat.

"Remember this?" I scream, waving my wrist in front of his face. "This piece of crap you had me stamped with today? Remember why you had this charade of a party?"

He has the audacity to smirk, and it makes me scream in frustration. "It's not a nice feeling, is it?"

"I'm crazy mad, Cooper." I suck in a shaky breath, not even recognising myself anymore. "I don't understand any of this. You make me this crazy woman who hates you one minute but can't stay away from you the next. I'm so fucking confused with all this bullshit. You claimed me and now you're sucking face with her?" I point to the woman who looks just as confused as her hair drips with the beer I threw.

"I really messed up last night, and it isn't an excuse, but you didn't make it clear. I thought we were casual, and Brick paid me attention, which is really sad and embarrassing, but he did, and I fell for it. But you never talk, Cooper. You don't say how you feel or what you want. I don't know if we're in this or not, but I know I'm tired, so fucking tired of games and arguments. I like you, and I think you feel the same, so let's just stop the drama and make this work, and if you can't, if this is all a show to let Brick know you've won, then tell me so I can leave. Because I'm so over this battle."

He links his finger around mine, moving in closer to stop others overhearing. "You're right. We've gotten into this crazy cycle of drama. But you fucking hurt me, Mila. I didn't think you could."

"If I could take it back, I would. I thought you didn't care."

He nods. "I care . . . way more than I thought possible. No more games."

I give a small smile. "I like the sound of that. No more games."

He tugs me closer and places a gentle kiss on my forehead. "I'm sorry for being a dick."

"Me too," I whisper.

CHAPTER ELEVEN

I feel myself being lifted and snuggled into a warm, hard chest. I must have only been asleep for an hour max. "What are you doing?" I mumble sleepily. I open one eye and it's still dark, so I'm pretty sure it's the middle of the night.

"You only sleep in my bed from now on," rumbles Cooper's voice.

I smile to myself. He is such a caveman. We go through a door and then I'm plonked down onto a cold bed. The sheets are pulled over me and then I fall back into a deep sleep.

I wake and sit up quickly. It takes me a second to remember I'm in Cooper's room and that he brought me here at some point during the night. I jump when Cooper coughs, bringing my attention to him. He's sitting next to me, propped up against the pillows, casually going through my mobile phone. I go to snatch it, but he moves it from my reach.

"So, the bruises?" he asks, placing my phone on his side of the bed.

"A run-in with Aaron," I say, eyeing my mobile phone and wondering how quick his reaction would be if I made a grab for it.

"Don't even think about it," he warns, like the mind reader that he is. "Aaron?" he repeats.

"To cut a long story short, I ignored you yesterday and went to see my parents. They weren't there, but Aaron was, and he was drunk. Things got out of hand, but luckily, my dad came back just in time."

"Lucky for who?" he asks, the vein in his head pulsating, indicating he's about to explode.

"Let's not go over that," I say with a forced relaxed smile. I lift myself to sit on his knee, facing him and run small kisses along his strong, square jaw, his rough stubble prickling my lips.

"What did he do?" he persists.

I kiss his lips, running my tongue along the lower one before taking it between my teeth and gently tugging. "Nothing that I couldn't handle." I rub myself against him and feel him stiffen beneath me.

"Stop trying to distract me," he growls, lifting me from his knee and plonking me down beside him. "Why didn't you tell me yesterday?"

"Because you were already mad at me, I didn't want you to hate me anymore."

I pull at his boxers, freeing his erection, and lower myself, running kisses down his hard abs. I peek up at him, checking he isn't going to stop me again before running my tongue along his shaft. He hisses and throws his head back.

It's been a week since Cooper marked me as his, and he's moved all my things into his bedroom, though it's more like a mini apartment.

It's weird but nice, even though Cooper is moody most of the time. Usually, by the time he comes to the bedroom, he's more chilled and nicer to be around. I assume he's very stressed during the day when club things need handling.

Like today, for instance. Something big is happening—he hasn't told me that, because apparently ol' ladies don't get to know club business, but I can tell by the important phone calls he shields me from and the fact that he stomps about barking orders at the guys.

Max was supposed to be taking me and Asher shopping today—the groceries are running low and Asher loves to help me shop—but as usual, Max got called away by Cooper to go on a short run. Normally, I would ask Cooper for someone else, but he's super grumpy today, so I decide I'm going to nip out without any of the guys. They're all too busy to babysit, and I'm perfectly capable of running out to the grocery store.

I'm fastening Asher into the car seat when Brook skips over. "Hey, you off? Where's Max?"

"Erm, he's just coming. I said I'd get Asher settled," I lie, mainly because Brook would insist on coming and I could do without Tanner overreacting when he realises we're both out without our escort.

The store is only a few streets from where the clubhouse is based, so I reach it in record time. I sit Asher in the trolley, even though he insists he's too big for it now, and we head inside. I'm halfway through the shop when my mobile rings. It's Brook.

"Hey," I answer.

"You lied," she says, sounding hurt.

"Huh?"

"You said Max was going with you, but Cooper said Max is on a run."

"Oh yeah, right. Does Cooper know I'm out?"

"Yeah, he's next to me now. Who's with you?" *Oh great, this is not going to end well.* I don't know what he expects to happen to me in the store.

"It's just me and Asher. I've almost finished, so see you in a short while." I quickly disconnect the call before she can relay that back to Cooper. I'm almost at the checkout when Cooper calls my mobile for the eighth time. I roll my eyes, ignoring it again. *How ridiculous.*

I'm packing the car when it rings again, and I'm about to answer, because I'm pretty sure Cooper is having some kind of breakdown, when I'm approached by a shifty-looking guy. His hood is pulled up and his head is down, so I can't see his face, but I instantly feel on edge. When he reaches me, he looks up, and I gasp.

"Aaron," I whisper. His face is a mess, bruised and swollen with cuts. He has stitches across his eyebrow and the top of his cheek bone.

"Mila," he mutters.

"What happened to your face?"

He glares at me for a few seconds. "Like you don't already fucking know. Your boyfriend is very handy with his fists," he snarls, and I rear back. Surely, he doesn't mean Cooper.

The loud rumble of an approaching bike engine is enough to send Aaron on his way before I get to ask any questions. I'm still staring after his retreating form when Cooper's bike pulls up in front of me. He jumps off, pulling his helmet from his head in a rage. "Answer the goddamn phone," he yells.

"You beat on Aaron?" I ask, confusion apparent in my voice.

This stumps him as he presses his lips together in a tight line, thinking what to say next. "You saw Aaron?" he snaps, looking around the car park.

"Yes, I saw him, and he's a mess." I don't know why I feel so angry. Aaron tried to attack me, but I certainly don't need Cooper jumping in to defend my honour. And the fact he didn't even tell me pisses me off. We're supposed to be a couple. I slam the car boot. "I didn't ask you to do that," I snap.

"Forget Aaron, he isn't your concern anymore. Why did you leave without a prospect?" I can't believe he's just dismissed Aaron like that. I yank the driver's door open, and he holds it while I climb in. "I'm not happy you left without an escort, Mila," he snaps.

"And I'm not happy you beat up Aaron, Cooper." I pull the door closed and drive off, leaving him looking mad and frustrated.

By the time I pull into the club, Cooper is dismounting his bike. I get Asher out of the car and take him inside, setting him down at the bar. "Go through to the clubhouse, baby, while l bring the bags in."

Cooper is ordering the prospects to unload my car when I get back out, which frustrates me more.

"I can do that," I argue. Cooper snatches my hand and pulls me around to the side of the building, and even though I protest, he doesn't stop. He takes me to a side door and punches in a code to unlock it. Inside is a cold, damp out building. It smells of wet leaves with a metallic tinge in the air. It's only small, but the space has an eerie feel to it.

He drags me over to a blood-stained chair sitting by a wall. "This is where your ex sat last night and told me he was going to fucking rape you. He told me he won't stop until he's raped you repeatedly and films it so that I can replay it on loop," he yells. Tears fill my eyes. Why would Aaron want to do that to me? He was never aggressive or violent, especially in the bedroom. "So, yes, I beat the shit out of him. He's lucky he walked out of here because I really wanted to kill him. So, next time you leave this fucking building, you take someone with you, are we clear?" he shouts.

When I don't reply, he leans in closer. "Are. We. Clear. Mila?" He punctuates each word slowly.

"Yes," I say quietly, tears rolling down my cheeks. He storms out, leaving me staring at the chair and wondering how he always turns shit around so I'm in the wrong.

Later, Brook comes into the kitchen holding Asher on her hip.

"Hey, chica, Asher was upset, so I brought him in here. Cooper is stomping about out there like a great big grizzly bear." I continue to chop vegetables. I don't think any of the guys had ever eaten vegetables until I took over the cooking. They were all sceptical at first, but now they eat whatever I cook and often ask for seconds.

"He wasn't happy I left without an escort," I mutter.

"Ah, explains a lot," she says with a smile.

I sigh. "I don't think I'm cut out for all this ol' lady shit."

She laughs and places Asher on a stool. "So, what, you're going to just walk away? Do you think it's that easy?" I shrug. I hadn't really thought about any of it. All the other ol' ladies seem to swan around here without a care in the world.

"He's mad at me all the time, and when he isn't mad, we're having sex. That's the extent of our relationship, fighting and fucking," I say quietly so Asher can't hear.

Brook laughs even harder. "Sweetie, what other type is there? That's exactly how it should be. Trust me, it's fucked up, but it works. You wait till you fight while fucking. Best sex ever!" She grins.

"I hate feeling like this all the time. I'm walking on eggshells. He's like the Hulk, one wrong word and he loses his shit."

"Mila, you need to toughen up. Don't let him walk all over you. How about I arrange drinks with the girls? We can give you tips on how to keep your hulk under control," she suggests.

I smile. Maybe advice is just what I need because I like Cooper, a lot, and I want it to work.

Cooper is in his office, so I lightly knock and wait for him to invite me in. "What?" he snaps. I gently push the door and poke my head in. I'm pleased when his furrowed brow eases and he almost smiles.

"I just wanted to check if it would be okay to leave Asher with Max this evening."

His brow furrows again. "Where are you going?"

"Brook arranged for me to have drinks with her and some of the ol' ladies." He pauses and looks thoughtful.

"Why has she arranged that?"

I shrug my shoulders. "Maybe she wants to include me in all the ol' lady stuff now we're tattooed together?"

Cooper sighs. "Fine, but Mila, don't be talking about our private shit," he warns. I nod while wondering what private shit he means. It's not like he tells me anything anyway. "Now, come kiss me," he orders with a smirk.

I'd like to be strong and deny him, but my feet are moving towards him before my brain can stop them. I lean down and peck him on the cheek. He shakes his head and then pulls me down onto his knee, parting my lips with his demanding tongue. He kisses me until my breath almost stops and my toes curl. Damn, this man can kiss. It doesn't escape my notice that all our disagreements are resolved in this way. We don't discuss it or talk it through. He shouts, we stomp off from each other, and then he kisses me like this, and we move on.

―—⁃ℓℓ⁃—―

When I finally enter the bar that evening, Brook has managed to secure us some tables at the back of the room. She's pushed them together and roped off the area like we're VIPs. Harper is working tonight, so I head to the bar first to catch up with her. She looks annoyed as she stares at her phone like it's the most important thing she's ever seen. Kain is sat at the bar watching her.

"Hey, Harper. You okay?" I ask. She looks up at me and smiles, tucking the phone away into her back pocket.

"I am now you're here. What can I get you to drink?"

"Gin, obviously." I smile, and she sets about to make me a gin and pink lemonade.

"You and Kain still not speaking?" I ask. She glances over to him, gives him an annoyed scowl, and then turns back to me. "He's back together with Ginger."

"Oh, wow. I thought he hated her?" Brook and Harper had filled me in on the drama that used to be Kain and Ginger's relationship. He eventually broke it off after she slept with a biker from a rival club.

"I'm sick of hearing about them. Everyone is ecstatic that they're giving things another try," she huffs.

"I thought that you two would get it on. You both behave like you're married," I say, because they seriously fight like they're in a relationship.

"Hey, Harper, any chance of a refill?" shouts Kain from the other end of the bar. She glances in his direction and then turns back to me, completely ignoring him.

"Clearly, he only goes for cheap whores," she mutters.

"Harper!" he yells again.

"I mean, have you seen her hair? Those extensions look like she had them done at the cheapest place in town," she continues.

"Harper, I swear to god, if you keep ignoring me, I—" She spins around before he can finish his sentence.

"You'll what, Kain? What the fuck are you gonna do?"

"You have a serious attitude problem," he snaps.

"Only with you," she snipes back.

"Marshall tells me you and he are going out on a date," he says casually.

Marshall is a new club member, only patched in a month ago, and he's already got the girls swooning at his feet. At six feet of pure muscle, even I try to get a good look whenever he walks by.

"What's it to you?" she snaps, refilling his glass.

"Nothing." He shrugs coolly. "Maybe we can double date, me and Ginger, you and Marshall?"

"I don't want to date Marshall . . . I want to fuck him. I can't do that on a double date," she says with a wicked grin and then walks back over to me.

"Maybe he and Ginger are into all that." I smirk, and she screws her face up in disgust.

"I know I say this at least five hundred times a week, but I am so done with bikers. I'm moving on to better things." I laugh because she really does say it that often.

I take a seat at the table with Brook. Connie and Kim, ol' ladies to a couple of the older members, have joined us so far and both are nice. We order a few bottles of Prosecco and chat about Asher. They both have children older than Asher, but they give me tips on sleeping because he is really struggling at the moment.

A few others join us, and Brook introduces them as Katie, Milly, and Tammie. Katie is five months pregnant and wastes no time in moaning about pregnant life and how her old man, Rocky, won't leave her alone for a second, in and out of the bedroom.

"Think yourself lucky that he likes your gorgeous, changing body. Some men hate their women getting fat," laughs Milly.

"He loves my body, can't get enough of this bump. He also loves my new massive boobs, but I just need a break. He wants it all of the goddamn time, I'm not kidding. He even wakes me in the night, sometimes twice," she screeches, as the rest of the girls fall about laughing.

"So, Mila, tell us, is the king himself as horny as we think he is?" asks Tammie, grinning and leaning closer. I feel myself blush. Cooper asked me not to discuss our private life, but I want to be like the rest of the girls and share.

"He doesn't get tired easily." I grin, and they all squeal with delight.

"In fact, ladies, Mila here is struggling to tame our wild beast and needs some tips," cuts in Brook.

"Good luck with that one. If we knew how to tame Cooper, one of us would have bagged him," says Tammie, and another fit of giggles erupts.

"He's so moody. But he always has been." Connie sighs. "He is under a lot of pressure, and I guess that's also what makes him so sexy. Everyone likes a brooding beast."

I nod. "So, how do I help with that, the pressure? He won't tell me anything that's bothering him, so how can I help?"

"By spreading those legs," says Kim, laughing. "He needs TLC whenever he walks in that bedroom door."

"But that's all we ever do," I say with a chuckle.

"Then you're already doing everything right," Kim offers. "You're the ol' lady of one of the most important club members. He doesn't need grief off you, just someone to cook him dinner and fuck his brains out."

"And that's it? That's the secret to keeping his interest and making him happy?" I ask uncertainly.

"No, we don't mean be a doormat," says Connie, shaking her head. "You need to keep the bear on his toes. Make sure he knows what he's got waiting at home so he doesn't stray. Stand up to him every now and then. Mark your territory when girls need to know he's your man."

"Oh, yeah, guys love it when you get jealous," cuts in Tammie.

"Don't take his shit just to keep the peace, grumpy or not. If he's in the wrong, you tell him he is. These men love a bit of fire. And that wife of his, well . . ." It goes silent. Connie covers her mouth when she realises what she almost said.

"You knew her?" I ask, and she nods.

"Yeah, me and Tammie were good friends with her. Sorry, I didn't mean to bring her up."

"It's fine. I want to know more about her. Cooper doesn't speak about her."

"Let's talk about her another time. Tonight is about us getting to know each other," says Brook, topping up our glasses.

It's nice to sit here with girls who get it and understand what I'm talking about. Their men are just as frustrating and overprotective. If I told some of my other friends, friends who don't know this world, that Cooper tracks my phone or rings me every hour when I'm out, they would tell me to run a mile. They don't get that he's like this because his world is different from ours. He's constantly having to look over his shoulder to make sure rival clubs aren't coming after his men. He's protective because he likes me, and I like that. I sit back, listening to tales of club life over the years.

We must be laughing loud because Tanner comes over. "We could hear your cackling from inside the clubhouse," he rumbles, kissing Brook on the head. "Nice to see you all, ladies," he says, then he takes his place at the bar next to Kain. Cooper joins them not long after, occasionally glancing at our table when we laugh.

I'm in deep conversation with Tammie when Brook nudges me. "Isn't that the new club whore?" she asks, nodding towards a thin blonde currently running her hand up and down Cooper's back.

I nod. Cooper hired her from one of his strip bars, said she wanted to get out of the strip joint and still earn good money. He offered her Carrie's position because some of the guys were fed up with the same pussy hanging around—his words not mine.

"The girl needs to know her place," hums Tammie.

I notice Cooper isn't exactly fighting her off. "Remember what we said about showing bitches that he's your man," adds Connie.

"He's the one in the wrong. It's Cooper letting her put her hands all over him. She's new," I shrug, "so how is she supposed to know?"

"She won't ever know if you don't tell her," says Brook, just as the girl leans in towards Cooper's face, laughing with him. Tanner looks to his side, like he's checking out her ass, and Brook almost crushes her glass.

"Boy, I know you didn't just check out that whore's ass," she yells, and Tanner looks around in shock.

"I was just looking behind me. What are you talking about, you crazy woman?" he asks innocently.

"Umm, that's what I thought," she mutters, and he rolls his eyes.

Harper brings us over another two bottles of Prosecco. "She's trying her hardest to get your man in the sack," she warns me.

"And what exactly is Cooper saying to put her off?" I ask.

"Not an awful lot, but that's Cooper for yah, a man of few words." She shrugs with a laugh.

I make my way over to them. I hate confrontation, but I've had a few drinks and the girls have fired me up. I stand at the bar beside Cooper.

"You're the President. You can have me whenever you like," the girl says, giggling like she is the cutest thing ever.

"He has an ol' lady," I butt in.

"She doesn't have to know," she whispers into his ear.

Cooper looks at me amused, waiting for my next move.

"Cooper, most of these women would probably rag this bitch by her hair, screaming and shouting, fully blaming her even though she's new around here and she's still learning the ropes," I say calmly, staring at the drinks menu in my hand. "I am not most women. I'm fully blaming you for letting this whore touch what's mine because you know where you belong. If you continue to stray like a dog, I may have to castrate you like the responsible owner that I am." I walk back to the table as Cooper's laughter rings out around the bar.

"Okay, Lacey, hands to yourself, sweetheart. My ol' lady is psychotic," I hear him say, amusement in his voice.

The girls laugh at my triumphant moment. "I don't know why you worry, Mila. You're a natural," says Brook, smiling.

CHAPTER TWELVE

"A bit higher," I say for the hundredth time. Well, not hundredth, but it feels like I've been standing here forever trying to get the 'Welcome Home' sign hung inside the bar. The prospects, Kurt and Shane, are like the chuckle brothers, useless but funny.

There's a welcome home party for one of the oldest club members, Kirk, who's being released from jail today. After ten years inside, everyone is excited about his return. Cooper tells me that he was the accountant for the club years back, before Cooper was President. He got himself into some bother when his pregnant wife was killed. She was run down in the street, and it was listed as a hit and run, but Kirk was convinced it was another club. He went after the president of that club and was caught battering him. His original sentence was only half of what he served, but he couldn't keep his head down inside and ended up staying longer on other charges.

"The bar looks great, Mila," Harper says with a smile. She isn't on shift today, but she's come to give me a hand. I'm hoping she'll stick around for the party. As my best friend, the guys are getting used to seeing her hanging around the clubhouse rather than just at the bar.

"I feel like this is my first important duty as the ol' lady to the President." I grin, and she laughs because she knows I hate the title. I think the whole thing is ridiculous and a bit old fashioned. I mean, who in this day and age can lay claim to someone? Brook tells me they take this shit seriously, and sometimes, when an ol' lady tries to leave their man, they get forced back. I was tempted to try it just for fun, to see if it was true, but somehow, I don't think Cooper is the chasing type of guy.

"There's a lot of charters coming from all over today, so stick around. You may find the biker of your dreams," I say.

Harper shrugs her shoulders. I know she's still pining after Kain, even though he's back with his ex. Ginger seems nice enough, although she keeps to herself. I still catch Kain watching Harper, and Brook thinks he secretly wants Harper but he's too proud to admit it.

"The girls reckon Kirk was a bit alright back in the day. I bet he needs a night of fun after being away for ten years." I wink.

"You still looking for love, Harper?" It's Kain, his voice rumbling across the bar, and Harper jumps and spins around to face him.

"Actually, I'm seeing someone, but I guess it wouldn't hurt to look."

He smirks. "Yeah, and who are you seeing?"

"Marshall," she says proudly. Kain almost chokes on his drink, and I drop the pins I'm using to put the decorations up.

"What?" I screech. She hadn't told me.

"Marshall?" repeats Kain, looking furious.

"Sorry, I didn't say, Mils. It's just a casual thing. Neither of us are looking for anything but fun," she explains, looking sheepish. Kain is by her side before she finishes her sentence.

"Just fun? So, he's using you?"

"No, if anything, I'm using him. Anyway, it's none of your business. How's Ginger, by the way?" she snaps sarcastically.

"Great. Amazing, in fact. I don't know why we ever split in the first place," he snaps back, equally as sarcastic. I roll my eyes, the point scoring crap becoming annoying. It's clear, especially after this showdown, that they like each other way more than they're letting on.

"Didn't she cheat on you with one of the guys?" she asks "And that was before she ran off with a rival of this club," she adds, tilting her head to one side, like her comment was innocent.

"So, you've fucked Marshall then?" he asks, completely ignoring her comment.

"A lot. That stool you just sat on, he had me over that the other night after I closed the bar." She smiles as he glances back at the stool, his face turning red with anger.

"Practically like a club whore," he spits out. She rears back and slaps him hard across the face. I gasp because I can't believe she's lost her cool. This never happens to Harper—she is the queen of cool.

Kain snatches her wrist before she can move away. "Fuck this shit," he growls and drags her towards the clubhouse. I follow them, pleading with him to let her go, but Harper follows without putting up a fight. I think she's still in shock from the slap she dished out moments ago.

Cooper comes out of his office to see what all the noise is. He grabs my arm as I pass, halting me. "Mila?" he asks, waiting for an explanation.

"They argued again, and Harper slapped him across the face. Now, he's dragging her off somewhere," I tell him. Cooper pulls me into his office, but I protest. "No, Cooper, I need to help her."

"Baby, there's no helping that pair. Let them fight it out. He's probably taken her for a hard fuck, that shit turns him on."

I screw my face up, "Ew, too much information. Besides, she's seeing Marshall."

Cooper looks surprised. "You know what I love about being the President? I don't get dragged into all this gossip and drama." He pulls me over to his desk and sits me on the edge, running his hands up the sides of my face and pressing his lips to mine. "There's gonna be a lot of badass bikers around here for the next few days. You gonna be good?" he asks with a grin.

"I'm always good, Mr. President," I say, smiling sweetly.

"Don't make me crazy, Mila." He presses kisses along my jaw and down my neck.

"You drive yourself crazy," I mutter, running my hands down his shirt, feeling his abs bunching as he moves his hands down my arms.

"It's been far too long since I was inside you," he whispers, fiddling with the button on my shorts.

I smile. "That's a lie, try two hours ago."

"Exactly," he huffs, tugging at my shorts.

I leave Cooper's office flustered and run straight into Ginger. "Have you seen Kain?" she asks.

Shaking my head, I tuck my vest into my shorts. "Nope, not for the last hour."

She shrugs and carries on in her mission to find him. I pull out my mobile phone and try to call Harper, but it goes to voicemail, so I try again. When she doesn't answer, I type out a text.

Me: *Ginger is looking for Kain!!!!*

I head back into the bar and continue to get ready for the party. Ten minutes later. Harper comes in looking just as flustered as I did. I eye her suspiciously. "What?" she asks innocently.

"Tell me you didn't," I whisper-hiss. Harper isn't the type of girl to sleep with attached men.

"Okay then, I didn't." She smiles, not even trying to convince me.

"Oh my god, Harper, you did," I hiss. "He's with Ginger. Did she find you together?"

"No, I hid in his bathroom until he got rid of her."

"Oh, Harper," I groan. "So, now what?"

"I don't know, we didn't get chance to talk. I know I don't normally do that kind of thing, Mila, but you know how much I like him. And that's not an excuse, but I can't say no to the guy. I've wanted him for so long," she argues.

I sigh. "Well, let's hope he tells Ginger where to sling her hook then."

———

It's almost two in the afternoon before I make it into the shower to get ready for the party. Bikers had begun to arrive as I came upstairs, so I quickly shower and pull on my jeans and a vest top. One thing about a biker party is casual dress is a must unless you want to be mistaken for a club whore.

Harper is sitting at the bar when I finally get back downstairs. Max has been watching Asher, and they've become quite inseparable lately. Asher is currently running around the bar with another little boy, Kyle, Connie's son. It's nice to see him interacting with other kids.

Cooper comes up behind me and wraps his thick arms around my waist, nuzzling his face into my hair. "I can't wait to get rid of all these people and have you to myself," he grumbles, causing me to smile. He really hates socializing.

"You have a weekend of partying. Enjoy it," I say. Then I kiss him, and he swats my ass before heading in the direction of a group of men who have just arrived.

"It's busy already. How many members are actually in this club?" I ask, sitting next to Harper. She doesn't respond, her eyes firmly fixed at the other end of the bar where Kain is sitting with Ginger. They're laughing, and she's snuggling into his side.

"Oh, has he spoken to you?" I ask. She shakes her head and sighs.

"Why do I always get the bastards, Mils?"

"He really likes you, Harper. Brook and I both see it. I don't know what stops him from just admitting it. But Marshall's just arrived, so forget Kain for now, sweetie." She looks over to where Marshall is shaking hands with Cooper. He catches her eye and gives a wink.

She sighs. "I guess. Marshall is pretty fit."

"Harper, he is a god. While he wants some fun, take it. I know I would, if I wasn't already with my very own god."

More and more people arrive, and Cooper and Kain have gone to collect Kirk. Harper is proving hard to cheer up, so I'm starting to wonder if I can get away with slipping off to my room and reading my Kindle. I drag Harper over to the girls. "Help me sort Harper out—she's heartbroken."

"I am not. I just feel foolish, but hey ho, I'm over it," she protests.

"Yeah, sure you are," I mutter, sitting down.

"Is this because of Kain," asks Brook, "because like I keep telling you, that boy loves you. I can see it in his eyes."

Harper shakes her head. "He doesn't. He's made it clear he's with Ginger."

"Oh, I have gossip about that," says Katie, and we all turn to her, eager to get the gossip, "but I don't think I'm supposed to say anything."

"Katie, we're your girls. Of course, you're supposed to say something," screeches Brook. Katie opens her mouth to speak but is interrupted when the door opens and Cooper enters, followed by Kain and then a gorgeous man, equally as big and equally as muscly and covered in tattoos. Cheers erupt and the guy takes a bow, laughing as people whistle and catcall.

Some of the girls from our table get up to go and greet him, including Katie. "Damn it, I want the gossip," moans Brook.

Later, I'm helping behind the bar because it's ridiculously busy. Sam, Harper, Marshall, and I become a great team and we soon begin enjoying working the bar, bantering back and forth between doing shots of sambuca. Harper seems to have temporarily forgotten her heartache, which is good because Kain has never looked so loved up with Ginger.

A few hours later, Cooper announces that Max has the barbeque started out back, so we head off to the back of the clubhouse, the field giving us plenty of opportunity to avoid awkward moments between Harper and Kain.

Brook lays out a large blanket and a few of us girls claim it. It's a nice, chilled evening, everyone is relaxed, and the mood is happy and light.

We're laughing about Katie's moving baby bump when Kirk joins us, plonking himself down next to Harper. "You must be the lovely Harper? Kain's been telling me all about you." He winks.

Harper's smile freezes, and I think we both jump to the same conclusion because her happy mood soon disappears along with her smile. "All good, I hope," she says politely.

He doesn't answer because Cooper is shouting and banging his hand on the table, trying to get everyone's attention. When silence falls, he gives a cough to clear his throat.

"Okay, so, just a quick few words because, well, because Kirk is home with his brothers, where he belongs. It's taken ten years to get him here, what with his quick fists and his short temper," he jokes, and everyone gives a cheer, "but I just want to say, Kirk, we're glad to have you back, man. From the stories I hear, you'll be joining Woody as Enforcer of the Manchester chapter, but let's get you settled back into your freedom before we sort all that. While I have you all here, because let's face it, we only all get together at prison releases, weddings, and funerals . . ." Again, everyone laughs.

"Most of you have heard that I went and got myself an ol' lady." He indicates for me to stand, and Brook gives me a shove, so I go towards him. He grips my hand in his and there's whoops and hollers from the crowd. "Mila is crazy enough to put up with my bad moods and high sex drive," he grins, "as well as taking care of my nephew. So, there will be another get-together because I'm gonna marry her while she's at this loved-up stage."

I turn to him in shock because this is the first I've heard of it. He's never mentioned marriage. "I've spoken to Michael, and he can marry us in four weeks, so I'll be seeing you all back here on the twenty-eighth of August."

I hear the cheers and congratulations that are bestowed upon us, but it feels like it's muffled, like maybe I'm watching this happen to someone else. I suddenly feel sick and dizzy. He hasn't asked what I want or where I want to get married. Hell, he hasn't even asked if I'll marry him. I'm not even talking to my family. As if he senses I'm not reacting right, he pulls me to him, so to everyone else, it looks like a hug.

"What's wrong?" he whispers into my ear.

"You didn't mention any of this to me," I say.

"So, what did you think would happen? We are together." He says it like I'm being stupid. It makes me want to cry, but I fight the tears.

"It's just a shock, that's all. Usually, couples talk about this kind of thing."

"We're talking now," he huffs. We're interrupted again when Kain shouts for everyone's attention. He waits for people to calm down again before proceeding.

"As Vice President, I just wanted to congratulate Cooper and Mila on their engagement, and also, welcome back to Kirk. But while we're making announcements, I have one of my own." I inwardly groan, searching out Harper's pale face. "As most of you know, Ginger and I recently sorted out our differences and we're happy to announce that she's having my baby."

Cooper lets me go and rushes over to Kain and Ginger, patting him on the back in congratulations. I stare at Harper, her heartbreak written all over her face. Brook is talking in her ear, and she nods occasionally. This must have been the gossip that Katie had earlier.

I approach Kain, reaching up and placing my hands on his shoulders to make it look like a congratulatory hug. "What you just did to Harper is shitty. If I wasn't such a decent person, I'd tell Ginger exactly where you were this afternoon when she was looking for you," I hiss in his ear.

"You're too innocent for this life, Mila. You're kidding yourself if you think you and Cooper will live a fairy tale with no cheating or fighting. The things we do, they aren't the sort of things your tiny, innocent mind could ever understand. That blood your man comes home covered in, that's a life, a life we took, that he took. Ginger gets me, and sometimes that overrides everything else. Fairy tales don't exist for us, but if I can bag a woman who will lay down for me at night knowing I slit a man's throat an hour before, a woman who will look into a cop's eye and tell him she was fucking me all night despite knowing I was hauling guns across the country, well, then I'm taking that."

"The sad thing about all of that, Kain, is out of anyone, Harper is that woman, loyal to the bone. You would know that if you spent time talking instead of fighting your feelings."

I leave him to let that sink in and head over to Harper, who has made her way over to Ginger. Ever the good person, she gives her a hug and congratulates her. Kain eyes her warily, and she smiles at him, then stands on her tiptoes and gives him a quick peck on the cheek.

"Congratulations," she tells him, and he holds her close to talk in her ear. Ginger is too busy chatting to the next person in line.

Harper leads me straight to the barrel of ice and drinks and takes out a full bottle of vodka. We move away from the rest of the crowd and find a quiet spot looking out to the horizon. The sun is setting, but the guys have set up heat lamps which are giving off a warm glow.

She swigs straight from the bottle and then hands it me. "Well, what a fucking night," she says. We turn to each other and both laugh. We've been here so many times before, at the end of a night, feeling sorry for ourselves.

"No one could accuse us of being boring," I say with a smile.

"Seriously, what is it that men hate about me? I never get the guy," she huffs, taking the bottle back from me and drinking. "And you, you're getting married. Mila. Why didn't you say anything?" she asks accusingly.

"Erm, maybe because I didn't know. Cooper seems to think it's quite normal to book a wedding without proposing to me first."

Harper gasps. "No way. So, if he'd have asked, what would you have said?"

I shrug. "Probably yes, but that's not the point. He just announced it like that. He's actually spoken to the vicar and booked it. I'm not even talking to my parents. What are they going to say?"

"I'm sure they'll be fine. Cooper will just intimidate them into being fine," she says, laughing. When I don't join her laughter, she turns to me, seriousness on her face. "Look, if you don't want to go through with it, I will bust you outta here, trust me."

I smile. "Don't be so dramatic."

We clear half the vodka, taking turns drinking from the bottle. The area around me is starting to spin and I stagger towards Cooper, who is chatting to the new club whore, Lacey. I wrap my arms around his waist from behind and snuggle into him.

"Someone's had too much to drink," he observes, and I grin.

"Take me to bed, husband-to-be." Lacey gives me an annoyed look, and I don't like how she watches Cooper's every move. When I'm sober, I need to talk to him about it.

CHAPTER THIRTEEN

I shoot up in bed, my head spinning from the sudden movement. Cooper has been away for two weeks, and I can't get used to sleeping without him. I hear a loud bang and a groan, so I reach for the bedside light and turn it on. Cooper is in the room, rubbing at his head. It's the same scenario that I'm getting used to—Cooper standing before me with blood over his jeans and T-shirt, that same lost look on his face. Kain's warning that we wouldn't last flash through my mind.

I watch him strip off his clothes and chuck them under the bed. Blood has soaked through the material of his T-Shirt and onto his skin, but I don't tell him. He's too deep in his own head right now. So, I pull the quilt back and he climbs in, pulling me to him and burying his face in my hair, sniffing it like he always does when he's like this. I think the smell grounds him.

"You good, Cooper?" I whisper, and he nods but doesn't speak.

I feel his erection pressing into my thigh. Slowly, I roll him onto his back and climb over him. His hands roam up my body until he finds my breasts. I sink down onto him, and he lets out a sigh. I use slow rocking movements until I see him start to come back to me, the glaze in his eyes disappearing. Once I'm sure he's back with me, I pick up speed, panting until he reaches his climax, quickly followed by mine.

Cooper pulls me to lay on top of him but won't let me climb off. He keeps us connected like this for some time. Once I hear his soft snores, I move to his side and snuggle against him.

I lay awake thinking about what he's spent his night doing and who's paid the price. It would be easy to convince myself the blood belongs to a bad person, like maybe a rapist, but I know that's probably not the case. I'm not stupid—I know the Hammers MC isn't made up of stand-up citizens.

I'm still awake when the sun rises, so I decide to get up early. I head down to make myself a cup of coffee and then go out to the back of the clubhouse. I sip it slowly, savouring the bitter taste and enjoying the peace and quiet.

I'm not sure how much time passes before I hear footsteps behind me. It's Lacey. She's never approached me before, but as she sits down, her dressing gown rides up and I notice small bruises on her thighs.

"Hey, you're up and about early," I say.

"I haven't been to bed yet," she says, smiling. "Kirk is an all-night kind of guy." I smile awkwardly because what do you say to that. "Anna was my best friend," she blurts out. It takes a second for the information to reach my brain. "That's why Cooper helped me out with the job." I stay silent. "He loved her so much, like to the point of suffocation. He drove her insane, always checking her phone, constantly texting her and ringing her to see where she was and who she was with. He hated her talking to other men, so he kept her well away from the clubhouse. They had a huge place together, not far from here." I blink quickly because I can feel the threat of tears. "She was his queen, and he treated her like it. She would joke about his sex drive, said if he could be inside her every minute of the day, he would be. He couldn't get enough of her."

"Sorry, but why are you telling me this?" I interrupt.

"Because he may stand there and tell the rest of the world that you're his, but he doesn't feel it. It isn't there in his eyes. For a start, he's got you living here when he has a mansion five minutes away. Don't you wonder where he goes to for days on end?"

A tear rolls down my cheek. I thought we were doing well. We're getting on so well and he seems excited about the wedding in two weeks. He's arranged everything because he says he wants it to be a surprise for me.

Lacey stands. "I didn't want to upset you, I just think that if it was me, I'd want to know if I was second best."

I watch her walk away then remain rooted to my seat, staring out over the field for another hour, her words ticking over in my head. It explains the disappearing acts. I don't understand why he would keep his house from me. Is it a shrine to Anna? Is that why he hasn't ever taken me there? Why would he keep Asher here if he has a nice, safe house that he could live in?

It's noon before Cooper surfaces. I've taken Asher to the field for a picnic, although there're grey clouds looming, indicating a storm.

"Morning, gorgeous." He smiles, sitting down next to me and kissing my head.

"I've been thinking," I say, feeling brave. I've spent the last hour thinking of ways to drag information from this closed book.

"Oh dear, that's never good," he jokes.

"If we're going to get married, then we need a place to live. We can't live here forever, and I'd like a home for us and Asher. Maybe somewhere close by?"

He looks uneasy and fidgets. "What's wrong with here?"

"It's not a home, Cooper. Don't you want a place of our own?" I ask. "Have you always lived here?" He avoids my eye but nods. The lie hurts my heart, but I shrug it off. "Did Anna live here with you?"

"What is this all about, Mila?" he snaps defensively, like he always does when I mention her name.

"I'm just saying it would be nice to have a home of our own. Somewhere I can wash the blood from your clothes in the privacy of our own place." He stands up, the blood remark a step too far. But we never mention it, and I'm sick of acting like it's all normal, or worst still, that it doesn't happen.

"Two weeks until we're married and already you're nagging," he huffs, stomping off towards the clubhouse.

"Well, that went well," I whisper to myself.

When I go back inside, I'm told by Sam that Cooper left the clubhouse and no one knows where he went. I go to Lacey because I suspect she knows. "I want the address," I demand, and she laughs.

"Yeah, right, so he can slit my throat for talking? Not a chance."

"If you don't give it to me, I'll tell him everything you said and you'll be out of here. Give me the address and I'll keep my mouth shut forever. He won't know it was you. I'll tell him I stumbled across it because I'm looking for a house." She huffs in annoyance but grabs a piece of paper from the bar and scribbles down an address, handing it to me.

"Don't tell him I gave you this. He really will hurt me, Mila. He isn't that cute teddy bear that he shows you." I roll my eyes because I don't think I've ever seen the cute teddy bear side she refers to. Maybe it was the side he kept for Anna.

Ten minutes later, I'm on my way to the address that Lacey gave me. Max is safely locked in my old bedroom with Asher because I couldn't risk him following me and tipping Cooper off. I was real quiet turning that key, so I doubt he'll realise until he tries to leave. I gave Brook the key and asked her to let him out in ten minutes, just so I get a good head start.

I park a few feet up the road. It's very private, set back from the road and hidden behind a huge brick wall and large trees. Making my way to the high gates, there're security cameras dotted all around.

I buzz the gate, and after a few minutes, there's a crackle and a voice. "Can I help?"

"Hi, I'm here to see Cooper. It's his fiancée." There's a long pause, where I assume the person is checking out my story, and then, to my surprise, the gates open.

Taking a deep breath, I force myself to walk on through the gates. Backing Cooper into a corner isn't going to end well, but I can't pretend that Lacey didn't tell me about him and Anna.

I admire the lush green grass that sits evenly on either side of the gravel pathway. Flower beds are dotted about, overflowing with bright colours.

Someone must be taking care of this place because I can't imagine that Cooper does the gardening. It's so different to the clubhouse.

As I approach the large, white house, I take in its beauty. If I was going to choose a family home, this would be it, which begs the question, why doesn't he want to share it with me and Asher?

The double doors swing open and a man stands to one side. He's dressed in a black suit and he indicates for me to step inside. I find myself standing in a large entrance hall with a winding staircase to one side leading up to the second floor. There're three rooms leading off from this hall and I'm led into the first one.

I take a seat on the couch. The décor is modern but cosy. The couch fills one wall and could easily fit ten people on it comfortably. The television is on the opposite wall and it's large enough to compare to that of a cinema. There're photos of Cooper, his arms wrapped around Anna's waist. They look so happy and in love in each picture, but I resist the urge to take a closer look. Seeing it from here pains me enough and I brush a stray tear away from my cheek.

"So, who told you?" Cooper's gravelly voice makes me jump in fright.

I stand and turn to him. "Does it matter? Why didn't *you* tell me?"

He shrugs his large shoulders, remaining in the doorway and not approaching me. "I didn't need to."

"We're supposed to be getting married and you're still living in your home, the home you shared with your wife, the home you didn't want to even tell me about."

"I just needed a sanctuary, something that was mine. Somewhere I could come when I needed a break from it all," he explains. Somehow, that doesn't make me feel any better.

"Usually, people like to have a sanctuary filled with love and family, a wife, children," I snap. "I asked you today if you had always lived at the club and you said yes."

He stays silent for a few minutes and then lets out a sigh. "Come on, I'll take you back to the clubhouse."

"So, you don't even want to talk about this?"

"What's the fucking point? This place means something to me. It's mine, mine and Anna's, and it doesn't feel right you being here," he yells.

I press my lips together in a tight line and give a slow nod of understanding. He doesn't love me, not as much as he loved her, and that's okay, but I can't be in a relationship where I will always be second best. He can't let her go. He isn't ready. I stand, and Cooper moves to one side so that I can pass. He goes to follow me, but I spin around, halting him mid-step.

"No, stay, I'll make my own way back." The pain in my heart is so intense, it's hard to breathe. I press the area to try and rub the pain away, it doesn't help.

Cooper kisses me on the cheek like this is a normal situation. "I'll be home later," he whispers.

"You are home, Cooper," I mutter before turning and leaving.

When I arrive at the clubhouse, Harper is just finishing up her shift.

"I need to stay with you for a few days," I say in a rush, not stopping to explain. She follows me to my room, a million questions on her lips, and watches me gather my stuff together and shove it into bags. I fill her in on the house, and she confirms what I was already thinking—he isn't ready to move on. He's still living in the past, in his house with Anna's ghost. Asher runs in with Max on his heels. Apparently, Max wasn't happy about the whole locking him in my room, so he doesn't give me his usual smile. He clocks my bags and looks confused before realisation dawns on him.

"Mila, what the fuck?" I ignore him and crouch down to Asher.

"Guess what, I've got to go away for a bit," I announce with as much cheer as I can muster. He grips my shoulders.

"Why?" he asks.

"Well, because something really important has come up and I need to sort it out. Can you be a big boy for me and look after the guys?" He gives a nod, a look of pride on his little face because I'm trusting him with such an important job.

"Does the Pres know?" asks Max, pulling out his phone. I stand and gather my bags.

"Give me a head start, Max, please?" He pauses with his phone halfway to his ear, his thumb poised over the call button.

"Fine." He sighs, shoving it back into his pocket.

I kiss him on the cheek and then Asher. "Be good for Max and I'll come and see you soon," I promise, heaving a bag onto my shoulder and handing the other to Harper.

"Can I tell him where you're going?" asks Max hopefully.

"Like he won't be able to find me on his own," I reply with a half laugh.

I'm awoken by banging and slowly sit up, taking a second to realise I'm on Harper's couch and not in my comfy bed snuggled with Cooper. Another bang makes me jump with fright and I reach for my mobile phone to check the time—it's three in the morning. There're thirty missed calls from Cooper. I'd turned my phone to silent before I fell to sleep.

"Mila, Harper, open the door!" I'm not surprised to hear Cooper's voice. I sigh, pressing my face into my hands. Harper enters the room, tying a silk robe around her waist.

"Jesus, he's going to wake the whole damn neighbourhood!" She swings the door open. "Cooper, keep it down," she hisses.

"Where the hell is she?" he yells, completely ignoring her plea.

"Why are you covered in blood?" She gasps, dragging him into her apartment and slamming the door shut before her neighbours see. His eyes find mine, and I see that same lost look I always see when he's in this state.

Cooper makes his way over to me and pulls me to stand. "You weren't there," he rasps, pulling me into his hold. I push away, struggling but eventually freeing myself from his grip. He looks at me confused.

"No, Cooper, just go."

"What? Have you left me?" he asks, understanding hitting him finally. I assume that Max didn't call him then.

I sigh. "You aren't ready to move on."

"I am. I am ready, and I have moved on," he rushes out, taking my hand and pulling me closer.

"You still live in your house, Cooper. You leave me and Asher at that shithole, and you go there and surround yourself with Anna," I yell, taking us all by surprise. "And I get it, okay, you miss her, she was your one true love, but I can't live in her shadow. I hate that you miss her so much and that I'm not enough. I just can't carry on pretending that we're okay." He sits down, looking shocked.

"We are okay," he mutters. Harper quietly leaves the room, closing the door behind her to give us some privacy.

"Cooper, you only come to me when you need to be distracted from whatever you want to forget. Our entire relationship is sex and sleep. Anything out of that is off limits with you. I thought it was because you needed to be the boss in front of the guys, but now, I see it's because I'm not her. You used to spend every minute with her, and when you weren't with her, you would text and call her constantly."

He sighs and hangs his head in his hands. "I do miss her. I blame myself and I can't shake it." The truth hurts me even though I knew it already. "She went out one night, we argued because she said I was suffocating her, and she didn't come home. Brick turned up telling me she was dead, that she had overdosed." I let out a gasp. I thought she had been ill. "He said it was my fault and he banned me from her funeral. I was too broken to fight him on it, so I didn't even get to say goodbye. I don't keep you at a distance on purpose, Mila," he admits, meeting my eyes. "I'm so in love with you that it terrifies me. I'm scared that I'll suffocate you too and you'll hate me like she hated me."

I feel my heart break for him. He's carrying this pain around and blaming himself for her suicide. I move towards him and kneel by his side, wrapping my arms around his huge shoulders.

"I don't want you to hold back," I whisper, kissing his forehead. "I love you too."

Cooper pulls me so that I'm sitting in his lap, and my legs automatically wrap around his waist as he holds me close. "I'm sorry, baby. Please don't leave me," he whispers into my hair. I kiss him slowly, taking my time to show him how sad I feel for him and how I love him. He holds me tight, like he fears letting me go. "Come home with me, Mila. I need you in our bed." I stand, holding out my hand for him to take, then I show him to my bags that still sit by the door, unpacked.

"Take them to the car and I'll explain to Harper." I smile.

CHAPTER FOURTEEN

The last two weeks have flown by. Things are amazing between me and Cooper, and I like the real Cooper, the one who checks on me throughout the day or surprises me by turning up unannounced. He seems more relaxed now that he can let his crazy take over.

It's the night before the wedding and apparently bikers do it different. Fuck tradition, as Cooper says. So, instead of spending it apart, which Cooper was not willing to negotiate on, we're having a huge party. Just the Hammers family, of course, because tomorrow will be the biggest party.

I sent my parents an invite, but things aren't good between us after all that business with Aaron. I haven't heard from them, so I'm not sure if they will just turn up or if they won't bother at all. After all, they don't even know Cooper, so it would have come as a big shock to them. The fact that we haven't done things traditionally, like Cooper asking for my dad's permission, will have upset them greatly.

Cooper hasn't left my side all night so far, much to Harper's annoyance. I haven't had a hen night because Cooper wouldn't accept that he wasn't allowed to come or send a prospect to keep an eye on us. If I'm honest, I don't want to be away from Cooper anyway.

So, I'm sitting on his lap, chatting excitedly to Harper about the plans for tomorrow while Cooper is staring at his mobile, which isn't unusual.

Brook joins us, looking annoyed. "Lacey is being a mega bitch tonight. Haven't you noticed her glaring over at you for most of the night?" I shake my head. I've been having too much fun to care, but she's right, Lacey has been a cow for the last two weeks. It seems her little plan to divide us didn't work like she'd hoped. Cooper insists that she's harmless and probably just hurt that he's moving on from Anna.

I glance over, and she's typing furiously on her phone. "Ignore her. Nothing is going to ruin my last night of freedom." I smile, and Cooper kisses my cheek while Harper rolls her eyes in annoyance.

"You call this freedom?" she asks, pointing to Cooper's arms wrapped around me.

I laugh. She's just annoyed because Kain is still with Ginger even though he visits Harper's bed quite regular. And like a doormat, she lets him. Tomorrow will be hard for her because he's Cooper's best man and she's my maid of honour. They argue like cats and dogs, and as far as the rest of the world can see, they hate each other.

Kain makes his way over, handing a drink to Cooper.

"Oh, you seem to be missing your shadow tonight, Kain," says Harper sarcastically. He rolls his eyes, but I can see from his smirk that he's enjoying the public banter they have.

"It seems that everywhere I go lately, you're there snarling in my ear, so I don't feel like I'm missing a shadow at all."

"Jesus, I hope you two aren't going to be like this all day tomorrow," snaps Cooper. I kiss him gently, shushing him while they continue their spat. To be honest, I quite enjoy it. If these two started getting along, I'd worry.

Kain sits on the arm of Harper's chair and throws his arm around the back of it. "I can't help if you chose the worst maid of honour. I told you to go for someone nicer."

"At such short notice, we had to make do," jokes Cooper, and Harper scowls at him.

The night is going far too quick, I'm enjoying it so much, I don't want it to end. I'm sitting with the girls, listening to their tales of marriage disasters, and some of the stories are so funny that I've almost peed my pants several times. Cooper isn't too far away, chatting with Tanner.

Harper is telling us a story about a one-night stand she once had, and we're all riveted, so we don't notice the room begin to fall silent. Eventually, it's Cooper's expression that captures my attention. His face is pale as he holds his bottle to his lips, but he isn't drinking, or even moving for that matter. I hear Brook gasp, and she follows it up with, "What the fuck?"

My eyes follow the direction of Cooper's frozen stare and I find Brick standing in the doorway, his eyes fixed on Cooper. However, it isn't Brick who's caused all the tension in the room. It's the beautiful, petite women standing by his side, looking worried and frightened.

"Anna," whispers Cooper. It can't be her because she's dead, everyone knows she's dead, but this woman is the spitting image of the one I saw in the photos hanging in Cooper's shrine of a home.

I'm still trying to process what my eyes are seeing, convincing myself that Anna's doppelganger is standing in the same room as Cooper. But then, all hell breaks loose and Cooper flies towards Brick, shoving him against the wall and yelling a string of curse words.

"What the fuck is going on?" he demands. The woman places a hand on Cooper's shoulder, and he freezes, looking at it before dragging his eyes to her face.

"Cooper, it's me. I can explain everything," she says quietly. His arms fall to his sides, and she places her hand on his confused face. "Let's go and talk."

She leads him by the hand and all I can focus on is her tiny fist wrapped in his. Does my hand look that small in his? Does it fit as well as hers does?

Nobody in the room speaks as the pair head towards Cooper's office. Once they've disappeared, all eyes turn to me. I focus on my hands, wringing them in my lap. "What the hell just happened?" Harper mutters.

"Fuck if I know. Tom, get us a bottle of vodka over here, will yah?" shouts Brook. "The rest of you get back to fucking drinking."

"Anna is dead," I mutter, not looking up from my hands.

"Yes, she is, sweetie. We all grieved for her. None of this is making any sense," says Brook, rubbing my arm. A bottle of vodka is placed down on our table, and I reach for it first, unscrewing the lid and gulping down the nasty liquid. "I'll be back shortly. Tanner's disappeared and so has Brick."

A few of the other ol' ladies have made themselves scarce so that I'm left with Harper. "Harper, tell me it's going to be okay," I mutter.

She nods, taking my hand and giving it a light squeeze. "Of course, it is. Cooper will come out of there any second and explain it all. Then, tomorrow, you're getting married."

I've drank almost half the vodka by the time Brook returns. She looks sick to her stomach.

"Well?" I ask. "Did you find out what's going on, because it's taking everything I've got not to storm into that office."

She takes a deep breath. "Anna didn't die."

"No shit, Sherlock. Did you get that information from a real detective?" groans Harper sarcastically.

"Brick said she'd had enough of Cooper. She knew he wouldn't let her leave, so she got Brick to lie for her. She's been living it up in the Canary Islands." She looks almost as shocked as Cooper did when he first saw Anna walk in.

"What?" screeches Harper. "Who the hell does that?"

"Brick said she was desperate. She couldn't take Cooper suffocating her anymore."

"So, what is she doing back then? The night before he's about to marry someone else?" I snap.

"Exactly. Brick said she's been talking about coming back for a while now but hearing that he was remarrying made her mind up, and, well, here she is, undead and still very much married to Cooper."

"So, she wants to come back and carry on with the life she left?" asks Harper.

Brook shrugs. "Technically, he's still married to her."

"I bet you had a hand in this," I shout, glaring at Lacey. She gives me a smug smile.

I stand abruptly, because honestly, I can't listen to more. I make my way towards Cooper's office, and I can't hear anything as I approach. I thought I'd hear shouting or glass breaking or, at the very least, crying. Why isn't Cooper raging? Why is he being so quiet and calm? None of it makes any sense.

I find Tanner pacing outside the door. He looks up at me warily. "He doesn't want to be disturbed," he says, wincing because he must feel bad for me.

"I need to know what's going on," I snap. "Am I getting married in the morning?"

The door swings open and Cooper pops his head out. He looks tired and sad. "Go to bed, Mila. I'll come and see you when I've finished up here," he says firmly.

"Are you serious right now, you're sending me away? We're supposed to be getting married at noon tomorrow, or have you forgotten?"

He gives me a sad smile and then goes back into his office. This sends my blood rushing and I have a sudden urge to smash his sorry-looking face in. I charge towards the door, but Tanner stops me, wrapping me in his arms. "Mila, do as he says. He'll be up shortly, once he's sent this witch packing."

A sob escapes me. "He isn't mad," I whisper. "She won't be going anywhere."

I've sat in bed for a good hour and there's still no sign of Cooper. I snuggle down into the blankets and switch off the bedside lamp. It takes me all of a second before I'm sobbing into my pillow. I hate this waiting. I want answers. What does this mean for me and Cooper? Because he sure as hell can't marry me if he's still married to Anna.

I don't remember falling asleep, but I wake with a terrible headache from all the crying. Glancing at the clock, I see it's eight in the morning. The makeup artist and hair stylist are going to be here in fifteen minutes. I sit up as the realisation hits me again that I'm not getting married. I look to Cooper's side of the bed, it's unslept in. Cooper didn't come to bed last night. I check my mobile phone and there are no missed calls or texts. That never happens. He always sends me messages or calls me.

I head for the shower, hoping that maybe no news is good news. When I've finished, I find Harper and Brook in my bedroom. "Any news?" asks Harper, and I shake my head.

"He said he wouldn't be long, but he never came to bed. Have you heard anything?" I ask Brook, but she shakes her head.

There's a tap on the door and I rush to it, my heart racing. My heart sinks when I don't find Cooper on the other side of the door. Instead, it's the hair and makeup girls. I usher them in, and the makeup artist tugs a large trolley behind her. "Morning, beauties, are we excited?" She smiles, but when she's met with blank faces, she turns to me. "Is everything okay?"

I take a deep breath and decide there and then that I'm not ready to give up on my wedding, so I nod and smile. "Where do you want me?"

It takes over an hour to do my hair. I ordered Harper to go downstairs and get us a bottle of Champagne. I don't miss the way the girls keep glancing at each other and then at me, worry on their faces.

My makeup is getting the finishing touches and then the stylist is going to start on Harper. I wonder for the hundredth time if I'm losing my mind. I know today isn't going to go ahead, and I know I will need to admit this at some point, but right now, I'm not ready.

When I'm finished, I admire her work in the mirror. I look beautiful, flawless even. My hair is twisted up on my head, the ends curled and pinned into a tidy up-do. There're little crystals sparkling throughout and a few wispy bits are artfully pulled down to frame my face. My makeup is fresh, and it makes me look like I've been airbrushed. I take a selfie and upload it to my social media page. A false smile is plastered onto my face with the caption 'Wedding Day'. The picture doesn't show that my world is falling to pieces.

By the time the girls are all done, and the makeup artist and stylist have left, I'm starting to feel nervous. I haven't heard from anyone, and neither have the girls.

"What are you going to do?" asks Brook.

"Get my dress," I say to Harper, and she sighs. "I know, okay, I know you think I'm crazy, but I don't know what else to do. I can't just sit here waiting for him to turn up. He knows we're getting married in less than an hour. If I don't hear from him, then I'm turning up to that church because there are a lot of people going to be arriving there shortly," I snap angrily. "And if he turns up to break my heart, he can damn well do it while seeing me in this fucking dress."

"But what if you're left standing there, Mila? What if he doesn't show?" Harper asks quietly.

I'm trying not to think that far in advance. "Then I'll let the guests know what's happened and I'll go straight to the reception to get wasted on the Champagne I carefully chose even though I fucking hate it." Harper smiles sadly, then goes to fetch my dress from my old bedroom.

When I'm ready, I take in the image, the full-length mirror giving me the perfect view of my fitted, fishtail, white dress. A thin diamante belt makes my waist look tinier than my size six frame.

"Oh my god, Mila, you look amazing," gasps Brook.

Harper and Brook have matching pale pink silk gowns that reach the floor. They both look gorgeous, and I'm sad that we might not get to show off how amazing we look today.

There's a knock at the door and we all stare at each other. It's quarter to twelve, and I'm supposed to get married in fifteen minutes.

"Showtime," says Harper as she reaches for the handle and swings the door open. "Oh shit," she mutters.

Cooper walks into the room, and he isn't in the charcoal grey suit that I chose. His clothes from last night are crumpled and he has dark circles under his eyes.

He looks at me and sucks in a breath. "Wow," he utters. He scrubs a hand over his face, tugging at his beard as he takes me in. "You look amazing, Mila."

The girls sneak out, giving me a small wave and a smile as they pass. Cooper sits on the bed, his eyes fixed on me.

"You didn't come back last night, and you aren't in your suit," I observe. "I've spent hours being prepped and prodded, so you better appreciate the trouble I've gone to look great for my husband-to-be," I say lightly, joking my way through the gut-wrenching feeling in the pit of my stomach. There's a guilty look on his face and I clench my teeth so I don't break down.

"No, I didn't come to bed," he mutters. "It took longer than I thought."

"All night?" I ask, and he gives a nod, not meeting my eyes this time.

"So, ten minutes until I walk down that aisle, Cooper . . . tell me, are you going to be at the end waiting for me?" I ask, a false brightness to my voice. He stays silent, his head hung so that I can't see his face. "Come on, Cooper, you're the President of the Hammers Motorcycle Club. You rule this area, and you aren't scared to break anyone," I grit out, "so, break me."

He looks up and there's a dimness to his eyes that I haven't seen before. "I can't marry you," he mutters, spoken so low that I struggle to hear him.

"Say it so I can fucking hear you," I snap.

"I can't marry you," he repeats more clearly, staring at me, unblinking.

I press my fingers to my temples and begin to pace. My kitten heels clicking on his wooden floor. "Because you're already married or because you still love her?" I probe.

He sighs. "It's complicated, Mila."

"Make it so that I understand then, Cooper," I yell, my sudden rise in tone causing him to flinch.

"I never stopped loving Anna, you know I didn't. Seeing her last night has thrown me. I need to work through that. I wanted to come and tell you face to face," he says. Before I can stop myself, my hand crashes against his cheek, sending his head to the side. He keeps it there, his hand rubbing at the red mark that appears before my eyes, and I rub my tingling hand. *Damn, that hurt.*

"How fucking noble of you to turn up ten minutes before our wedding to dump me," I grate out. "Did you have sex with her last night?" He has the audacity to look guilty and a sob leaves my throat. He gets to his feet, gripping the tops of my arms.

"Mila, I am so sorry. I didn't want any of this. I don't know what the fuck I'm doing, but I have to sort this shit out. Marrying you will confuse the situation even more. I know you hate me right now, but please don't go. Please, just wait so I can sort myself out."

I laugh. Seriously, is he asking me to wait around while he decides what he wants? I pull away from his hold and storm from the room, picking up the bottom of my dress to stop from tripping. Honestly, whoever designed fishtail dresses did not keep in mind that the bride may need to run.

I stop when I get into the main room of the clubhouse. Tanner, Brick, Harper, and Brook all spin to face me. I don't know what to say, so I just stare back at them while my thoughts race a mile a minute around my head.

There're chair covers and a large table set out ready for food. There're balloons that must have been delivered this morning, all bobbing about together by one wall. No one bothered to spread them out because they all must have known this wedding wasn't going to happen.

I march over to the table where there're a few bottles of Champagne waiting to be opened. Everyone tracks me with their eyes as I reach for a bottle and release the cork, the pop ringing out around the room. I tip some into a glass and drink it down in one before topping it up again.

"Mila?" asks Harper, approaching me with caution.

"Tanner, the party is still on. Please go and let all the guests know there is no wedding today, but the party is still fucking on," I say, bitterness in my voice.

I find myself a spot by the dance floor, place two bottles of Champagne on my table, and seat myself. I pay no attention to the others, who all stand in silence, watching.

The guests begin to arrive slowly, but I stay at my table. There will be no hugs or greetings of congratulations. The mood feels awkward, so I drink more alcohol to compensate.

Harper sits opposite me. "Want to talk?"

I shrug. "There isn't a lot to say. Anna is alive, praise the fucking lord."

Harper smirks and it makes me laugh. "Talk about shit timing."

"He wants me to stick around," I say, fiddling with the bottle label.

"That's a big ask when the guy just cancelled your wedding with fifteen minutes notice."

I nod slowly. "I love him, Harper. What the fuck am I going to do now?" I almost whisper.

She squeezes my hand. "Party. Just party." She smiles. "We'll figure the rest out tomorrow." I look around at the people chatting quietly, and it feels like a wake rather than a party. I guess there's no rules on how we should celebrate the cancellation of a wedding.

"Harper, what I really need right now is for this to feel less like a wake and more like a party. I want to get stupidly drunk and make the important decisions tomorrow, after I've been sick and cried into my pillow."

She gives a smile and pats my hand. "Then let's get this party started!" She heads to the juke box and puts on a track, then she grabs my hand and pulls me to the makeshift dance floor. People stare as we dance around, my wedding dress restricting my movements. The other girls join us, Brook hugging me. The only time I leave the dance floor is to pick up a fresh Champagne bottle.

By the time evening comes around, I am suitably drunk, just like I wanted. All the girls, except Katie, are dancing and swigging straight from bottles. We have loads of Champagne to get rid of. Kirk has joined us, and he seems to be taken with Harper, but despite his best efforts, she only has eyes for Kain.

I finally drop into my seat, the restricting dress starting to irritate me at the waist. Brick joins us, and

I don't give him a friendly welcome. I feel like he's getting a lot of enjoyment from all of this.

"How are you holding up?" he asks softly, which really grates on me.

"I'm fine, Brick, thanks for asking," I snap.

"If you want to talk, I'm here," he offers.

"Seriously, you think I'm going to come and talk to you after everything that's happened?" I laugh.

He shifts in his seat, looking uncomfortable. "I couldn't tell you about Anna."

"So, you let me get to the night before my wedding and you think that's the ideal time for me to find out? I think you're enjoying every moment of this. You get to have a second go at revenge, fuck everyone else." Brick stands awkwardly. I don't think this was the conversation he was hoping for. At this moment in time, I hate him, I hate Anna, and most of all, I hate Cooper.

"I didn't mean for you to get hurt. I didn't want this either. I don't want Anna with Cooper and I tried to put her off—"

I wave my hand, cutting him off mid-sentence. "But you updated her on his every move because how else did she find out about me?" He doesn't bother to answer, but the guilt on his face tells me all I need to know.

"Please, just leave me alone."

He nods. "You don't realise it right now, but I did you a favour." I shake my head in annoyance as he walks away. *Arsehole.*

Over the crowd, I spot Cooper on the dance floor. He's talking to Kain, and he looks pissed off. My heart beats quicker, not expecting to see him tonight. Then it hits me that we should have been enjoying this together, as husband and wife, and tears spring to my eyes. As if he can feel my pain, he glances in my direction, and once his eyes land on me, he freezes. Marshall happens to be walking past me, so I make a grab for him. He looks at me in surprise. "Distract me," I plead.

Wrapping an arm around my waist, he pulls me to him, guiding me towards a space on the dance floor. I can see why Harper's got her eye on him. He isn't quite as big or as good-looking as Kain, but he has something about him. His strong arms feel safe, and I relax as we move together to a slower number.

"Thought it would be a good few years before I danced with a bride." He smirks, making me smile.

"Well, apparently, I'm available now, so if you feel like you get the urge to marry me, everything is booked and paid for, including the honeymoon." He throws his head back and laughs.

When I look back to where Cooper and Kain are, he looks sad. Maybe he's realised the same thing as me, that it should have been us here, dancing.

After the song finishes, Marshall releases me and carries on to wherever he was going before I stopped him. Cooper heads my way, and I'm too frozen in sadness to move. "Can I have a quick word?" he asks. He goes to take my hand, but I pull it free and fold my arms, following him through to his office. It's quiet in here, the music and loud voices fading. "Are you okay?" he asks cautiously.

"What do you want to say?" I respond coldly.

"I've moved your things back into your own bedroom for now. I didn't think it was fair to keep you in my room and that maybe you would like your own space again." I roll my eyes but keep silent. "I'm really sorry. I would appreciate you staying around for Asher. I can look for someone else if you want to leave, but please stay until I find a replacement." Before I can respond, the door opens and we both look up in surprise to find Anna bouncing in looking happy and carefree. Cooper closes his eyes for a second, in frustration or annoyance, I can't work out which.

"Whoops, sorry, baby. I didn't realise you were having the chat right now," she says, going to his side and touching his arm in a loving gesture.

"Anna, not now," he growls.

"Well, if she sticks around as the nanny, she needs to get used to seeing us together," she huffs. I grit my teeth, willing myself not to react.

"Is that all you wanted me for?" I ask calmly.

"I must say, Milly, you're taking this so well," Anna butts in, and I know she got my name wrong on purpose.

I smile coldly. "I'm used to it, Annie. Cooper is always fucking shit up at the last minute, but I'm sure you already know that."

"My name is Anna," she snaps.

"And my name is Mila."

Cooper sighs. "Look, ladies, I know this is going to be hard for you both, but I still have a club to run, and I don't want any drama. You need to be civil around each other, especially around Asher," he demands firmly.

"Quick question, before I head off to enjoy my wedding reception, where is she sleeping?" I ask. Anna smirks, giving me my answer.

"No drama, Mila. She'll be in my apartment but not in my bed. We have a lot of talking to do," he says. I want to throw something hard at him, but I refrain from grabbing the heaviest object and leave the office. Half of me wants to walk straight out of here and never look back, but the other half wants to stay, hoping desperately that he will realise what he's losing and pick me. It's sad and pathetic, but I can't help the way I feel. I love Cooper, and up until last night, I thought he loved me too.

As I head for the kitchen, Harper spots me and follows. "What the hell did he want?" she asks.

She watches as I search through the utensils drawer and pull out a pair of scissors. I pass them to her. "Cut this dress so I can move."

"Are you sure? It's a really pretty dress," she says, looking at me like I have lost my mind.

"Cut it," I repeat. She holds the bottom and begins to cut up, getting to just above my knee before she changes direction, cutting the material around my legs until the bottom flutters to the floor around my ankles. I step out of it and admire her handiwork. I've never come across a short wedding dress, but I decide it should definitely be a thing.

"So, what did he want?" Harper asks again.

"To let me know that I'm back in my old room," I answer, and she raises her eyebrows in surprise. "Oh, don't worry, his bed won't get cold. Anna is jumping straight back in from where she left off. Apparently in different beds," I say, using air quotes.

"Wow, what the fuck is he doing? I thought he just needed time?"

"Well, seems he got a taste of what he'd missed, and dead pussy obviously wins." I rummage around under the sink until I find what I'm looking for, pulling out a wrench and holding it up triumphantly.

Harper sighs. "Oh gosh, this looks like trouble."

"Stick around, the show is about to start," I mutter.

She follows me out to the car park, where I spot Cooper's pride and joy. The Harley Davidson Fat Bob shines brightly under a streetlight, its newly sprayed red paint polished to within an inch of its life. Cooper loves this bike. It's one of three, but this is his favourite. I circle the bike, running my pointer finger over the paint and trying to remember how much he said this thing cost him.

A few bikers are standing around having a cigarette. Jase, Max, Brick and Woody are eyeing me cautiously.

"I think this is a bad idea," whispers Harper. "I'm all for revenge and a woman scorned and all that, but I'm worried for your life if you do anything to this bike, Mila. I don't often say that ideas are bad, but this, well, this is definitely bad," she puffs out.

"Worse than being jilted fifteen minutes before your wedding?" I ask, taking a step back from the bike.

I raise the wrench, and Max pushes himself from the wall, "Mila, what are you . . ." His voice trails off when I bring the wrench down onto the bike. It clangs loudly, the echo bouncing off the surrounding buildings. There's only a small dent in the shiny red tank.

"*Fuck!*" yells Jase, opening the bar door and yelling for Cooper to get his ass out here. I bring the wrench down again, over and over, until the dent is big, the paint is scratched, and metalwork is now showing through. I run it over the sides, delighted as the paint scratches away.

Brick approaches, and I eye him warily. He holds out a metal bar and winks. "If you want maximum damage, you need something longer, get a better swing." I chuck the wrench to the floor and start hitting the bike with the bar. He's right, the dents are way better with this. I look up as I bring the wrecking bar down again and see Cooper standing there, frozen to the spot, his mouth open and a look of shock on his face.

"Mila, what the fuck are you doing?" I bring it down again, and he winces. "*Mila!*" he yells.

I don't know when the tears started, but I feel them running down my face and dripping from my chin. I really hope the makeup artist used waterproof mascara, or I'll look like some crazy Halloween bride.

"Someone stop this shitshow," Cooper shouts. Jase and Woody make their way towards me, their hands out in front of them in a placating gesture.

"Mila, come on now, put that down," says Jase gently. I wave it in front of me, warning them to stay back. "Mila, stop this now. You're making a show of yourself. This isn't you. I get you're upset, but you aren't this person," he pleads.

I hit the bike again and there's a crash as it falls onto its side.

"Oh Jesus," yells Cooper, running his hands through his hair in frustration. "You're crazy! You've lost your mind!" He reaches into his waistband and pulls out a gun, pointing it directly at me. "Put the bar down, Mila," he orders, using his President voice. I stare at the gun. I've never had one pointed at me, but it isn't really affecting me the way I thought it might. Maybe it's the alcohol, or the serious amount of pain I feel in my heart right now, or maybe it's just the adrenalin, but either way, I simply stare at it, contemplating if it would hurt less to have the bullet slice through my heart.

I feel arms wrap around me gently from behind and a face nuzzles into my neck. I close my eyes and press my cheek towards the comfort. "Drop it, baby girl, the damage is done. You did good," Brick whispers, his gravelly voice in my ear. I drop the bar and it clatters to the floor. "Let's move away slowly, so that crazy bastard doesn't let that gun off," he adds, moving me back away from the bike. When I open my eyes, there's quite a crowd watching. I hadn't noticed them before. My eyes meet Cooper's—he looks pained, and it hits me hard. The fact that I am cradled in Brick's arms must hurt him and I'm glad, he deserves to feel some pain for what he's done to me today. I turn myself in Bricks tight arms so that I have my back to Cooper. I wrap my arms around his neck and bury my face into his hard chest.

"Take me to my room, Brick. I can't be near him," I whisper. Brick scoops me up in his strong arms like I weigh nothing and takes me inside.

"This isn't done with, Mila. You need to pay for that little display," snaps Cooper.

I press my face harder into Brick's body, not able to face Cooper right now. "She did pay, shithead. You did this to her, you and my fucking sister," Brick replies.

He places me on my feet at the top of the stairs, brushes the loose strands of hair from my face and smiles down at me. "Remind me never to get on the wrong side of you, Mila Coin."

I reach up and kiss his cheek gently. "Thanks for getting me out of there."

He gives a nod. "Go get some rest. All this will seem better in the morning." I turn and head towards my room. I doubt that very much.

CHAPTER FIFTEEN

It's late, sometime in the early hours of the morning, and I'm lying on the bathroom floor. I'm so cold in this stupid, cut-up wedding dress, but it's too hard to get myself up. I feel too dizzy, too weak, too exhausted. The Champagne was not so nice coming back up. I groan and attempt to sit up, but when the room spins faster, I lay back down. The light flicks on and it's too bright, so I groan louder and cover my eyes.

"What the hell are you doing in here? I thought someone was in here fucking, with all that moaning and groaning," snaps Cooper, his voice harsh.

I moan again. "I wish." I ignore the panic rising in my chest, as the last time I was near him, he had a gun pointed at me. "I could do with that gun pointed at me right now, to put me out of this misery," I joke.

"Don't tempt me, Mila. That show back there could have gotten you killed. I've murdered for much less," he snaps. "Fifteen thousand that bike cost me, and you need to come up with a way to pay for the damage."

"You have to be kidding," I mutter. "You deserved that and more for what you've done to me. Maybe you're lucky I didn't pull a gun on you."

Cooper bends to grip my wrists, and in one swift movement, he hauls me up onto my feet. I fall against him, the room spinning faster.

"Mila, why did you get yourself into this state?" he snaps. "I'm not worth this." He spins me around until I'm facing the mirror, and I wince at the girl staring back at me. My hair is half up and half down, clips hanging out in various places. I have panda eyes where my makeup has run, and I'm pale from all the vomiting. I try to turn my head away, but he grips my chin, forcing me to look back at myself.

"This is not you. You should be relieved I didn't get you down that aisle because I'm a fuck-up. I would have hurt you somewhere down the line and we both know it," he growls. Tears run down my face, causing my makeup to start running again. "After tonight, no more tears. You hold your head high, so I know exactly what I'm missing."

"It hurts too much," I whisper. Cooper wraps his arms around me and rests his chin on my shoulder, staring at my reflection in the mirror.

"She's my wife. I thought she was dead, but now she's back, I can't turn my feelings off. It's fucked up, I know it is, and if I could turn it off, I would. I don't know what to do or how to feel, and that's shit for you, I get it, but I couldn't marry you today. Apart from the obvious legal shit, it wouldn't have been fair to you."

My head hurts, my heart aches, and I look a mess, but I find myself nodding. He gives me a small smile and then makes a grab for my makeup wipes. He takes one out and hands it to me, watching as I begin to wipe away the mess. He unhooks the fastenings on the back of my dress before stepping away.

"I'll leave you to get some rest," he offers.

"Wait." The word is out even though I didn't plan on saying it, not out loud anyway. He stops, and we stare at each other for a few seconds. He has that look in his eyes, like he's the predator and I'm his prey. I take a step towards him. "Show me the gun," I whisper. I'm not thinking straight, and I just want him to stay.

Cooper eyes me suspiciously. "Why?" he asks, and I shrug my shoulders. Cooper sighs and pulls the gun out. I take his wrist and guide it up until it's pointing at my chest, gently digging it into my skin. His breathing gets heavy, his chest rising and falling while his eyes run over me. He places the gun on the counter and grabs me by the wrists, hauling me against him. Our mouths clash together in a hungry, passionate kiss as his hands push into my messed-up hair.

"Just one last time. I need one last time," I pant, pulling at his belt.

Cooper pulls down the front of my dress and it falls to the floor. He takes a step back to look at the lace underwear I chose especially for him, matched perfectly with suspenders and stockings.

"Fuck," he groans. It's not romantic and he doesn't take his time. We rip each other's clothes off and fuck against the wash basin like animals. I just want him to see. I want him to remember that he loved me, that he wanted to marry me, and most of all, I want to go back in time and pretend that Anna never walked through those doors.

By the time Cooper climaxes, I'm crying, silent tears running down my face. He wipes them away with his thumbs and kisses me on the forehead.

"I'm sorry, Mila," he whispers, and then he's gone. Pulling up his jeans, he leaves in such a hurry that he forgets his T-shirt. I press my face into it, using it to muffle my sobs. I just made the pain worse.

The next few days pass by in a blur. I keep myself busy with Asher, and now that Cooper isn't around to distract me, I find that I get so much more done. Asher is due to start school in two weeks and we've managed to get his uniform sorted and squeeze a few day trips in, with Max as our escort, of course.

Cooper's been staying out of my way. It's a relief really, even though I'm missing him terribly. Wherever he's hiding, probably in his nice house, I assume Anna is with him because I haven't seen her either. Nobody mentions them to me, and I don't ask.

It's Thursday evening and I'm sat cross-legged on my bed browsing the internet, looking for another job. I feel like looking after children isn't what I want to do anymore and maybe a change is just what I need. I open a job description for a personal assistant when my bedroom door creaks open and Cooper pops his head in. I'm not expecting him, so it surprises me, and I almost knock my laptop off my knee.

"Hey," he whispers.

"Hey, is Asher okay?" I ask, because why else would he be here.

He nods. "I think so. I looked in on him an hour ago and he was asleep." He steps into my room and quietly closes the door.

"I need . . ." He stops and sighs. "Can I just sit?" I nod and point to the end of my bed.

"Is everything okay?" My stomach starts to tie itself in knots. Maybe he's going to fire me before I've even found a job or somewhere to live.

"I shouldn't ask, and I know you hate me, but I just need to be near you sometimes," he admits. "These last few weeks have killed me to stay away." I frown in confusion. "I sound like a pussy, and if the guys could hear me . . ." He trails off again, shaking his head. "You stop the noise. No one else can do that, and I need just ten minutes of quiet," he explains, the frustration clear in his tone.

He hates that he needs to come to me for this. He's told me so many times that I stop the noise in his head. He has too much responsibility, and his life is shrouded in violence and death. It gets too much for him, so he would often lay with me to feel calm again, but I can't have him lay with me this time—I'm too weak for him, and I can't put my heart through any more pain.

"You can stay and talk to me, but you can't touch me," I say firmly.

He smiles. "I didn't plan to, just needed to be around you." I continue to click through the website on my laptop.

"What're you doing?" I hesitate but decide to be honest. I have nothing to hide, and I didn't cause any of this.

"I'm looking at jobs."

Cooper nods slowly. "I thought you might."

"It makes sense. Asher is doing well now, and he starts school in two weeks, so I'll have too much time on my hands. I'm sure Anna can handle bedtime routines and dinner time." I give him a forced smile because saying her name kills me a little inside.

Cooper scoffs. "I think Max can step into that role. Maybe you can show me the bedtime routines and I can give it a try when I'm around?"

"Asher would like that. He really looks up to you now." That isn't a lie, Asher is always asking questions about his uncle and wanting to spend time with him.

"I'll miss having you around here, though, so will a lot of the guys," he says.

"I'll miss being here too. I've loved it, but it's time to move on."

"I guess, if you stick around here too long, someone is going to want to claim you, and I won't handle that too well," he admits with a laugh.

It's too soon to make jokes like that, so I continue my job search. "I think I've had enough of bikers to last me a lifetime. Besides, can anyone else claim me with this on my wrist?" I ask, waving my tattoo at him. Cooper snatches up my wrist and looks closely at the tattoo of his name, rubbing his thumb over it gently. He presses a kiss against it, but I pull my arm free. "You said you wouldn't touch me," I whisper, holding my wrist to my chest like he's burned me.

He stands. "Sorry, I didn't mean to, it's just . . . well, I guess it's habit." I watch as he leaves, the ache in my chest rising again. I have to stop letting him walk all over me.

elle

Friday morning arrives and I'm on a mission, a mission to forget Cooper and I ever had a thing. I manage to talk Max into watching Asher for an hour and I head out for the same tattooist that Cooper took me to. If I ever want to escape his hold, there's only one thing for it.

Jay looks surprised to see me. He's sitting at the front desk with his feet up, reading a newspaper. "Mila," he says, dropping his feet to the floor with a thud, "Cooper not with you?"

I shake my head. "Sorry I didn't ring ahead. Not sure if I'm supposed to book an appointment?"

"No, it's fine, I'm free and I'd always make time for club members and their ol' ladies."

"Actually, that's what I've come to see you about. I need this covered. Is that possible?" I ask, holding up my wrist. Jay looks shocked.

"Does Cooper know you're doing that?"

"It's not up to Cooper, it's my body."

"Yeah, I know, but if you haven't run this by him and I do it, he'll come for me, and trust me when I say no fucker wants your old man after them."

"He isn't my old man, not anymore. His choice, not mine." He thinks about it for a minute and then seems to make a decision.

"Give me a minute," he says before disappearing into the back room. He reappears a few minutes later. "Come on then, follow me." I sit in his chair while he preps the needle and ink. "What were you thinking to replace it?" he asks.

I shrug. "Maybe a rose or something pretty?"

He taps his chin in thought and then grabs a pen and begins doodling on my wrist over Cooper's name. When he's finished, I admire the freehand artwork that is now a rose with vines. "You won't see the name once it's all coloured in," he explains.

"I love it. Thanks Jay." I sit back and let him get on with his art. With every stroke of the needle, I feel a little freer.

I get back to the club an hour later. Harper texted me to say she was working the bar today, so I go there first. I stop dead in my tracks when I find Cooper sitting on a bar stool chatting to Harper. She could have warned me. He never comes in here anymore. Cooper eyes me as I approach, and I take a seat at the other end so I'm not near him.

"Are you gonna show me then?" he asks. Of course, Jay would have told him. I was stupid to think he wouldn't. I wave my covered wrist at him, showing him it can't be seen because of the bandage.

"What have you done?" asks Harper, placing a coffee in front of me.

"She's freed herself," says Cooper, taking a swig from his bottle of beer, bitterness lacing his words.

When I don't respond, Cooper stands and moves towards me. I pretend not to notice and take a drink of my coffee. When he reaches my side, he takes my wrist and gently unwraps the covering. He examines the rose, sadness in his eyes.

"Did you hate it that much?" he asks quietly. I'm taken aback because I love him so much, but I hate what he's done to me, and I can't spend the rest of my life branded to him.

"We don't belong to each other anymore. How would I ever explain another man's name on my wrist when I meet someone else?" Cooper glares at me, his jaw ticking like it always does when he's annoyed.

"You want to move on so badly, job hunting, tattoo removals, it's like you can't wait to get rid of me from your life."

"Cooper, you moved on or back, however you choose to look at it. I wore the wedding dress you chose, was willing to turn up to the church you booked, I had the tattoo that you wanted to brand me as yours, and then after all of that, you chose Anna. You told me you'd moved on, that you were ready, and then you made a fool of me. I can't be tied to you. I need to move on."

"I didn't choose Anna over you. It wasn't even a choice, at least not one I thought I'd have to make. What was I supposed to do when the wife I thought was dead turns up? I didn't stop loving her, we didn't split up . . . I didn't think I'd ever see her again and then she came back to me."

"The fact that she even left should tell you something," mutters Harper, wiping a cloth around the bar top nearby.

"It was a bad time back then, so I get why she left. I was young and immature," he defends, looking pissed.

"She didn't just leave though, Cooper, she pretended to die. Who the hell does that?" Harper asks. "You'd have to be pretty messed up or desperate."

Cooper leans over, grabbing Harper by the wrist. She lets out a surprised squeal as he hauls her half across the bar so their faces are inches from each other. "Who the fuck do you think you're talking to? You're a bartender in my fucking club, so you don't get to speak to me like shit," he growls.

Kain rushes over, stopping by Cooper's side, and speaks quietly into his ear until Cooper eventually releases his hold on Harper. She lands back on her side of the bar, looking flustered as she rubs her wrist.

I push my barstool back and it screeches in protest, bringing Cooper's attention back to me.

"Who the hell do you think you are, treating women like that? Harper was saying what your own brothers are too scared to tell you. She has more balls than any of them. I'm glad Anna came back and showed me what a complete ass you really are. I can do better than you," I say calmly, then I walk away, going towards the clubhouse.

"I told you that from the beginning," I hear him yell after me, followed by glass smashing.

CHAPTER SIXTEEN

Brook has managed to talk me around to joining her and a few of the ol' ladies tonight for a Friday night grill. Club members often throw impromptu parties and today has had some exceptionally warmer weather for September. There's been no sign of Cooper or Anna, much to my relief.

The night air seems cooler now that the sun has set, so I head over to a couple of large logs where Brook is perched, keeping warm by the fire. We're distracted when Harper storms out from the clubhouse screaming and shouting with Kain hot on her heels. We aren't close enough to hear what's being said, but it looks heated.

"That doesn't look good," Brook says, wincing. I stand, deliberating whether I should get involved, but then Harper makes her way towards us.

"Everything okay?" I ask.

"No, no, it isn't. He just punched my date!" she screams, jabbing a finger at Kain angrily.

"He isn't your date. He's a club member and he's out of line. He deserves it and he knows exactly why," yells Kain.

"Why are you even getting involved in my life, Kain? We aren't together," screams Harper. "Fucking me behind your ol' lady's back is not the same as a relationship, so you don't get the same rights," she yells, stamping her foot in frustration.

"While you're carrying my baby, I'll interfere. What kind of self-respecting mother goes out on dates? You should be at home resting up," he shouts.

As the news filters to my brain, my mouth falls open in shock. Harper had failed to tell me she was pregnant, and as she turns to look at my shocked face, she bursts into tears. "Oh god, Mila, I am so sorry," she whispers.

"You're pregnant?" I ask slowly, and she gives a small nod. "By him?" She nods again and sobs.

"You had so much going on with the wedding and whatever, I didn't want to add to your stress."

"Harper, you're my best friend. You can tell me anything and it will always take priority."

"If he carries on like this, there will be no baby. I can't spend the next seven months like a nun." I grin at her dramatics, but Kain spins her around to face him.

"Don't even joke, Harper," he snaps. "That's not funny."

"Then back the hell off before I find our dirty little secret slipping out while Ginger is around," she warns.

I glare at Kain and screech, "You're still with Ginger?"

"I tried to end it with Ginger, but she told me not to bother," he replies, pointing to Harper.

"I will not be your pity wife, the second best," she scoffs, folding her arms.

"Oh my god, what the hell have I missed? Come with me," I huff, dragging Harper by the arm towards the clubhouse.

Once inside, I head for Cooper's office. It's the only room where we won't be overheard or disturbed. Luckily, the door is unlocked, so we head on inside and I switch on the office light. "Now, tell me what's going on from the beginning."

Harper sits on the worn sofa and places her head in her hands. "It's all such a mess," she moans.

"How long have you known?" I ask. Harper is terrible at keeping secrets.

"I found out the day before your wedding. I originally didn't tell you because it was your day and I didn't want to steal your thunder, but then all the drama happened and it just didn't feel right telling you when you were so hurt." She sighs. "Only you and Cooper know."

Great, so Cooper knew and didn't tell me. Harper must read my expression because she quickly jumps to his defence. "I told him not to tell you yet. We've all witnessed the pain you've been in."

"I've been fine," I say defensively, and she gives me a sympathetic smile.

"You've put on a good act, but you look terrible. You've lost weight, and you look like you're in constant physical pain."

"Great, and you didn't think to share this observation so that I could put on a better act?" I snap.

She smiles. "You're allowed to be hurt. Anyway, I didn't tell Cooper, Kain did, mainly because he flipped out when I first told him. He didn't cope very well at all. Ginger is further along than me, but only by five weeks. She doesn't know about me, by the way."

"But he offered to be with you and leave Ginger?"

She nods. "Yeah, but only because of the baby. Before that, he was happy to keep me on the side. I feel like he offered because he thought he should, rather than actually wanting to. As soon as I told him I didn't want that, he shrugged it off, and then the next thing I know, he's in the bar with Ginger playing happy couple."

"Oh, Harper," I sigh, "why do we pick the worst kind of men?"

She shrugs. "And now I'm saddled with him forever. He's determined to be in this kid's life."

"How do you think Ginger will take the news?"

"I don't think he plans on telling her. He said it's his business and she isn't his ol' lady officially, so he doesn't need to explain any of it to her."

"Wow, what a keeper," I mutter, and she smiles.

"Things any better between you and Cooper?" she asks.

"I hardly see him, or Anna. I think they avoid me."

"I see her in the bar sometimes, just passing through, but I haven't seen her with Cooper at all. Weird, really," she muses.

"I don't think they're living at the clubhouse. They have an amazing house together. Anyway, I'm moving on. I have a couple of job interviews lined up and an apartment viewing on Sunday, and with the money I've saved from living here, I can put a deposit down as well as a month's rent. That should keep me going until I find a better job."

"Why don't you just move in with me? The place is lonely and far too big for just me," Harper suggests. It would be nice to have some company. Harper has a huge apartment overlooking the river that her rich father pays for, even though she never sees him. "Think about it and let me know. I honestly would love to share with you."

We head back outside to join the others. It's getting late, so I'm thinking of going to my room, but Harper begs me to stay for one drink so she doesn't have to face Kain alone. We get as far as Brook, who is still sitting by the fire, before I realise that Cooper is sitting opposite, with Anna by his side. I inwardly groan. *This is going to be so hard.* Pretending not to notice them, I take my seat. Brook gives my knee a quick squeeze, letting me know that she's here for me.

Kain sits by Harper. "Sorry, okay, I shouldn't have gone off like that," he says. She shrugs him off, and he sighs, clearly frustrated. "Harps, I will try to reign it in, okay. It'll be hard, but I will try. Just please don't go on dates with any of my brothers, it's all I'm asking. Marshall, of all the guys, is a real whore."

"That's why I like him," she huffs, and he growls.

"You do this shit to wind me up, I swear."

I don't take much notice of their back and forth sniping after that because I can feel Cooper's eyes on me.

"Wow, if he could eat you with his eyes, you would have been devoured by now," Brook whispers with a giggle.

I glance up and see Anna is talking to him, but he's still staring at me. She gently rubs his arm, but he doesn't respond.

"So, guess what," says Harper, talking over me to Brook. She says it extra loud, and I look at her confused. She gives me a wink and a smile. "I have a new roomy."

Brook smiles. "Wow, you only said yesterday you wanted company."

"It better not be a guy," snaps Kain. Harper rolls her eyes, and we both laugh.

"No, it's the one and only Mila."

Brook lets out an excited squeal. "Oh my god, I'm so jealous. You guys will have so much fun living together."

"Well, technically, I didn't agree to it yet. I have a viewing on Sunday," I say, glancing to Cooper, who looks fit to burst.

"And how will you look after Asher? You just gonna abandon us?" Cooper asks, making me flinch.

"Technically, you abandoned her first, so . . ." Harper butts in with a smug smile.

"Does your smart mouth not learn?" Cooper snarls at her. I touch Harper's hand, telling her without words not to respond.

"I'll give notice as soon as I find a job. I won't move out until then," I say firmly. He will not make me feel guilty about this when it's all his fault.

"Asher needs you," he huffs.

"No, he doesn't. He has you, and he has Anna now too," I say, the words almost choking me. Anna looks up in surprise, she was busy looking at her phone.

"Me?" She almost laughs.

"Well, yes, Cooper has parental responsibility and you two are married," I point out.

Anna shrugs. "He's Cooper's responsibility, not mine. Remind me, why are you here anyway? I thought this was a club family grill."

"She is club family," snaps Brook, jumping to my defence. Cooper gives Anna an annoyed look, and she shrugs at him like she was asking an innocent question. I'm still taken aback by her lack of compassion for a small child who's been orphaned. She clearly doesn't have a maternal bone in her body. I silently panic that I'm leaving Asher with a terrible stepmum and guilt hits me again.

Cooper stands, flicking a cigarette into the fire. "I want proper notice, Mila. I expect you to make it as easy on Asher as possible. You break his heart, and I will break yours," he snaps and then stomps off inside.

"You already did," I mumble, more to myself than anyone else, but I notice Kain wince, indicating that he heard me.

―――*ℓℓ*―――

The weekend passes quickly. I decide not to go to the apartment viewing. I like the idea of staying with Harper, and we've agreed on a monthly rent which is more than affordable. This means I don't have to stress too much about my monthly wage and can be a bit choosier about what jobs I apply for. This inspires me to apply for more office-based work.

By Sunday evening, I've sent emails off to several companies and I'm feeling more optimistic. I haven't been with Asher today since Sunday is still my day off and I suggested that Max take him to see Anna at their huge home so he can get a feel for the place. Cooper can't leave him living at the clubhouse now that he's hardly ever around. Max texted me to say he ran the idea past Cooper, who said no, so I plan to speak to him about it when I feel like I can spend more than a minute in his company without wanting to smash his face in or have a full-on breakdown.

I'm reading my Kindle when the bedroom door crashes open, making me jump out of bed in fright. It's Jase, looking panicked and stressed. "We need your help, Mila," he puffs out.

"Jesus, Jase, you scared the crap outta me," I screech, clutching my chest.

"It's Cooper! He's going mad, and no one can get near him. Brook suggested you, said you can calm him," he explains.

"Call Anna. He's her responsibility now, not mine," I say.

"We did, but she didn't answer the call. Please, Mila, I wouldn't ask if I wasn't desperate." I pull on some shorts and rush after Jase, who is now running ahead. *This man is driving me to insanity.*

As we near the office, I hear crashing and glass smashing. A few of the guys are in the hall outside the office. Woody, the club's enforcer, maybe one of the scariest bikers in this club, looks worried. Jase pushes through them, clearing the way for me to follow, and I gasp when I get to the front. The office is completely trashed, and Cooper is just about to tip the heavy oak desk over.

"Pres, Mila is here," shouts Jase, but it isn't enough to break through the mood that Cooper is in. I take a deep breath, knowing there is only one way to get him back. I head into the office cautiously. "Mila, are you sure?" Jase whispers, worry marring his face. I nod and then push the door closed behind me.

My heart is almost beating out of my chest. What if he is too far gone and he attacks me? The desk crashes to the floor, making me jump back. Cooper stands before me, his shoulders heaving up and down with the exertion. His back is to me, and I don't think he's aware that I'm in the room. I slowly run my hand across his back to let him know someone is here, and when he doesn't move, I wrap myself around him, lifting up onto his back to wrap my arms and legs around him. His body sags, and I squeeze tight until I feel his hands run along my legs. He gently guides me until my body is at his front and then he buries his face into my hair, inhaling deeply over and over. Something bad has happened—I feel it in the way he grips me tight against him.

We stay like this for at least ten minutes, completely silent, him just breathing me in. I stroke my hand idly up and down his neck. Eventually, he lowers himself to the floor so he's sitting and arranges me around him so that I'm still wrapped around him.

"She's gone again," he eventually whispers into my hair. I don't speak because it hurts me. He destroyed his office because Anna has left him again. It makes it more real that he loves her. "I messed it all up and she left."

A stray tear slips down my cheek, but I swipe it away furiously so it doesn't run onto him. I don't want him to see me cry over him anymore. There's been too many tears.

We stay quiet for a few minutes more before I try to free myself and stand, but he keeps his grip on me. "Don't go, please," he mutters, holding onto me tight.

"Cooper, I just came to stop you trashing the place. I can't be your sympathetic ear about Anna. Please understand." He releases me, and I stand. "Look at this place. You left me on the morning of our wedding, and I didn't smash the place up," I joke, picking up a chair.

"Is it too late?" he whispers.

"Is what too late?" I ask before realizing what he means. "Please don't say us, Cooper. Please don't say that."

"I fucked it all up. I thought I was doing the right thing, but I was having doubts. Anna wasn't happy about that."

"Cooper, it's way too late. I can't believe you could even ask me that after everything, and to do it the minute Anna leaves you? Way to make me feel special."

I leave him sitting on the floor looking lost, surrounded by destruction. Opening the office door, I find Kain and Jase pacing. They stop and look at me. "Is he okay?" asks Kain.

I nod. "Anna left again," I say as way of explanation before leaving them to pick up the pieces.

The next morning, I'm making Asher his breakfast, now that he's hooked on scrambled eggs and bacon. His little face is full of concentration as he practices his reading while he waits patiently.

"You know, I think your new teacher will be so impressed with your reading skills, Asher," I praise him, and he smiles proudly. He really can't wait for school. I've made sure that we spent time with other children, mainly from club members' families, but it's progress from where he was when I first came to work with him. I don't think he'll have any trouble settling into school. He's ready to start learning now.

Kain enters the kitchen looking worn out. I didn't hear another thing from any of them once I'd walked away from Cooper last night. "Morning. Would you like some breakfast?" I ask. He waves a white piece of paper at me.

"We have a problem."

I plate up Asher's breakfast, and Max joins him while I follow Kain into Cooper's office. It's still a mess and there's no sign of Cooper. "So, I went looking for Cooper this morning only to find this," he says, waving the piece of paper again. "He's gone. Said he needs time to clear his head and doesn't know when he'll be back, but I'm in charge of the club."

I raise my eyebrows in surprise. Cooper loves his club more than anything, so it must be bad for him to walk away and leave someone else in charge, even if that someone is his Vice President.

I sigh. "Wow, Anna really did a number on him."

"I don't think this is down to Anna, Mila. I think he realises that he lost you because of her, and now he can't win you back."

"Don't put this on me, Kain. He chose her, and she left. I can't just decide to forgive and forget because he put me second," I snap. "Where does this leave Asher?"

He shrugs his shoulders. "He has you and Max."

"I'm not going to be around for much longer, Kain. Cooper knew this. I can't stay just because he can't handle his shit."

"Well, I guess I'll have to find another nanny or something," he huffs.

I leave Kain to sort it out. How selfish can Cooper get, just up and leaving the nephew he's supposed to be looking after? My annoyed mood stays around all day, and by the time I put Asher to bed, I'm so pissed that I decide to call him and give him a piece of my mind.

The call goes straight to voicemail, which angers me even more, so I leave a message. "How dare you run? You have responsibilities here with Asher. You have a week to sort your shit out and get back here for him. He needs you." I disconnect the call. I never thought Cooper would run like this. He's the type to stick around and get stuff done.

The news travels fast around the club that Cooper is gone and Kain is in charge until he returns . . . *if* he returns. Some members seem to think he's had some kind of breakdown.

Later that evening, once Asher is safely tucked up in bed, I head out to Cooper's house. I feel a rush of hope when I buzz the intercom and the gates immediately roll open. As I reach the house, the front door swings open and a man in a suit approaches my car. I lower the window, and the man smiles. "He said you would call by here."

"So, you've spoken to him?"

The man nods. "He doesn't want to be found. He needs to clear his head."

"But he has responsibilities. He needs to look after Asher."

"He needs time, that's all."

I feel my fury ignite again. You can't just take time out when you feel like it, not where children are concerned. "Do you know where he is?"

"No. He took his bag and bike, and that's all he needs. He'll be back when he's ready. For now, I suggest you take care of that little nephew of his. He'll be forever grateful."

I roll my eyes. I love Asher and it breaks my heart to leave him, but Cooper needs to step up and be a man.

It's been almost two weeks and there's been no sign of Cooper. No one has heard from him, and there's no indication that he will be returning anytime soon.

I re-read the email, confirming that I have the new job as a personal assistant for a small modelling business. I'm excited and scared all at the same time. It's something I've never done before, but the woman who interviewed me has never had a P.A., so it will be a learning curve for us both.

I knock on Cooper's office door. Kain did a good job clearing up the mess and redecorating it. He shouts for me to enter, and I find him staring intently at a laptop. He glances up at me. "How can I help?"

"Any news?" I ask hopefully, but he shakes his head. "Erm, well, there's no easy way to say this . . ." I start. He looks up at me, irritation clear on his face.

"Spit it out, Mila."

"I have a new job." He chucks his pen on the table and leans back in his chair, steepling his fingers in front of his mouth.

"No," he says firmly.

I give a nervous laugh. "Yes, I start in a week."

"Mila, seriously, I haven't got anyone to replace you. Asher needs you in his life. His uncle's gone AWOL and now you want to leave him too?" he snaps.

"It isn't my responsibility," I argue. "I told Cooper I was leaving."

"You're both selfish bastards, you know that?" he yells.

"How am I selfish? Asher isn't my nephew."

"But you call yourself a nanny. You're supposed to care about that kid but now you want to abandon him, leave him in this hellhole with a bunch of drunken bikers."

He's right, the thought of leaving Asher here without me breaks my heart, but what am I supposed to do? I can't stay here. This isn't my life anymore.

I promise Kain that I will come up with a solution that suits us all until Cooper returns, but I'm not sure what that solution is. Asher starts school tomorrow. I have his little uniform laid out and I find myself feeling heartbroken that Cooper won't be around to see this important milestone.

I dial his mobile number, but as usual, he doesn't pick up. "Hey, Asher starts school tomorrow. I wish you were here to share it with him. Come home, Cooper. He misses you."

Later, I call Harper and tell her about the new job and ask for her help on a solution to the whole Asher situation. "You could always bring him with you."

I laugh. "Yeah, right. I need some serious advice here, Harper."

"I am being serious. Bring him here. He's at school in the day, then one of the guys can do the school run and bring him to me at the bar until you finish work. That way, he gets the security of having you but still sees the guys."

"I don't think that was the solution Kain was looking for."

"Well, it's all I've got, and it's only until Cooper shows up again. The guy is sulking, how long can that go on for?"

"I guess it wouldn't hurt to run it by Kain. He wasn't in a very good mood earlier, so I'll speak to him in the morning."

"I annoyed him with a parental agreement," giggles Harper.

I sigh. "It almost sounds like you enjoy upsetting him."

"Mila," she huffs, "he dumped me for Ginger. He deserves every bit of stress I can possibly cause him, and you're supposed to be on my side, not his."

"You're right. I just wanted you guys to make it, and I thought a baby might get you back on track."

"He had more than one chance. He thinks I'm only good for one thing and wants to put Ginger and her kid on the back of his bike, so fuck him, I'm worth more than that."

She's right—he was using her knowing full well that he wasn't going to stop seeing Ginger.

The following day, I put my solution to Kain over breakfast. He looks at me sceptically. "You're gonna take him with you, to live with Harper?"

I nod. "Between us all, we can look after him. I love Asher, and if it helps while Cooper is away, then I'll give it a go."

"Fine, if you're happy to do that. I'll make sure your wage doesn't stop, that should cover any costs." That's good news for me. It'll mean I have a double wage coming in, which will help me save for my own place. I'm happier knowing it's all sorted and that Asher will be looked after.

I spend some time helping Asher get ready for school. It's a private school, so he has a blazer and little hat to wear that make him look adorable. I brush his floppy blonde hair away from his eyes and put the cap on his head. "You look amazing."

"I wish my mummy was here," he says softly, and I pull him in for a hug.

"I know you do, baby boy, me too. But I'm pretty sure she's in heaven watching you with a huge smile on her face right now and wishing she was here too." I then make a big fuss of photographs. Cooper may regret missing it, so at least he will have the pictures, and Asher needs to look back on this time and remember it.

We make it to school with five minutes to spare. I buzz at the main gates and we follow the secretary down the halls towards Asher's new class. Stopping outside a blue door, I look through the glass window and see lots of small children playing. They all look happy to be there, which makes me feel a small relief.

I crouch down to Asher's level. "Now, remember what I said. Have fun and be kind to everyone. I'll pick you up at three o'clock." I kiss his head, and he wraps his arms around me tight.

"I really love you, Mila," he whispers, and I blink a tear away.

"I love you too. You're gonna have the best day, Asher. I can't wait to hear all about it."

The secretary takes his hand and leads him into the class. I watch through the window, my heart bursting with pride. I really do wish his mum and Cooper were here to see this.

When I return to the clubhouse, I spend some time cleaning to take my mind off how Asher is doing. Being brought up around all these men means that he often picks up bad habits and I'm really hoping he doesn't display any of those today. I text Cooper a picture of Asher in his smart new uniform, but as usual, he doesn't answer, which disappoints me. I'd hoped he would at least acknowledge his nephew, even if it was just a good luck message.

Then I decide to pack some stuff. Now that I'm taking Asher to stay with me, I can move into Harper's anytime I like. I'm in the middle of deciding what clothes to pack for Asher when I get the sudden urge to vomit. Making a dash for the toilet, I almost knock Max over in the process, and he looks alarmed as I shove him out of the way. He follows me, which is mortifying, but I can't close the door and vomit in the toilet at the same time, so I pretend he isn't there.

He hands me some tissue, and I wipe my mouth. "You hungover?" He smirks.

"No, I think it's all the worry of Asher starting school. He told me he misses his mum today."

"Poor kid. I'm glad he's got you to help him through." He smiles. "I came to see if you need a hand packing anything. I have a spare hour." I take him up on his offer and leave him to choose some things for Asher.

By the time I've finished packing my room up, it's time to get Asher. Max comes with me, and Asher is delighted to see us both waiting for him in the playground. Once his teacher dismisses him, he makes a run for Max, who picks him up and swings him around. The teacher follows, smiling.

"You must be his uncle, Cooper?" she asks, smiling.

Max puts Asher down. "No, ma'am, I'm Max, a family friend. Cooper is away on business, so it will either be myself or Mila here to collect and drop off."

"Well, Asher is settling in lovely. He's had a really great day and seems to be making lots of friends."

I notice that she's ignoring me and speaking directly to Max, a twinkle in her eyes. Max seems oblivious, though, choosing to fuss Asher instead.

"She had a thing for you," I say with a smile once we're in the car.

He shrugs. "She isn't the type of girl who gets our lifestyle."

"Neither was I, but I fit in okay, don't I?"

"You were always that type of girl, which is why you fit in. That's why Cooper turned you away first off. He saw it in you and he knew he was gonna fall if you stuck around."

"I wish I had walked out that day and never looked back," I mutter.

After Asher goes to bed, I call Cooper again. Once his answer message kicks in, I sigh. "Hi, it's me. Again. Asher had a good day today. He misses his mum, which is why you needed to be here. Anyway, I'm calling to tell you that I have a new job and I'm moving out tomorrow. I just thought you would want to know."

The text comes almost as soon as I disconnect the call.

Cooper: Don't leave Asher.

That confirms that he is receiving my messages.

Me: Where are you? Answer my calls.

I try to call again, but he doesn't answer. I growl in frustration and throw my phone. It clatters across the carpet and the battery flies out.

There's a knock at my bedroom door and I open it to find Max. "Is everything okay?" he asks, concern across his face. I shrug and shove the door open wider so he can come in.

"Cooper texted me. When I tried to call him, he ignored it. Why won't he speak to me?" Max sits down, looking huge on my bed. Not as huge as Cooper, but still.

"He just needs time. He does this sometimes, but he always comes back. It's a tough job running a club and I guess he needs to be away from it for a while."

"It's a shitty move, to run when things get tough. I didn't run when he stood me up on our wedding day, and I stuck around for Asher despite having to see Cooper and his wife together."

"Good point." He smirks, laying back and putting his hands behind his head. I sit down and lean against the headboard.

"Talk shit with me, Max. Take my mind off him." I sigh and that's what he does. We talk until the early hours and laugh about stupid things we've done in the past. By the time Max leaves, I realise I haven't thought of Cooper once, and it's a good feeling.

—*elle*—

I drop Asher at school the next day and decide to try Cooper one more time. I need to tell him that I'm taking Asher with me. If he doesn't answer me this time, then I won't try again. He will have to find out from Kain whenever he decides to return.

It rings a few times and then it connects. I take a breath in surprise, waiting for him to speak. I'm disappointed when it's a female voice that greets me. "Yeah?"

"Is Cooper there?" I ask.

"He's asleep. You want to leave a message?" she asks. I disconnect the call, squeezing my phone tight in my hand, mainly from anger, I think. I unlock the screen and, taking another deep breath, I scroll through my contacts until I land on his name. I hover over it for a minute or two before finally forcing myself to delete his number.

"No more, Mila. No more," I whisper to myself. I can't waste any more time on Cooper. I have to move on. With the decision made, I load up my car with mine and Asher's things and head for our new home. It's a fresh start and a chance for me to put the last year behind me.

Harper helps me unpack our stuff. We each have a room because Harper's apartment is huge. I feel like Asher is going to love staying here. He hasn't experienced this kind of lifestyle before, and even though

I don't know the ins and outs of what happened with his mum, Cooper told me she was a drug abuser, so I can't imagine she gave Asher a top-notch lifestyle.

By the time Max drops Asher off after school, his room is set up and ready for him. He looks around the apartment in awe and comments on the normal sized television since the clubhouse shares one huge screen in the main room. He snuggles down on the sofa with Harper and watches a children's television show while I set about cooking us all dinner.

This is going to work. I have a good feeling.

CHAPTER SEVENTEEN

My new job comes around far too quick. It's a struggle getting ready for work while trying to juggle Asher and getting him ready on time. Without Harper's help, I don't know how I would manage, and I curse Cooper for the hundredth time for putting me in this predicament.

I finally enter the office at nine a.m. My new boss, Isla, greets me with a warm, friendly smile that eases me instantly. She shows me to my desk, which sits opposite hers. It's a small office, but I instantly love it. She spends the morning showing me what to do and how to input data into her client lists and her accounts. By lunchtime, I feel slightly overwhelmed, but I know I can do this.

"Let's go and grab some food. I'll show you the deli I go to, it's amazing," suggests Isla. "I know this all seems overwhelming now, but it's easy to get to grips with, I promise."

We find a table near the window and I tuck into a salmon and soft cheese bagel. She's right, it really is amazing here. Isla is filling me in on her best client, a new magazine that's only had three issues but is already popular. She's really excited about all the upcoming shoots they want to do and is on the hunt for new models. The whole time she's talking, I can't shake the feeling that I'm being watched. I glance out the window numerous times, but all I can see is the hustle and bustle of people rushing back to work from lunch breaks.

By the end of the day, I'm overloaded with information to read, clients to research, and model applications to go over. "Go home, rest. We'll work through that pile tomorrow," Isla says, smiling.

As I get my things together, I feel a rise of excitement. I know this is going to work out for me.

I get to the club bar to collect Asher just after five. He's reading a book to Max, and I smile at the scene before me. Asher is sitting on the bar, concentrating hard on his words, and Max is sitting in front of him, listening well with pride in his eyes.

"You having a story?" I ask, sitting next to Max. He gives me a kiss on the cheek, something he seems to do a lot lately. Not that I mind, it's sweet.

"So, how was it?" asks Harper excitedly.

"A-maze-ing!" I sigh, and she does a little happy dance.

"I knew you would love it."

"I have to confess, Mila, I was secretly hoping you would hate it so you'd change your mind and come back to us," smiles Max, "but I'm glad you enjoyed it."

At home, once Asher is in bed, I open my laptop and research some of the companies that Isla spoke about today. I have no knowledge of the fashion industry, so I feel like I need to arm myself with as much information as possible.

By the time Harper gets home from her shift at the bar, I'm half asleep.

"Good shift?" I yawn as she throws her keys on the table.

"If you can call Kain being a complete dick to me all night good, then yeah, sure," she mutters, pulling her boots off and flopping down next to me.

"He still mad about you and Marshall?"

"He sits there glaring at me with her on his fucking arm. What am I supposed to do, stay single for the rest of my life?"

"Tell Ginger," I suggest, and she looks at me like I've lost my mind. "He's cheated on her, Harper, so tell her. I would want to know, wouldn't you?"

"She's pregnant with his kid. I can't ruin her life like that."

"You're pregnant with his kid too. Why should you get all the grief? He's sitting pretty with his wifey and kid on one arm and his dirty secret on the other. Who does he think he is?"

Harper raises her eyebrows sceptically. "Wow, who upset you tonight?"

"No one. I'm just sick to death of men, especially those Hammer men, lording it around like they're the kings and we're their peasants. Picking and choosing women like they're in the candy store. Well, fuck them all. Bring his castle down around him." I realise I'm getting irate and I'm not really sure where it all came from. Maybe the fact that I miss Cooper so bad is beginning to get to me.

"We need a night out. We could go for a meal and a few non-alcoholic drinks on the weekend, celebrate your new job," suggests Harper. She's right, of course, I need to get my life back on track, to forget about Cooper and start socialising again. Now I have two salaries coming in, there is no reason to sit at home every night.

The following day is pretty much the same as the first. We go through the list of potential models and arrange for them to come and see us. Isla needs several for a wedding shoot that's coming up. I manage to book a studio room for the shoot on Friday, which I get to attend so I'm excited.

Isla is in a meeting at lunch, so I decide to nip out to the deli she took me to yesterday and grab us each a sandwich. I'm looking down at my phone as I enter the deli, trying to get onto my social media page, but it says my password has been changed. I look up just in time to avoid crashing into someone exiting, also with their head down.

"Sorry," I utter as I go to hold the door. The person looks up, and I take in a deep breath to hide my shock. It's Aaron.

"Mila," he stutters like he's just as surprised to see me. I try to move past him, but he puts his arm across the door, halting me.

"I've been wanting to see you, to apologise for everything."

"Now is not the time, Aaron," I mutter.

"It's the perfect time. Let's walk," he says forcefully, taking my hand and pulling me from the deli.

"What the hell are you doing? My boss is waiting for me," I snap, trying to pull my hand free, but he grips it tighter. He marches me across the street to a small park area, then he sits on a bench and pulls me down beside him.

"You aren't with him anymore," he states, as if he already knows the answer.

"It's none of your business."

"I saw him a few days ago with another girl, so if you're still with him, then he's cheating on you too," he says smugly.

This gets my interest and I sit up straighter. "Where did you see him?"

He smirks. "Stalker much?"

"This isn't a game, Aaron. I have his nephew staying with me, so I need to see him to get him back home and go back to my normal life." I'm lying, because I love having Asher around and I can't imagine the day when I have to give him back. But I have this need to see Cooper, just to know that he's okay. What if he's had a breakdown and that's what's keeping him away?

"He seemed happy . . . a little out of it but happy. I guess most men would be happy with the little blonde he had all over him."

"Just forget it, Aaron. Why did I think you would possibly be adult about this?" I huff, standing.

He grabs my wrist again and pulls me back down. "I haven't finished. You know, your little sob story got me thrown out of your parents' house. Your dad talked your mum into kicking me out," he states, annoyance in his voice.

"Good. You came between us when you should have just walked away. Did you tell Cooper that you were going to rape me?"

He grins. "I'd say anything to piss him off. It worked—he really cracked my jaw after that comment."

"Look, it's been fab catching up, but I really have to go," I snap.

"He was in the Town Bell Inn, if you want to know. He often goes in there because the girls are easy and looking for a big bad biker to throw them around the bedroom. He looks like the kind of guy to do that," he muses. "I do want to apologise for my behaviour back then. It's not an excuse, but I had a lot on, so I'm sorry." I nod and stand, and this time he lets me. "For what it's worth, he looks broken," Aaron adds.

That last comment plays like a loop in my head. I hate to think that Cooper's broken, because I know how that feels.

By the time Saturday night comes around, I've hatched a plan. I need to see Cooper—not to talk, not even to bring him home, but it's an urge I have to see him with my own two eyes. Harper and I are going out for dinner, and I've booked the restaurant that sits next door to the bar Aaron spotted Cooper in. Maybe if I can catch a glimpse of him, I'll get it out of my system and move on.

Harper screws her nose up in disgust. "Where did you find this place?" she asks, looking around.

"Someone told me about it a while ago. I've been wanting to give it a go for some time," I lie. She's right to screw her face up, it looks terrible. It's a rundown Chinese restaurant and I'm praying I don't give my pregnant best friend food poisoning.

We choose a seat by the window, mainly so we can run if the food is bad, and order a mocktail each. I feel bad for Harper, so I decide not to drink to support her.

"I thought about what you said, about telling Ginger."

"Look, Harper, I shouldn't have said that. I was being a moody cow. You were right, it isn't fair to break Ginger's heart."

"What?" screeches Harper. "Well, I wish you'd have said that earlier."

"Oh gosh, why, what have you done?"

"I've told her. I sent her a text a few hours ago."

"*A text?*" I hiss, leaning closer to Harper. "You told her that her man cheated on her by a goddamn text? That's a real shitty move, Harper," I snap.

"Well, you said to tell her, so I did," she hisses.

I groan. "What did she say?"

"She didn't reply, and I haven't heard from Kain either."

I put my head in my hands, sighing loudly. "Shit, Harper. Read me the text you sent her."

"I don't want to," she huffs. "I feel awful now."

"Harper, read me the damn text," I demand.

She rolls her eyes and pulls out her phone. She dramatically unlocks it and brings up her messages before handing me the phone.

I scan the message. "Oh wow . . . oh gosh . . . this is terrible. What made you think that texting it was a good thing?" I groan. "I mean, seriously, I'm pregnant by Kain too! Really, that's what you put?"

Harper snatches the phone back and stuffs it in her pocket. "Well, what was I supposed to say?"

"Gentle and kind would have been at the top of my list to keep in mind when breaking someone's heart," I snap just as the waiter comes to take our order. "Actually, I'm not feeling too good," I say, standing. "I need the bathroom."

Once inside the cubicle, I empty the contents of my stomach into the dirty toilet. This keeps happening to me. I think it must be all the stress. When I return to the table, Harper has her coat on. "I paid for the drinks. I'm not feeling too great either, so can we skip food and head home?"

I nod and link arms with her. "It wasn't that bad, the text," I tell her.

She smiles gratefully at my attempt to make her feel better. "It was awful and a shit thing to do. Kain is going to kill me."

We head out into the cool night. The street is fairly busy, and it crosses my mind to suggest the bar in case Cooper is in there.

"Well, well, well, what are the chances?" A deep voice from behind us startles me. We turn to find Kain and Cooper looking menacing.

"You tracking me, Mila?" Cooper asks, and I shake my head. He looks good, dressed in a white shirt and jeans, without his cut.

"I saw your little text," says Kain, dangerously quiet. Harper fidgets uncomfortably next to me, and I grip her arm tighter.

"She had a right to know," Harper mutters.

"It's lucky that I saw it first then, isn't it?" he snaps.

"You deleted it?" Harper gasps.

"Damn right, I fucking deleted it. You're on dangerous ground, Harper," he suddenly yells, making us both jump. "Don't fuck with my life!"

"Then stop fucking with mine," she yells back.

I step to one side, closer to Cooper. "You're alive then?" I ask him.

He nods. "Getting there. I'm back for a few days for a wedding. Hitting the road again on Monday."

"What?" I gasp. "And what about your nephew? Who, by the way, is fine, in case you're interested."

"He's doing great with you. He looks so happy."

I take a step back. "When did you see Asher?"

Cooper suddenly looks guilty. "I checked in on you guys a few days ago."

"You were watching me when I went to lunch with my boss the other day, weren't you," I accuse. I knew I was being watched—I *felt* him. "So, what, you came back for some wedding, but you couldn't come and say hi to your nephew?"

"I didn't want to upset him. You both look like you're doing well."

"You're supposed to be looking after him. Not me . . . *you*!"

"And I will. I just need some time," he says, sighing.

"No," I snap, shaking my head for added effect. "You don't get to have time out. You took him on, now step up."

Two girls stumble out of the nearby bar, laughing. "Hey, guys, we were wondering when you would show," says a tiny blonde. I glare at Cooper, who has the decency to look ashamed.

"Time for whores but not us, hey?" I ask, disappointment hanging from my words.

"She isn't a whore," he defends quietly, which stings a little.

"Well," I sigh, "enjoy your trip. Come on, Harper, let's leave these love birds to it." Stomping off, I call over my shoulder, "Oh, and Kain, tell Ginger you're going to be a daddy times two or I will. Your threats won't work on me, and I won't be sending her a text. I like to deliver bad news face to face."

"Don't threaten me, little lady," Kain yells after me.

"Tell her or I will make sure you never set foot near this kid ever," I yell angrily.

Who the hell do they think they are? They treat us like crap, then turn up when they feel like it. I hate them and wish we'd never heard of the Hammers MC.

CHAPTER EIGHTEEN

The weeks seem to roll into one. Christmas is looming, and I'm so underprepared. I still haven't spoken to my parents. My father has left a few messages on my mobile, but I've been so busy trying to make a good impression at my new job, running around after Asher, and trying to kick this sickness bug, that I haven't replied.

I'm on the way to meet Brook. I haven't seen her in weeks and friend guilt kicked in when she texted to call me out on my excuses. Entering the bar, I see her perched on a stool. Tanner is hovering in the far corner, pretending to stare at his mobile phone even though I know he's watching Brook's every move. I don't know how it doesn't drive her insane, and it's the first thing I say to her after I've hugged and kissed her in greeting.

"You get used to it." She shrugs with a laugh as I take my coat off.

She gasps. "Wow, when were you going to tell me?"

"Tell you what?" I ask, taking a seat and waving to get the barman's attention. "Gin and lemonade, please," I order.

"Not gin, just lemonade," Brook butts in. The barman shrugs and heads off to get me a lemonade.

"Why? Aren't you drinking tonight?" I ask.

"Yes, I am, but I'm not pregnant," she scoffs.

"What are you talking about, Brook?" I laugh. "You're full of riddles tonight."

"Oh my god, you don't even know yourself," she hisses, and I give her my best annoyed look. Seriously, she's driving me crazy with her odd chatter tonight. "Mila, you're pregnant!"

I almost choke on the lemonade, spitting it down my chin. I rub at my shirt and snap, "What the hell, Brook?"

"I'm never wrong. My ma always said I have a nose for it, and I am telling you, you're pregnant," she insists. Her serious expression makes me feel nauseous. She's crazy. I *cannot* be pregnant. She waves at Tanner to come over and smiles sweetly as he approaches. "Baby, do me a favour. There's a twenty-four-hour pharmacy not far from here, can you take us there?"

He nods, and she jumps off her stool, but I remain rooted to the spot.

"We don't need a test, Brook, because you're wrong," I huff.

"Prove it." She grins, and I sigh as I hop off the stool. Fine, I'll prove it just to get her off my back.

We pick up a couple tests. Brook insists that getting different brands is best just in case one isn't very good. Before I realise what's going on, we're pulling into the clubhouse car park.

"Why are we here?" I ask, panic setting in. I haven't been back here since I moved out, and I don't know if Cooper's back on the road or not, but he hasn't been in touch. Max picks up and drops off Asher so I can avoid this place. I know Asher has seen Cooper a few times, but Cooper keeps going back on the road, so we haven't discussed him taking Asher back. If I'm honest with myself, I've not brought up the subject because I'm quite happy to keep him.

"Relax. If Cooper is around, he'll be in his office. It's where he always is these days," says Brook confidentiality. "We can drop you off later."

We head inside, and I'm relieved to see that Cooper isn't in the bar area. We enter the clubhouse and I'm greeted by various bikers, all of whom tell me they miss seeing me around the place, which is nice to hear. Brook wastes no time dragging me to the bathroom and locking us in. "Right, go do your thing, I'll wait here." She grins.

"You could look a little less smug." I sigh, locking myself in the toilet stall. Once I've peed into a plastic cup, I dip both sticks and unlock the door. Brook is pacing back and forth, then she halts and looks at me expectantly. "I've only just done it. It says to wait a few minutes."

"Is it Cooper's?" she asks excitedly.

"I am not pregnant, but if I was, then yes, it would be his. But I'm not because I was on the pill," I reassure her. After two minutes, I hand the tests to Brook. "You look, so I can watch your face when you see you are so wrong on this," I say.

She turns them over and looks at me wide-eyed. "I told you I'm never wrong," she says with a satisfied grin.

"What?" I yell, snatching the sticks from her and looking for myself. "This can't be right," I mutter. Both tests are positive. "I haven't slept with Cooper since August, on our failed wedding night."

"Haven't you had any signs, like sickness or tighter clothes?"

I shrug my shoulders, suddenly feeling foolish. "Well, yeah, but I thought I had a bug, and I've been eating loads because Harper said I'd lost too much weight," I say defensively.

"What are you going to do now?"

"I have no idea. You've seen how he is with kids, Brook. He has no commitment. He hasn't even checked in with me about his own nephew."

"Maybe he'll be different with his own child," she suggests. I can't imagine that. He never spoke about having children, and Anna didn't seem the type to want kids.

We head back out of the bathroom. Tanner looks up, as if waiting for an announcement. "You told Tanner?" I whisper-hiss, and she nods.

"I tell him everything. Besides, he wanted to know why we were doing a pharmacy run so urgently."

Tanner approaches and gives me a tight hug. "Cooper's in his office if you want to talk to him."

"He'll know what to do, Mila. Despite what he's been like lately, he'll know what to do," says Brook, and I admire her confidence in him.

Maybe I should just say hello. I don't have to tell him anything yet, but my head is reeling. Perhaps telling him while I'm in shock will be easier than telling him when I'm thinking straight and have had time to really think about it.

I knock on the door, but there's no reply. I wait for a few minutes, trying to decide what to do, when Lacey comes down the stairs. "He's in his room. Go on up, the door is open," she says, grinning, a mischievous glint in her eye.

I hesitate, knowing what I'll find if I go up there. He's with a woman, and that's why Lacey wants me to go up, but I find my feet moving forward. It's like my heart loves the pain that he causes me, like I'm addicted.

Passing my old room, the door is open slightly so I glance in. It looks the same as when I left it. Cooper's apartment door is wide open, and I hear panting and screams coming from inside. I place both hands on the doorframe, working out if this is really what I want to see. Following the sounds to his bedroom, I find him lying on his bed, completely naked, half asleep, with a porn movie blaring out from his television.

"Fun night?" I ask, making him sit up quickly and grab for his gun. When he sees it's me, he lets out a sigh of relief.

"Shit, Mila, don't sneak up on me like that." I note that he doesn't cover himself but lies back down, muting the television. "What are you doing here?"

"I came back with Brook and Tanner," I explain. "Lacey saw me knocking on your office door and sent me up." He sits up slightly, resting his head against the headboard. He doesn't take his eyes off the film that's playing.

"You coming in or are you just going to stand there and watch?" he asks.

"Can you cover yourself up at least? I need to talk to you."

"Do you miss it?" he asks, not making any attempt to cover himself or the fact that his cock is beginning to harden.

"Miss what?" I ask, licking my lips. It's a natural reaction to his body, and I can't help but want to go to him. He takes his cock and gives it a stroke, finally bringing his attention to me.

"Us."

I watch him, shifting nervously from one foot to the other. "I just need to talk," I say feebly.

He grins and pats the space next to him. "Then come and talk."

I bite my lip. if I go to him, it's possible he'll put me under his spell, the one where I get naked and do things I should not ever do with him again. My body is screaming at me to go to him. I haven't had sex with anyone since him—not because I couldn't, but because my traitorous body craves him. "I can't do that," I reply stiffly.

"Mila, come," he commands. My heart flutters, along with other parts that have no business fluttering. I slowly walk to him and sit, making sure no part of me touches any part of him. He reaches for the television remote and turns it off. "I never needed to watch that crap when I had you."

I watch as his hand gently strokes himself. "I miss it, all the time. Nothing comes close to feeling you, to being inside you," he admits. He takes my hand and guides it to his hard cock. "You miss it, too. I can see it in your eyes. You get this flushed look when you're turned on," he says, wrapping my hand under his and continuing his movements.

He reaches his other hand around the back of my neck and gently pulls me towards him. When my face is inches from his, he leans in and runs his tongue across my lower lip. "Just one more taste, Mila," he whispers. I open my mouth slightly, and he thrusts his tongue inside, pulling me in for a mind-numbing kiss.

Things begin to speed up, and before long, he's pushing me onto my back and trying to lift my skirt. It's at my waist when Cooper pulls back, taking in the lacey purple thong I'm wearing. Months ago, he would have asked me who I was wearing this for, but now, he doesn't want to spook me by asking questions. I watch him battle with himself before growling and burying his face between my legs. I hiss, not expecting him to be so eager. It takes him all of sixty seconds to have me screaming his name while pulling his hair and thrashing about.

Cooper doesn't let me recover before he's flipped me over and buried himself deep inside me, slamming into me with such force, I'm pushed farther up the bed. "I swear, this pussy has me bewitched," he pants, picking up his pace. I know how he feels. This pull we have to each other, despite the pain we cause, has me questioning my state of mind right now.After a few minutes of him slamming into me, he pulls out and guides me onto my back, then he pushes my legs over his shoulders and continues where he left off. He makes a grab for my breasts, but I realise they're too sensitive and I wince, making him stop. "You okay?" he asks.

I give a wiggle, encouraging him to continue, and he eyes me suspiciously before picking up his pace again. He stares into my eyes, and I know the moment he's going to come because he grips my face, forcing me to look directly into his gaze.

Cooper lets my legs drop back to his sides but doesn't move from me. He runs his tongue across my chest and over my breast, taking my nipple into his mouth. I wince again, but he doesn't stop. I pull his face away and kiss him to hide the fact that I didn't like him touching me there, then I feel his cock begin to swell again and he gently moves back and forth. The man is insatiable. "I didn't use a condom. Are you still on the pill?" he asks, and I nod.

"It doesn't matter anyway," I mutter. He pulls out and taps me to turn over, making me kneel on all fours before pushing back inside me again.

"Why?" he asks, wrapping his fist into my hair and giving my head a tug back until we are cheek to cheek.

"Because I'm pregnant," I pant. Cooper stills, gripping my hair tighter in his fist. I wince as it pulls at the roots.

"What did you say?"

"I'm pregnant," I repeat.

There's an uncomfortable silence. He still has my hair in his fist and he's still inside me, but he isn't moving . . . or talking. I press my lips together, the silence making me want to laugh. It's a nervous reaction. "Cooper, say something." This seems to bring him back down to Earth, and he releases my hair and pulls out of me. I turn to face him as he stands by the bed, I daren't speak again because he looks like he could explode at any moment.

"How long?" he whispers.

"How long what?" I ask. Of all the questions he could have asked, I'm a little disappointed by this one.

"How long have you known?"

"Oh, erm, I just did a test. Well, actually, Brook made me do two, downstairs."

"Brook knows?" he snaps.

"Yeah, she guessed and made me get the test because I didn't believe her. Look, there are more important things to discuss than how long I've known and who knows."

"Yeah, you're right, like what the hell happened to 'Cooper, I'm on the pill'." He mimics me, his voice becoming high-pitched.

"I really don't sound like that, and I am on the pill."

"Is it mine?"

I scoff, standing and adjusting my clothes back into place. "Wow, really, Cooper?"

"Yes, really. We haven't been together for ages, and now you show up telling me you're pregnant while I'm fucking inside of you? How do you know it's mine?"

I resist the urge to slap him. We're both in shock, and he's entitled to ask that, so I take a deep breath. "Because I haven't slept with anyone since you, since our wedding that you stood me up on, so I know the baby is yours. Look, don't worry, okay. I wasn't expecting you to suddenly step up and be happy about this—God knows I'm not—but it's happened, and I thought you should know. So, there, you know."

I head for the door, and Cooper doesn't chase after me. I think that disappoints me more than his shit line of questioning. I don't know what I expected. I mean, normal couples get excited about this kind of thing. They announce it on social media these days, like it's not official if it's not on Facebook or Twitter. There're even gender reveal parties. But those couples are together, and they're happy, and most of the time, those babies are planned. This one isn't, and we're not, and it makes me sad.

Brook is cuddled up with Tanner in the main room of the clubhouse. She disentangles herself from him when she sees me and rushes over. "You were gone ages. I thought he might have killed you, but Tanner wouldn't let me come and check."

"Thanks, Tanner," I huff. "Let's just say he's in shock."

"As in he didn't take it well, or it's just taking a while to sink in?"

"As in I'm going home and I don't expect to hear from him anytime soon," I say firmly.

"No, Mila. Cooper will come around. Just go back and see him. I'm sure he was just shocked," Brook pleads.

Cooper enters the room, and we fall silent. I really wanted to leave before he came down. He stands in his low-cut jeans and boots, with no shirt, all tats and muscle, watching me, and I feel my knees go weak. How can this man reduce me to a mess just by looking at me?

"Anyway, I should go," I find myself saying to Brook.

"No, you aren't going anywhere," Cooper cuts in.

"Why?" I sigh, because it's not like he's overjoyed.

"Because I fucking said so, Mila, and because I'm the boss around here. And because you can't just drop shit like that while I'm in the middle of fucking you and then walk out like it's nothing." He ends with a raised voice that grabs the attention of several other guys who are hanging around. I shuffle my feet nervously, keeping my eyes to the ground. I know my cheeks are now flushed with embarrassment.

"Asher is at home, so I need to get back," I mutter.

"My office, now," he orders, storming into his office, leaving the door open.

I look at Brook, who gives me a helpless look. "Maybe he wants to celebrate," she offers weakly, and I scowl at her before stomping into his office and slamming the door.

"Well, that was embarrassing," I huff.

"What happens now?" he asks, leaning back in his chair and slamming his feet up on the desk.

"I go home and work out what the hell I'm going to do with my life? Maybe work out how I feel about the whole thing." I didn't realise I was worried. Maybe it was the adrenaline pumping, but I suddenly feel anxious, and before I can stop it, I'm sobbing into my hands.

Cooper dives up and rushes over to me, wrapping his huge arms around me. "Mila, you aren't on your own. I'm here for you, and for the baby."

I wail, "Like you're there for Asher?"

"I'm a shit uncle, that's why I hired a nanny, but I can be a good dad—"

"You dumped me on our wedding day! You're hardly mister reliable." I sniffle. "I should hate you."

"But you don't. I messed up. Seeing Anna again was a huge shock, but the feelings weren't there, not like the first time around. I felt like I had something to prove when she came back. It was my fault that she left, and I wanted to show her I could be better, but my heart wasn't in it. I spent all my time thinking about you and who you were with and what you were doing. I was distracted and she knew it. That's why she left again . . . because she knew I was in love with you."

"No," I snap, "don't do that. Don't spout bullshit to try and win me back now. You left me. You broke my heart."

"I realise it's going to take you time to trust me again, but I will spend every day working at it if you'll let me." I shake my head, but he continues. "Just think about it, baby. We were good when we were together, and if we're having a baby, don't you think it will be easier to do it together?" he asks.

"You hate kids, and now, all of a sudden, you want to create a family life? You're unbelievable. You think having a baby together means I have to forgive you and let you back into my life? I'll always be wondering if Anna will come back and turn your head again."

"She won't. I'm not interested in her. It's always been you, Mila," he says.

"Has it?" I yell. "It wasn't me on the twenty-seventh of August, the night before our wedding. If it was me all along, then there is no way you would have treated me so badly, Cooper. I can't ever forgive that. You humiliated me, and the worst thing is that even now, after everything you did, I still can't turn you away, I still let you get me into your bed, and it makes me hate myself."

"You can't help how you feel. It's your heart telling you that you belong with me."

"Let's get something straight, Cooper. This baby does not mean that I forgive you. It doesn't mean that I want to take you back. You have to stop using my weakness for you to get me into bed. It isn't fair. We need to meet to discuss what we do about this baby, but I can't do that right now. I have responsibilities waiting at home."

Cooper nods. "Okay, you're right. I'll prove myself to you though, Mila, I promise. I'll step up with Asher and prove I can be a good parent."

"I'll look forward to you changing my opinion."

By the time I get home, I'm exhausted. I have just enough energy to break the news to Harper about the baby. She grins, excited. "We can be baby mum friends."

"Well, at least you're excited. How do I know if Cooper just wants to be with me for the baby?"

"At least he wants to be with you. Who cares about the reasons? I can't even get Kain to answer my calls," she huffs.

I smirk. "You haven't tried to tell Ginger again then?"

"No. If he wants to be with her, then let him. I'm sick to death of him and the drama he brings. I'm going to keep meeting Marshall and I'll just keep it secret so he doesn't find out." Personally, I know she doesn't like Marshall as much as she tries to convince us all that she does, but if he helps her get over Kain, then who am I to argue.

CHAPTER NINETEEN

I don't hear from Cooper for the next few days. I refuse to text him because I don't want him to feel obliged to be in contact with me, but I'm disappointed that he hasn't been in touch. Work is busy and it takes my mind off things, which helps. I'm doing the lunch run when I finally see his name flash on my phone.

"I know it's short notice, but can you make an appointment at a private clinic at six p.m.?" he asks.

I choose to ignore the fact that he hasn't even started our conversation with 'How are you'. "Yes, that's fine. Text me the address."

"I can pick you up," he offers.

"No, I can make my own way, Cooper, just text me the address." I feel silly for being snarky with him, but I can't help being annoyed, and these hormones do not help me at all. I'm getting upset over the smallest things.

"Fine," he mutters, "whatever you want."

When I stop the car outside the address that Cooper texted me, I realise it isn't a normal clinic. It looks more like a mansion. Cooper is waiting outside, pacing back and forth.

"You're late," he grumbles.

"By two minutes. Is this a real doctor?" I ask.

"Of course, it is. I'm paying private for this."

I raise my eyebrows. "Wow, aren't I special?" I mutter sarcastically.

Following him inside, the reception area is brightly lit, the walls all white and clinical. The young-looking brunette at the desk stands and gives Cooper a hug and a kiss on the cheek. "Hey, stranger, how are you?" she greets, looking genuinely pleased to see him. I stand behind him, feeling like a spare part as usual.

"I'm good, Kei. How are you?"

She shrugs and gives a flirty smile. "Good. Did you lose my number?"

He steps aside and her eyes fall to me. "We have an appointment. It's under the name Ms. Mila Coin," he says.

She gives a curt nod and goes back behind her desk. "Fantastic. Take a seat and the doctor will be with you shortly." We sit, and a second later, the door opens and a doctor shouts us through.

"Did you sleep with her?" I whisper, and he glares at me.

"No, of course, not. She's harmless, just flirty."

The doctor asks me to get on the bed, then he sets about squirting cold gunk on my stomach. After a few minutes of him fiddling with buttons, he finally presses the camera to my stomach and a grainy image flickers to life.

"Wow, you didn't realise you were pregnant, Mila?" the doctor asks, looking surprised. "Because you're a little further gone than we usually like first-time mums to go without seeking medical attention. I'd put you at about three and a half months."

I nod in agreement. I'd worked out already that this was the case because it was August, my wedding day, when I last had sex with Cooper.

"So, can you pinpoint a date?" Cooper asks.

"A due date?" asks the doctor, clicking some more buttons.

"No, a date of conception. Like can it be put to a precise date?" I whip my head to glare at him. Is he seriously questioning whether the baby is his, here, in front of the doctor?

"Well, not exactly, but it would have been sometime at the end of August."

"How would a DNA test work?" Cooper presses, and I bite my tongue. I want to explode, but I stare at the white ceiling instead, thinking of ways to murder him. I block out the rest of their conversation because, quite frankly, it's like I'm not even in the same room. I get the impression this is one of the doctors who work privately for the Hammers MC, as Cooper seems to know him very well.

By the time we've finished, the doctor hands me a few photos of the scan and some leaflets on vitamins I'll need. I stomp out while Cooper finishes off chatting.

I'm almost at my car by the time he comes out. "Mila, wait," he huffs out, running to catch up with me. I whirl around to face him and slap him hard across the cheek. He winces, rubbing the spot. "What the fuck was that for?" he growls.

"How dare you embarrass me like that. I felt like some cheating whore. I have not had sex with anyone since you. And I don't lie. I'm not like you!" I yell.

"I was just asking," he argues.

"You were insinuating that you think I'm lying. Do you think out of all the men I know, I'd choose you to be my child's father?" I scream. He takes a step back, and I can tell that my remark has hurt him. But I'm hurt too, and I can't hide it.

"I need to go before I say something I'll regret" he mutters.

"Yeah, go, you're good at that. When are you coming to collect your nephew, by the way?" He walks away, shaking his head, and I burst into tears. What the hell is wrong with me, screaming in the street and then crying? I feel like a hormonal mental case, but the guy drives me mad.

I sit in my car, crying for a few more minutes. I can't drive while sobbing like a demented fool. I grab my handbag and search for a tissue, knowing I have some in here. Suddenly, the passenger door of my car opens and a hooded figure dressed in dark clothing gets in.

"What are you doing?" I ask, surprised. Clearly, he has the wrong car. He pulls something from his pocket, and it takes me a few seconds to see it's a gun, then he presses it into my side.

"Start the car," he orders. He looks up as a car drives towards us and the headlights illuminate his face.

"Aaron?"

"Drive, Mila," he growls. My hands are shaking far too much, but I manage to turn the keys and start the engine.

"What's going on?" I ask.

"Do what I say, or I swear to God, I will pull this trigger," he warns. My mind is racing as fast as my heart. *Why did I sit in the car for so long? Why did I push Cooper away? Why is Aaron doing this? What does he want?*

I drive into traffic. "Where are we going?"

"I'll give the directions. All you have to do is drive."

"What do you want?" I ask, but he doesn't respond. All the while, my mind is still racing with unanswered questions. We drive in silence for at least an hour before he directs me to turn onto a dirt track. It's very secluded and I try not to let the panic show. I keep looking around for signs or a way to escape.

"Stop just over there," he orders. Once I stop the car, he leans across and pulls the keys out. "Get out." I don't move, too busy looking around in a panic. This is the perfect place to kill or attack me. No one is around, and I doubt anyone would hear me scream.Aaron gets out and walks around to my side of the car, yanking the door open. He reaches in and grips my arm, pulling me from the car.

"Aaron, talk to me, you're scaring me." He has a rucksack which he empties onto the floor. Zip ties and rope fall out, and I begin to struggle, crying and begging for him to let me go. Eventually, he gets tired of me fighting and delivers a swift backhand across my face. When that doesn't calm me, he hits me harder. The last thing I see is him laughing as I fall against him.

It's cold and dark. I try to lift my head, but it hurts too much. I wiggle my hands because there is no feeling in my fingers, and I realise they're zip tied together as are my ankles. I wiggle about and discover that I'm on a bed, but it doesn't feel soft and comfortable like a normal bed. The mattress is thin and I can feel the springs digging into my skin. It smells damp, like wet leaves and earth.

I'm not sure how long I lay there before I hear the clanking of a chain and then a dim light shines through as a door opens. There's a buzzing noise and then the room fills with illuminous bright white lights, making me flinch and bury my face into the mattress.

"Sleeping Beauty, finally, you're awake." I know that voice, but it isn't Aaron's. I peek out and see a large figure heading towards me. The light is still too bright to make out his face, but once he gets closer, he grabs the top of my arm and pulls me to sit. I notice the mattress is dirty and I shudder, knowing I just had my face pressed into it. "Open those pretty little eyes, darling." I open them and find myself staring into gorgeous blue eyes that once turned me on so much.

"Brick? Thank God you're here. Aaron took me." I burst into tears.

He brushes a stray hair from my eyes and then leans in and kisses me. I turn my head away, but he roughly grabs my chin and kisses me until I'm almost compliant. "Just how I remember you," he whispers with a smile.

"Help me get my hands free," I plead desperately, but I think I already know he isn't going to do that because he isn't here to help me. He's the reason I'm here.

"I can't do that, darling."

I let out another sob. "Please, Brick, please don't do this. I haven't done anything." He runs a finger across my collar bone and down my chest, between my breasts.

"There's something about you looking all vulnerable and sad that makes me want to fuck you," he growls, suddenly gripping my shirt and ripping it apart. The buttons fly off in all directions.

"Brick, I don't know what you want, but keeping me here like this is not going to achieve anything," I say in a hurried tone. He pulls at one of my bra straps until my breast is uncovered. He gropes it hard, and I close my eyes, trying to hide my disgust. "I don't want this," I sob as he bends to take my nipple into his mouth.

He's interrupted by a loud bang and looks behind as Aaron enters. "What the hell are you doing?" he yells. Brick stands, his build dwarfing Aaron.

"We didn't say we couldn't enjoy this," says Brick calmly.

"That's my girlfriend," Aaron snaps.

"Technically not," laughs Brick, "and for this plan to have full impact, this needs to be done."

"Look, just do what you came in here to do. Get it over with," Aaron mutters, and then he turns to leave. I panic because being alone with Brick seems dangerous and Aaron may be my only option.

"Aaron, don't leave me. I want to talk to you."

He stops and turns towards me. "About what? You didn't want to talk before." Brick is undoing his belt.

"About us," I say, adding a nervous smile.

"So, now there's an us?" he asks sceptically.

Brick opens the button on his jeans. "Hurry the fuck up and get out, will yah," he snaps at Aaron.

Aaron goes to leave again, but I blurt out, "I'm pregnant." It wasn't planned. In fact, I laid here thinking how I shouldn't tell him, because if he finds out the truth, he might hurt me and the baby. They both pause.

"Aaron, I know how much you wanted a baby and I kept putting it off, but Brick here, he made me have unprotected sex and he got me pregnant. I don't want to be with him, I want to be with you, and now I know you feel the same about me, I can tell you how I really feel," I lie.

Brick grabs me by the throat and pulls me to stand. Without my arms, I can't loosen his grip and I start to panic. "You lying little bitch, I didn't force you to do anything, and I used protection," he roars.

I make a few choked sounds. "Man, put her down. What if she is? You'll kill the baby," snaps Aaron. Brick lowers me so that my feet just touch the ground. He looks at my stomach, seeing that I do have a small swelling.

"Aaron, we can raise this baby together. Being around these bikers, it's not good for a baby. Think how happy my mum would be." He ponders it, and I can see him forming the picture in his head. He always did want kids, but after an accident when he was younger, he was told that his sperm count was exceptionally low, meaning he would probably have to go through IVF to have his own kids.

"Fuck this bullshit. She's lying. If we want to hit Cooper where it hurts, then I need to fuck her. Just for that bullshit lie, I'm going to make it all so much worse. Aaron, get out your phone," Brick snarls, pulling at my jeans. He cuts the zip ties from around my ankles and pulls my jeans off.

"Please, Aaron, what if he hurts the baby," I beg.

"Just be gentle with her," mutters Aaron.

"No," I scream. "Please, Aaron, you do it if it has to be done, not him. I don't want Brick to do this." Aaron looks torn, like he wants to intervene but can't.

"Fuck that, it's me he hates. Once he sees this, he won't touch her again, and then you're free to keep her and the damn kid," Brick snaps, and then he's inside me. I scream out, grasping at the mattress to keep me upright. I glance at Aaron, who looks pale.

"Film it," yells Brick.

He grips my hair and pulls my head back. Somewhere in the room, there's a bright light, and I realise Aaron is doing as Brick ordered and he's filming this. I sob uncontrollably.

Brick isn't being gentle, and I panic because I never asked the doctor if it was safe to have sex while pregnant. I feel my mind begin to shut down, slowly closing off from my body, and I no longer feel his rough, unwanted touch anymore.

I think about babies and little clothes. I picture Asher and my little baby together. He'll make a good big brother because, let's face it, I see him like my own now. The thought makes me smile inside and I make a note to tell Cooper that I love that kid and I want to keep him with me. I can't give him back now he's settled.

I'm shoved onto the dirty mattress. I'm naked and cold, and I'm sure Brick didn't use protection because I can feel him on the inside of my thighs. Bile rises in my throat, and I fall to my knees just in time to be sick all over the dirty, cold floor.

"Jesus, Mila," Brick groans in disgust. "Do you want to have a go, too?" he asks Aaron, who shakes his head but hands the camera to Brick.

Brick snaps a photo of me on my knees and then he fastens his jeans and looks at the phone, clearly playing back the video. "Shit, this will kill him," he says, grinning. He fiddles about some more, then turns to me. "You know he got you a house? Told my sister he didn't love her anymore because he loves you. He sold their house and paid her off and then bought you some condo near the beach. Spent weeks doing it up, leaving everyone else to run the club while he took a break to make it all nice for his queen. What will he do now he's seen you fucking me again?" He smirks and grips my hair, making me wince in pain as he pulls me to stand. "You'd better hope he pays me quick cos I have a high sex drive. I can fuck two, three, even four times a day, and every time I do, he's gonna get a video."

"I need a shower and some clothes," I whisper, looking at Aaron desperately.

"This isn't a hotel, and you aren't the queen here," snaps Brick, heading to the corner of the room. I realise too late that there's a hose there. "Get her over here."

Aaron pulls me to my feet, marching me over to where Brick stands. He turns it to me and then I'm doused in freezing cold water. After a few minutes, the phone rings and Brick pulls it from his pocket.

"It's lover boy. Took longer than I thought." He smiles as he answers. "I didn't interrupt you and Lacey again, did I?" he asks, connecting the call. I can hear Cooper shouting down the phone, but I can't make out what he's saying.

"Now, you listen to me, Mr. President. You speak to me like that again and I'm gonna keep sending you little reminders of what I have here, naked, in front of me." There's more yelling and Brick turns the phone camera on me. I'm wet through and shaking from the cold. "Live action for you, Coop. Don't yah just love modern technology?" Brick taunts him.

"I'm coming for you, baby girl, I promise," yells Cooper.

Brick puts the phone back to his ear. "I just want what's mine, and until I get it, I'm taking what's yours. Although, I'm a fair guy, so I'm gonna share with Aaron next."

Aaron turns the hose off and leads me back towards the bed. He gets a grey blanket and wraps it around me. I'm so grateful to be covered up that I don't care it's itchy and rough on my skin.

"Please help me, Aaron. This isn't you. You're better than this." I sob, my body shivering violently from the cold.

"You ruined my life, Mila," he says.

"I didn't mean to, but you hurt me. We can sort it out if you just get me away from here."

He shakes his head. "Once Brick has got his money, he'll go and I'm keeping you here. If I take you back there, you'll go straight back to him, and I can't have that."

"I won't. Cooper and I are done. Please, Aaron, you have to see how insane this is. This is kidnapping. Take me home to my parents and we'll forget this ever happened. We can work through the rest."

"I can't risk it. You have to prove to me that you're mine again. Until then, I'm keeping you here, where he won't ever disturb us."

I cry hard. How has it come to this? Aaron strokes my cheek gently while I sob and then sits next to me on the bed, wrapping me in his arms. He eventually urges me to lay down, unwrapping the blanket and pulling me against him. "I miss this," he whispers into my hair, gently kissing me on the head. "I want us to go back to this."

"I've got some errands to run. I'll leave you to get reacquainted." Brick grins, leaving us alone.

We lay together for a long time, and he falls asleep wrapped around me. My hands are still bound, but they left my ankles free. I wriggle to see how deep in sleep Aaron is, but he groans, making me freeze. After a few minutes, I poke a toe out and move it around until I find the floor. Once I have balance, I move my other foot out and begin to disentangle myself from Aaron.

Standing, my heart races so much that I have to breathe slow so I don't wake him. I take a couple steps towards the door and then look back, finding he's still asleep. When I reach the door, it's open and cold air blows through. I push it gently so I can slip out of the gap. It leads to another room, this one carpeted, and I get halfway across the room when I hear a cough.

"Going somewhere?" asks Brick, stepping out of the shadows. I eye up the door. The space between us is about even, but I can't give up now, so I make a run for it. I don't make it far—I'm too cold and my legs aren't functioning right. Tripping on a small rug, I crash to the floor, smashing my forehead hard on the ground. Brick is on me before I've fully landed, and I let out a cry of frustration. He laughs and licks up the side of my face.

"I was just about to wake you for round two." I let out a scream, and he covers my mouth, laughing at my feeble attempts. I thrash about, trying to buck him off, but he's too heavy and large for my little frame.

"*Get off me!*" I scream against his hand, kicking out with my legs.

Aaron comes running in. "Get off her, Brick. You had your fun, now stop," he shouts, pulling at Brick's arm. Brick pushes himself up from the floor and grabs Aaron's T-shirt, shoving him back against the wall.

"Who the fuck are you talking to? Do you forget who I am?" he growls. Aaron's face pales, but he shoves back at Brick's chest. He must get lucky because Brick loses his footing and stumbles back slightly. It's enough for Aaron to move away from the wall and come towards me. He reaches his hand down, and I take it. As he goes to pull me, we both flinch at the shrill sound of a loud bang. Aaron's face twists in agony and then he stumbles forward and falls to his knees.

"Aaron? Aaron! What's wrong?" I panic, scrambling onto my knees. His eyes are wide, like he's in shock, and then he falls forward, landing with a thud on the dirty floor. I shuffle back, away from his crumpled body, scraping my knees on the rough carpet. There's blood on the back of his T-shirt and lots of it.

"Aaron?" I squeak, watching the crimson fluid spread, and then I look to Brick, who is tucking a gun back into his waistband. "What have you done?" I whisper, gently leaning forward on my tied-up hands and pushing myself up onto my unsteady feet.

"I can't have him speaking to me like that, Mila. He's a nobody. I just needed him to do the dirty work."

"My god, you are insane," I cry. "You've killed him!"

"Don't judge me. You think that lover boy hasn't done this a million times over?" He laughs. "And trust me when I say, some of them didn't deserve it."

"Are you going to kill me?" I'm beginning to panic. There's no way he's going to let me walk away from this. I've seen too much now.

"Well, Cooper has until midnight to make the transfer, so there's time to save you yet." He grins and reaches for my hands, yanking me back towards the bedroom. Despite my struggles, he shoves me onto the dirty mattress and then storms out, slamming the door and locking it.

I wait until it goes silent outside the door before reaching for the mobile phone from the floor. Aaron must have dropped it when he came from the room. My heart is racing as I punch in the code to unlock it. *Access denied.* Damn him for changing his code. I need to think . . . what would he change it to? I try the date we met, but access is denied again. I have one more attempt before it will lock me out for half an hour. I try my date of birth, just because that's his bank code, and I breathe a sigh of relief when it unlocks.

Tears begin to fall with the relief I feel right now. My fingers shake as I dial Harper's phone number, not knowing Cooper's without my own phone. It rings and rings, but there's no answer. It probably shows up on her caller display as Aaron, so she won't answer. The voicemail clicks in. *'Hey, this is Harper. Leave me a message and if I like you, I'll call you back.'* Her singsong voice makes me cry harder. "Harper, it's me, Mila. Pick up." Within seconds of me disconnecting the call, the phone vibrates in my hand and Harper's name flashes on the screen.

"Harper," I sob.

"Hold on, I have Cooper here," she says.

"Mila, have you got away? Are you safe?" The relief in Cooper's voice is short-lived.

"No, I'm in a room. We drove north for an hour, then stopped at a dirt track. It was on the left side. Then I blacked out, so I don't know if he's got me somewhere along that dirt track or if he drove me somewhere else," I whisper quickly.

"You drove straight, no turnings?"

"No, it was straight. Cooper, I'm so sorry about what I said," I sob.

"Shh, Mila. It's okay. Save the apologies for when I get you back."

"You will get me back, won't you, Cooper? He said you have until midnight."

"Don't worry about that either. I promise I'll get you back. Is it just Brick and Aaron?"

I let out another sob and cover my mouth. "Just Brick . . . he shot Aaron."

"Good, saves me a job. I'm coming, baby. Hide the phone somewhere so Brick doesn't find it. We can track the signal. Make sure it's on silent and turn the vibrate off."

I find myself nodding, even though he can't see me. "I love you, Cooper," I whisper.

"I love you too, baby," he replies, and my heart sings. Suddenly, nothing matters. Everything he did to me seems so small compared to this, and my need for him is so strong. I'd give anything to see him right now.

I hide the phone under the mattress. My wrists are sore from the zip ties and I try to rub the plastic against the metal of the bed to snap it, but it's not as easy as it looks in the movies. I wander around the room as the light bulb keeps flickering, but at least he left it on this time.

There's nothing much in here—a wooden chair in the corner and some wires hanging out of the wall. I sit back on the bed, hoping that Cooper finds me because I know Brick isn't going to let me walk away from this. Not now he's killed Aaron and I'm the only witness.

Sometime later, I jump up into a sitting position. I must have fallen asleep, but something woke me. I look frantically around the room—there's no one here but me. I can hear hushed voices, so I rush to the door and press my ear against it.

"There's no one here." It's Brick's voice.

I bang my hands against the door and scream, "I'm in here! Help me!"

"Shit," comes a woman's voice. "Open the damn door, Brick."

There's a click and then the door opens. Anna stares at me, taking in my naked body, and turns to Brick, slapping him hard across the face.

"He's going to fucking kill you, you stupid idiot," she screeches.

"I need that money, Anna. It's the only way to get it," he snaps.

"Please, help me. I'm pregnant, Anna," I cry.

She turns back to me, shock written over her face. "Cooper's?" she whispers, and I nod. "Does he know?" I nod again, and she lets out a frustrated scream. "You stupid, stupid fool! What were you thinking?" she yells at Brick. "You think he'll let you walk from this?"

"He doesn't have a choice. I'll kill her the minute I get the cash and laugh while I do it. He deserves it after all the shit he's done, what he's put you through."

"So, what's your big plan then, super brain? Kill the girl, watch him crumble, and walk away with the cash? You'll spend the rest of your life watching over your shoulder because once he's pieced himself together, he will come for you and probably me and everyone else you have ever loved," she snaps.

"Smart girl, your sister." We all turn towards the door where Cooper stands, pointing a gun at Brick.

My body sags with relief. "Told you I was coming, baby," he says to me with a wink.

Anna grabs me by the hair, and I stumble, falling to my knees. It all happens so fast. I feel cold metal press at my temple, but then a loud bang rings out for a second time today and Anna falls to the floor, spluttering and gurgling. I scream and fall onto my naked ass, bringing my knees to my chest and hugging them tight.

Brick shouts out, the pain in his cry raw. He pulls a gun from his waistband, but before he can raise his arm to aim it, he's in a pile next to Anna. The ringing in my ears hurts, but it shuts out everything else. I can hear a distant wailing, and as the ringing dims, I realise it's me. I feel arms around me, sweeping me from the cold floor, and then I'm held tight against warmth. My eyes feel heavy as my head rolls back.

***

I hear whispering, but it isn't clear enough for me to make out the words. I feel like they all blur into one. I try to open my eyes, but they feel sticky and it's too difficult, so I give up and drift back to sleep.

***

I can tell it's light even though my eyes are closed. I feel the warmth of the sun on my face. This means I'm not in that room anymore because there were no windows there. I try to lift my arms to see if they're still bound together, but they feel heavy and I don't have the strength to lift them. I let my body pull me back into sleep.

I hear voices again, but they don't sound so distant this time around.

"Mila, please wake up. I need you so much." Someone is crying, and it sounds like Harper.

"She's doing much better today. All her vitals are stable. I told you she just needed to rest." That's Cooper's smug voice.

"Don't speak to me. This is all your fault," Harper snaps. "The best thing you can do is leave her the hell alone." I don't want them to argue. I love them both. But I can't open my eyes or move or talk. I try, I really do, but I'm too tired.

"Mila . . . Mila, it's time to wake up now." That's my mum's voice. I wonder why she's here. She didn't come to my wedding, and I haven't seen her in so long. I wonder if she knows about Aaron and what he did. *Oh god, Aaron.* His wide eyes flash through my mind, and I hear a loud beeping noise. It's so loud, it hurts my ears, *What is that? It's so annoying.* My fingers twitch. It takes some effort, but I can feel them twitch. "That's it, sweetheart, wake up," my mum gently encourages.

"She moved. I saw her hand!" That's Harper sounding excited.

I squeeze my eyes tight before slowly opening them and blinking. The light burns my eyeballs, so I squeeze them closed again. "Close the blinds," Mum orders. "Try again, sweetie." I open them again, and this time it's not as bright. I blink a few times and Mum's blurry face comes into view. She's smiling and there's tears in her eyes. "You had us all worried there for a minute." I move my eyes to look around, but I can't move my head, it hurts too bad. Harper comes into view, but there's no Cooper, and my heart squeezes with disappointment.

"Mila, I'm so happy to see those eyes open," whispers Harper. She takes my hand and squeezes it.

The room is decorated in a pale grey colour, it looks cold and depressing. There're machines at my side beeping and flashing.

"You're in hospital. You were shot," Harper gently explains. The machine beeps faster, and my eyes dart around in panic. How did I get shot? I don't remember that. What about the baby? Harper pats my hand, "You're okay. You and the baby are okay," she reassures me and the beeping slows. I try to talk, but my throat burns.

"Drink," I choke out. A straw is placed against my lips, and I slowly suck up the cool water. The relief is immense as it hits my throat. "Cooper?" I whisper. Mum looks at Harper, who gives me a fake smile.

"He'll be here soon."

I'm not convinced by her facial expression. I have a faint memory of Harper telling Cooper to leave. He never listens to anyone, so I find it hard to believe that he would have left unless he wanted to.

CHAPTER TWENTY

"Why didn't you call me? How dare you try and shut me out!" That's Cooper shouting.

"Get out! She doesn't want to see you," hisses Harper. I open my eyes and see them standing toe-to-toe at the foot of the bed. I smile at Harper, who looks small with him towering over her, but she doesn't back down. Cooper catches me watching and immediately moves to my bedside, taking my hand.

"Baby, you're awake." He smiles, kissing my forehead. I give a weak smile in return.

"Where were you?" I whisper.

"I needed to sort some stuff out. Harper promised to call me if there was a change," he says, giving Harper an annoyed look.

I squeeze his hand. "Don't leave me again." He kicks off his boots and pulls off his jacket, throwing it over the chair.

"I'm going nowhere, baby." He climbs onto my bed, pulling me against him. "Goodnight, Harper," he says smugly.

She kisses me on the head and stomps out, giving Cooper her best pissed-off expression.

It's been two weeks. I'm packing up my bag and waiting for Cooper to come and get me from the hospital.

I've learnt that Cooper fired two shots at Brick, the first hit me in the thigh and caused me to bleed out. The second hit Brick in the head, killing him instantly. It's lucky they got me to hospital when they did because I'd lost a lot of blood. An infection then took hold, and all in all, it's been eventful, but I am so relieved to be going home.

I reach for my crutches and hobble over to the chair. The doctor enters and smiles. He's about my age and good looking, and Cooper has been rude to him numerous times, but the doctor hasn't let it bother him. He must get used to possessive assholes working in here. "You look so much better today, Mila. Is it the thought of getting out of here?"

I nod and smile. "It's been great and all that, but I need my own bed."

He hands me my paperwork. "It's been a pleasure treating you, and if you . . ." He trails off when Cooper enters, a stern look on his face.

"If she what?" Cooper growls under his breath. It comes out menacing and I roll my eyes.

"Never mind. Take care, Mila." He winks and then leaves the room.

"He can't do that. You're his patient, and he can't hit on you like that," mutters Cooper.

I smile, annoying him further. "He didn't hit on me. You interrupted him before he got a chance," I tease.

"I'm taking you home before you piss me off more and I kill the doctor," he grumbles, picking up my bags.

"You have anger issues." I grin, following him.

Cooper draws to a stop outside a large set of metal gates, and I eye him suspiciously. "I thought you were taking me home?" He presses a button on his keys and the gates slowly begin to open. He follows a gravel drive that curves up to a large, white house. He parks the car and turns to me.

"When you woke up in hospital and I wasn't there, I was here, sorting this place."

"And this is?" I prompt, taking in the large double front door and the pillars standing either side of it. It's a dream home, like a fairy tale castle of the modern kind.

"It's our new home." He smiles as I stare at it in awe. It's the kind of place you imagine buying when you're four years old and think everything costs a few pounds.

We step out of the car, Cooper rushing to my side to help me. He walks beside me slowly since I can't race around on these crutches. We take the steps one at a time, and when we reach the door, he lets us in with his key.

Standing in a huge marble-floored entrance hall, before us is a winding staircase that leads to a second floor. He opens a door to his left and we're in a living area. It's fully furnished with huge comfy sofas and a television big enough to be confused with a cinema screen.

"Wow, this is huge," I gasp, taking it all in.

"I've made mistakes, Mila, too many to list, but I want to get this right. From now on, I want us to get it right. I want us to share a family home—me, you, our baby, and Asher." It's the first time we've broached the subject of 'us' and I take a seat on the couch. Tears spring to my eyes. Asher has missed me so much, he came every day to the hospital and cried each time he had to leave me there.

"Cooper, this is amazing. I love it, but we didn't discuss this. I had a lot of time to think while I was in hospital and—"

"So did I, and I realised how much I messed up. It was always you . . . always. I know it's going to take so much more than my words to make you see that, and I am fully prepared to work hard for the rest of my life making you see how amazing you are. I'm ready to take on my responsibilities, and I know I'm a little late to the party and all, but you have to believe me when I say you are the only one for me. I love you so much, and knowing how much I've hurt you kills me. I deserve for you to leave me, to take my nephew and my kid and leave me, but I'm begging you not to. Just give me one last chance." He lets out a long breath, like he's been waiting so long to say all that and he's relieved he got it out.

"Loving you was never the problem. Knowing you chose her—"

"I didn't. Not in the end, Mila. When it came down to it, I chose you."

Anna falling to the floor fills my mind, and I close my eyes briefly. "Did it hurt you to pull that trigger?" I ask quietly.

Cooper takes my hand, kneeling in front of me. "Not as much as it would have hurt for her to pull it and take you. After Anna left the second time, I was relieved. Me smashing up the office was because I realised there was no way you were going to forgive me, that I'd messed it all up for nothing. When I saw her holding that gun to your head, it wasn't even a thought in my mind. I pulled that trigger because I chose you, and from now on, it will always be you."

I squeeze his hands, tears running down my cheeks. I love him so much, and hearing him say all this makes me want to fall into his arms so bad. I take a deep breath and say, "Maybe you should show me around this castle." I need a minute to think straight.

Cooper leads me from room to room, each one as grand as the one before. By the time we reach the upstairs, I'm overwhelmed. I love this place and I know Asher will too. It feels like a real home.

Cooper opens the final door at the end of the landing, and I burst into tears. It's a nursery. The crib sits against the cream-coloured wall, a toy hanging above it. There're murals painted across the walls of Disney characters. A small white wardrobe and a baby change unit rest against the opposite wall, and I walk over, running my hand across the unit and then opening the wardrobe. There are tiny clothes inside, folded neatly.

"I don't know whether you will like them, but I got a few things to start us off." I feel the soft material between my fingers.

"This is all so perfect, Cooper." I smile through my tears.

"You deserve the best. I'm just sorry it took me so long to see it." He comes up behind me and wraps his arms around me, his hand gently rubbing my ever-growing baby bump. "I don't want you to feel any pressure. You can move in here with Asher, and I can stay at the clubhouse. We don't have to rush any of it. You being open to having me around is enough for me for now."

"I love you," I whisper, resting my head against his chest.

"I love you too, Mila, more than you know." For the first time in months, I feel like I belong right here, with Cooper, Asher, and our baby.

Of course, I know it won't be easy sailing. Cooper will mess up, just like I will, but after everything we've been through together, we're stronger than ever. If I don't give him this chance, then I will forever wonder if I made the right choice.

One thing I do know is we belong together, and I owe it to Asher and my unborn child to try.

THE END

KAIN – The Hammers MC

CHAPTER ONE
Kain

Cooper stares into the eyes of each and every one of us. "Mila's only just begun to talk to her family again, and I don't want to give them any reasons to think I'm not good enough for their daughter." He pauses and then turns to Tanner. "No drama with Brook," he warns, pointing a finger in his face. Tanner tries to hide his sheepish grin.

Marshall laughs, which brings Cooper's attention to him. "And you can stay the hell away from Harper today." Marshall's smile disappears, and I bite my inner cheek to stop me grinning from ear to ear. Serves the fucker right. He's been after my ex-hook-up for weeks now, and despite my fist hitting his face on more than one occasion, he still hasn't taken the hint.

Harper's pregnant with my kid. It wasn't planned, but we were happy to carry on with the hook-ups, until she tried to reveal her pregnancy to my ol' lady. Since then, I've kept my distance. "I don't want him upsetting," he adds, pointing in my direction.

Cooper, our club President, takes a minute to look around the semi-circle of brothers awaiting his further instruction. He's marrying Mila today, the woman he was always supposed to be with despite life getting in the way on a few occasions. He's nervous, not that he'll admit it, but I can tell by the way his fingers twitch and by the rants that he keeps reigning down on the brothers.

Mila wanted a huge wedding this time around. She's not usually the type to be a diva and make demands, but the last time Cooper was supposed to marry her, his ex returned, ruining their plans. Mila was taking no prisoners this time. She insisted that if Cooper wanted to marry her so badly, then he could spend his money on a big white wedding. That way, if he decided to let her down again, he was out of pocket a good few grand. Cooper isn't one for fuss, preferring to marry her in a quiet ceremony and then whisk her away on their honeymoon, but he needed to prove to her that he was serious this time around and that he wasn't going to fuck it all up again.

"Brothers, I need this day to go without a glitch. If you spot something about to go off, then you need to squash it. No drama, no fighting, no fucking." We all snigger at that one. Mila has cousins and friends coming who haven't met us before, and she's already warned us that no one from the MC can hit on them.

We take turns slapping our President on the back and wish him luck. The brothers step out the back room and into the church, leaving me and Cooper alone.

He begins to pace, and I smirk. "You nervous she's gonna leave your arse standing there this time?" I joke, and he glares at me, his expression anything but amused. "Relax, Coop, I was kidding," I say. "Mila loves you. She's gonna be there."

Checking my watch, it's a few minutes after when Mila should have arrived and Cooper is twitching. "Call her and find out where the fuck she is," he growls, close to my ear. The church is packed out with no seating space. Mila really did go all out on the invites. I spot Harper's parents towards the back of the church. They don't know me, but I've seen their pictures around Harper's place. Rich and pompous is how she described them.

"I'll go and take a look outside. Relax," I whisper.

Stepping out into the church grounds, I breathe a sigh of relief when I spot a white Rolls Royce coming to a stop at the entrance. The driver gets out and rushes to open the passenger door. I watch as Harper steps out in a long, silk lilac gown that's fitted perfectly to her gorgeous pregnant figure. She wobbles on the heels, and the driver steadies her, causing my eyes to zone in to where their hands connect, and I scowl. I hate any man touching her to the point I want to break his damn fingers, but she'll only remind me she doesn't belong to me.

She might be pregnant with my kid, but we've done too much to each other to ever make things right between us. When she texted Ginger to break the news that she was pregnant, I was furious. Not only because Ginger is also pregnant, but because Harper was the one who told me she wasn't interested in me and that I should live my life with Ginger. Women are so confusing.

Harper's eyes connect with mine and that familiar burning in my chest flickers to life. I love everything about this woman, from her gorgeous bright blues to her perky little backside. She keeps me on my toes with her fiery temperament, and I find it hard to resist that usual pull that draws me to her whenever she's nearby. My body craves her, but her blank expression soon brings me back down to Earth. It's like she's flipped a switch and now she looks at me with nothing—not love, not even hate, just nothing.

"Is Mila on her way, because Cooper's in there busting a nut with stress," I say light heartedly.

"Yes, she's in the car behind us. She should be here any second," she says politely, and I hate that indifference in her tone.

Brook is next to step from the car in a dress matching Harper's. She smiles wide when she sees me. Tanner's ol' lady is something else, always laughing and smiling. She reaches up to me and kisses my cheek. "You look so handsome, Kain," she says, rubbing her lipstick stain from my cheek.

"Damn, lady, if you weren't with Tanner, I'd be all over this arse today," I say with a wink, and she playfully taps my shoulder. "Don't tell Tanner I said that," I add. That guy is bat shit crazy when it comes to Brook, and he'd beat my arse before he heard me out.

I head back inside, and Cooper looks up with a hope that soon fades when he realises it's just me. As best man, I should mess with his head a little, but I can see the guy is in pain with nerves, so I pat him on the shoulder. "They're arriving now. Photos and all that," I say, and he sucks in a deep breath, nodding.

A few minutes later, the music begins and everyone stands. I take my place by Cooper's side as we move to the front. I turn and watch as the bridesmaids begin their descent down the aisle towards us. I can't help but admire Harper's beauty, and the fact that her perfectly rounded pregnant stomach makes her even more beautiful to me. My heart squeezes, and I wonder if this would eventually have been us if we hadn't messed it all up. I've never considered marriage before, but I would for her. I feel eyes burning into the side of my face and I see Ginger watching me carefully. I smile at her, but she doesn't return it. She's obviously noticed me staring at Harper. I'll pay for that later, I'm sure.

KAIN – The Hammers MC

CHAPTER TWO
Harper

Why does he insist on staring at me like that? Before, when no one knew about us, it was sexy and appealing, but now, it makes me want to slap him hard across the face. Ginger will no doubt have noticed because she's like a damn hawk-eye whenever we're all in the same room together. She doesn't know this baby is his, but I think she suspects. She'll never voice that out loud and face up to it though, not if it means she might lose Kain.

I take my place across the altar from Kain and Cooper. Glancing back, I watch my best friend since forever walk towards her future. She looks amazing in her Vera Wang wedding gown. I laughed when she told us she was having such a large wedding cos it wasn't Mila's usual style, but I'm pleased she went big. Not only does she look stunning, but the whole day so far has been magical. We've all been pampered and preened to within an inch of our lives. It's the first time I've ever looked at myself in the mirror and gasped.

The ceremony is beautiful, and my face hurts from the smile I have plastered on my face. There's just something about weddings that brings out the happiness inside me.

We gather outside for photographs. The church grounds are picturesque, and Mila's paid extra to have some photos taken despite Cooper's protests about him being too big and bad to have photos. I stand patiently while we are swapped back and forth, pictures taken with the bride and groom, pictures taken with just the bride and bridesmaids . . . the list is endless, and I can feel my ankles beginning to swell. Marshall stands just behind me. "Baby, you look so hot," he whispers, and I smile to myself.

Marshall is one of the brothers from the Hammers MC. Before I realised that I was pregnant, he was a hook-up. At first, I used him just as much as he did me. I needed to get over Kain, and he needed to fuck—it was that simple. Kain became jealous, and once the news of my pregnancy came to light, I've tried to tone down the flirting. Kain begged me not to get with any of the club brothers, and although he doesn't deserve my word, I don't want to upset him because we've caused each other far too much pain as it is.

"Back away, Marshall," I mutter, hardly moving my lips, and he laughs.

"I'm on my best behaviour today. Cooper warned us all before the wedding, but I just wanted to tell you that I think you look amazing and that you're the only pregnant woman I've ever looked at and gotten a hard-on," he says. I laugh out loud and watch as he saunters away. I catch Kain's eye, he's unhappy about the exchange, I can read it on his face, but I'm not going to ignore Marshall completely. We're still friends.

"Okay, can I have Harper and Kain," shouts Mila, and I wince. This will cause problems between Kain and Ginger, and I have no doubts that Mila's done this on purpose. I take a deep breath and make my way to the large oak tree. I stand on Mila's side, and Kain moves to Cooper's side. We smile for the photographer, and he clicks away before Mila steps away, pulling Cooper with her. I glare at her, and she smiles at us innocently.

"I'd like a picture of my best friend and Cooper's Vice President," she says, and then she lowers her tone. "Besides, don't you want one picture that you can show your child once it's here?" she adds, and a pang of guilt hits me.

My child will have to share his or her daddy with a child just one month older than itself. The thought has kept me awake at night, and as awful as it is, I've often wondered if I've made the right decision by keeping this baby. I subconsciously place my hand on my tiny little bump, and Kain moves next to me, placing an arm around my waist and tucking me closer to him. I force an awkward smile, mainly because I can feel Ginger's eyes on us and I know she must feel so much hatred towards me. She won't cause an issue because she has no solid evidence other than knowing we had a thing before she came back into Kain's life, but as a woman, she must sense it. I must set off her alarm bells whenever I'm near her man.

"Are you feeling okay? We've been standing around for a long time," he whispers, and I nod. I don't tell him that my feet hurt bad but I can't bend to remove my shoes, or that my back is also hurting, because he'll try and take care of that for me, and I don't want questions coming from Ginger. Not on Mila's day. Once the photographer gives us the nod, I move away from Kain quickly and make my way through the crowd.

I feel my father's eyes on me as I approach. I didn't want them here today, but Mila's mother insisted on inviting them. They've been friends since Mila and I were born, although they don't tend to see each other these days, not unless there's a special occasion like this.

"Sweetie, you look lovely," says my mother, kissing my cheeks.

"Seven months already," my father mutters, also swooping down to kiss my cheek. I shudder involuntary and fold my arms over my chest before stepping back from him.

"Are you staying for the party, or do you have to jet off?" I ask hopefully. My father is always flying off for business, and usually my mother goes with him.

"Actually, we'll be staying around for the next week or so. It seems odd being in the house and not a hotel." My mother smiles. "We don't have to be anywhere until the end of next week, so I can spend some time with you," she adds excitedly.

"Yay," I mutter with less enthusiasm, but my mother doesn't react. I don't know if that's because she doesn't understand my sarcasm or she just doesn't care.

"Harper, I had the accountant put some money into your bank this week. Have you received it?" asks my father. I nod and force a smile. He often deposits money into my account, but I never touch it. I don't want his guilt money, but I don't tell him that. Instead, I pretend I've spotted someone important and make my excuses to leave.

I ease the shoes from my swollen feet and haul my legs up so I can rest them on the seat next to me. I glance around the large white tent decorated with twinkling lights and fake flickering candles. Mila hired a team of people to put up the tent on the clubhouse grounds so the guys could drink themselves stupid and then not have far to crawl to their beds. Plus, she reasoned no hotel would be happy with a bunch of rowdy bikers partying in their establishment. Looking around, you wouldn't know we were at the clubhouse.

Marshall approaches and takes a seat next to my feet. "Your cankles giving you grief?" he jokes, and I scowl at his name for my swollen ankles.

"Why aren't you drinking shots and chatting up Mila's family?" I ask, and he shrugs his huge shoulders.

He trails a finger over the top of my foot and then looks me direct in the eyes. "They don't interest me, Harper," he says seriously. "Not like you do."

"Marshall, don't," I warn. "We talked about this. It was fun, but as you can see, I have other priorities now," I say, pointing to my bump.

"I can't help how I feel, baby." He sighs, taking my foot in his large hand and gently massaging it. I close my eyes because this seriously feels better than sex right now. My brain is telling me to stop him, but my poor feet are screaming in delight as he rubs away the pain.

"Marshall, did you not hear the Pres today?" asks Kain, his shadow looming over us. I sigh and open one eye as Marshall gently places my foot back on the chair.

"Yes, VP, I did. I was just helping her out," Marshall says, standing.

"Well, that ain't your job, is it?" asks Kain firmly, and Marshall salutes him before walking away. "Cheeky fucker." He sighs, taking the seat that Marshall vacated. "If you're tired, why don't I get one of the prospects to take you home?"

"Because it's my best friend's wedding, and we still have," I look at my watch, "an hour before she leaves for the airport."

"There's lots of bedrooms free here if you want to stay over," he offers, and I shake my head. The last time I stayed here at the clubhouse, we ended up starting an affair.

"How's Ginger coping?" She's a month further on than me, and I noticed she's carrying her weight differently. Kain fidgets, which he does a lot when he's uncomfortable, but I'm trying to make this whole situation easier on us both. I don't want to be bitter and jealous, and I don't want to be the other woman anymore. I made it clear from the beginning of my pregnancy that I'm not expecting anything from Kain. I chose to keep the baby, and by that time, he'd already announced Ginger's pregnancy. Once he found out about me, he tried to come crawling back, but it felt like a pity thing rather than love, and I was sick of being his second choice.

"Ginger is fine," he says, his tone clipped.

I sigh. "I'm not asking to be a bitch, Kain. I was being polite."

"Well, it's weird, my knock-off asking about my ol' lady." The words sting, but I cover it well. He's never referred to Ginger as his ol' lady, not to me anyway.

He realises what he's said and runs a hand over his neatly trimmed beard. "Sorry, I didn't mean it like that. It's not official. Ginger and I haven't said it . . ." He trails off. "Anyway, I came over here because—"

This time, I cut him off. "Because you saw Marshall talking to me," I say coldly. I know his game, always ready to intercept any potential lovers. He must think low of me if he thinks I'd be having sex with Marshall right now at seven months pregnant.

"Well, that too, but no. I came to see if you need anything for the baby. Cooper mentioned that you'd asked for extra shifts behind the bar. I know babies cost a lot. Ginger's spent a fortune kitting out the bedroom and . . ." He trails off again, and this time, he winces, realising his words are messed up again.

Working at the clubhouse bar is ideal, but it doesn't pay great, and although I've been saving throughout the pregnancy, I need the extra cash for the baby things that I'll be needing soon. "No, it's fine. I have everything." I stand abruptly, grimacing as my feet pinch. I grip my shoes in one hand and my bag in the other. "See you around," I say brightly, and I go to find Mila. I shouldn't be upset. It was my choice to step away from the whole situation, and I honestly think Kain would have stepped up if I'd have let him, but I also think he'd have kept both me and Ginger, and I wasn't prepared to continue to be the other woman. I should never have been that in the first place.

My father grips me by the arm as I pass him, halting my steps. "Why haven't you touched any of the money in your account?" he hisses. I pull my wrist free and rub it.

"Because I've told you over and over that I don't want your hush money. I have a job."

"It isn't hush money. Don't be so dramatic." He takes a calming breath before adding, "Gloria would like you to come over for lunch tomorrow, and I told her you'll be there."

I groan and don't bother to hide it. The fact that my parents will be in the same town as my stepmother is awkward and I can't relax. "I don't want to come over for lunch. Why can't you leave me out of it?" I snap.

"I'll send a car to collect you at twelve," he says, kissing me on the forehead. "I've booked your mother into a health spa. She needs a rest." *Of course, you have,* I think to myself bitterly.

To continue, head here...https://mybook.to/Kain

A note from me to you

Cooper was originally released under the name Splintered Hearts. Amazon was constantly getting the book confused with another author's work and so I decided to redo the cover, change the name and re-edit the original works. I hope you enjoy it.

If you enjoyed Cooper, please share the love. Tell everyone, by leaving a review or rating on Amazon, Goodreads, or wherever else you find it. You can also follow me on social media. I'm literally everywhere, but here's my linktr.ee to make it easier.

https://linktr.ee/NicolaJaneUK

I'm a UK author, based in Nottinghamshire. I live with my husband of many years, our two teenage boys and our four little dogs. I write MC and Mafia romance with plenty of drama and chaos. I also love to read similar books. Before I became a full-time author, I was a teaching assistant working in a primary school.

If you'd like to follow my writing journey, join my readers group on Facebook, the link is above. You can also use that link if you're a book blogger, I'd love you to sign up to my team.

Popular Books by Nicola Jane

The Kings Reapers MC
Riggs' Ruin https://mybook.to/RiggsRuin
Capturing Cree https://mybook.to/CapturingCree
Wrapped in Chains https://mybook.to/WrappedinChains
Saving Blu https://mybook.to/SavingBlu
Riggs' Saviour https://mybook.to/RiggsSaviour
Taming Blade https://mybook.to/TamingBlade
Misleading Lake https://mybook.to/MisleadingLake
Surviving Storm https://mybook.to/SurvivingStorm
Ravens Place https://mybook.to/RavensPlace
Playing Vinn https://mybook.to/PlayingVinn

The Perished Riders MC
Maverick https://mybook.to/Maverick-Perished
Scar https://mybook.to/Scar-Perished
Grim https://mybook.to/Grim-Perished
Ghost https://mybook.to/GhostBk4
Dice https://mybook.to/DiceBk5

The Hammers MC (Splintered Hearts Series)
Cooper https://mybook.to/CooperSHS
Kain https://mybook.to/Kain
Tanner https://mybook.to/TannerSH

www.ingramcontent.com/pod-product-compliance
Ingram Content Group UK Ltd.
Pitfield, Milton Keynes, MK11 3LW, UK
UKHW021330310725
7175UKWH00033B/323